DARK LEGACY

KNIGHT'S RIDGE EMPIRE #12

TRACY LORRAINE

Copyright © 2022 by Tracy Lorraine

All rights reserved.

No part of this book may be reproduced in any form or by any electronic or mechanical means, including information storage and retrieval systems, without written permission from the author, except for the use of brief quotations in a book review.

Editing by Pinpoint Editing

Proofreading by Sisters Get Lit.erary

Photography by Wander Aguiar

Models - Zakk Davis & Ivenize Ruiz

1

CALLI

Everything is fuzzy when I wake.

My head feels like it's been stuffed with cotton wool, and my body is weak. Too weak.

I swallow, ripping my tongue from the roof of my mouth. Somehow, the taste of that godawful whisky Emmie made me drink is still coating my tongue. My stomach turns over, but it quickly settles before I have to make a run for it. Thank God, because I'm pretty sure my legs wouldn't hold me up right now.

My mind churns trying to come up with anything but the whisky.

Why did she make me drink it any— fuck.

"Daemon," I cry, sitting up faster than my head can cope with. It spins, making the world feel like a freaking merry-go-round.

"Calli," a broken voice whispers.

Looking to my side, my breath catches in my throat

when I find Jocelyn there, holding my hand, her eyes filled with unshed tears.

The sight makes whatever is left whole in my chest shatter into a million pieces.

"Tell me it was a dream," I whisper, pain ripping through me once more. It's the most hopeless feeling I've ever experienced. And it leaves me broken and bleeding out in its wake.

"Oh Calli," she sobs, pulling me into her arms, finally giving in to the tears I'm sure she's been holding onto all this time.

Dad.

Nico.

Daemon.

Sobs rip from my throat. It's like knives against my raw skin, but I can't stop. The pain is too unbearable.

My entire body trembles, ice rushing through my veins as my mind tortures me by replaying pivotal events from last night.

Until it locks on one face, one person.

"Where's Alex?"

Jocelyn releases me, her hands lifting to my face and allowing me to see my empty room.

"Where's everyone?"

"They've all gone back to the country club to search."

Silence stretches between us as I try and process what that means.

"Th-they're not de—" A hiccup erupts from my throat, cutting off my final word.

Taking both of my hands in hers, she stares me dead in the eyes.

"I don't know everything, only what they explained before they left again." I nod, swallowing nervously but equally needing to hear everything. "Nico is okay." All the air rushes from my lungs at that news.

"Oh God," I sob. "W-why didn't he come back?"

"He refused to leave and stop searching for your dad, for the others."

"O-others?"

Sadness passes through her features that makes my stomach sink.

"They can't find Daemon, and—"

"No," I cry. "No."

Tugging my hands from hers, I push from the bed.

"No, I refuse to believe it. He wouldn't go like that. He wouldn't. He's better than letting some building fa— NO," I bark, storming across the room and swinging the bathroom door closed behind me hard enough that it makes my entire body jolt with the bang. "NOOO," I scream. "NOOOOO."

Sobs wrack my body, but I don't let it stop me, I use the bathroom and then splash my face with cold water. Anything to try and crack through the haze of despair that's surrounding me.

"Calli," Jocelyn calls from outside the room. "Calli, please."

Ripping the door open, I storm past her and straight to my wardrobe. In a second, my dress from the party is on the floor and I'm dragging on a pair of leggings and a hoodie.

"Calli, what are you—"

"I'm going to help. I'll find him, I know I will."

"Calli, please. You need to—"

"I need to what?" I snap, turning to face her.

Jocelyn's eyes soften, the pain in them undisguisable before they drop to my belly.

"He would want you here and safe," she says, her tone a low warning that leaves very little room for argument. I find it, though. When it comes to Daemon, I always will.

"Right now, he needs me. He needs all of us. And I'm not going to sit around here feeling sorry for myself when I could be out there helping, looking for them."

Shoving my feet into my trainers, I pause at my clutch that's sitting on the counter, but I push aside thoughts of what's hiding inside there and rush past, swiping my car key from the hook on the wall as I go.

"Calli, please. They told me to—"

"I'm done with doing what I'm told, Jocelyn. They're my family too. I have every right to fight for them too."

I don't hang around long enough to hear her response—I'm already running through the house and out the front door. The late afternoon burns through the black hoodie I tugged on. My brows pinch as I consider just how long I've been out of it, but I don't have time to worry about such meaningless things like that.

"Calli, wait," Jocelyn cries from somewhere behind me, but I don't so much as look her way as I throw myself into my car and jab my finger into the start button.

The engine of my Mercedes grumbles to life and I throw it into reverse, damn near wheelspinning out of the driveway and leaving Jocelyn standing in the middle of it with a hopeless expression on her face.

Tears silently fall from my eyes and drip from my chin, but I refuse to give in to the despair that's trying to rip me apart.

Caving to it and crumbling into a heap is going to help no one.

And I need to help. I have to do something

I have to find them.

My entire body trembles with my restraint, but I swallow all of it down.

I fly through the street, my decision-making way riskier than it's ever been, but my need to get there to be useful is more important than scratching my car right now.

The sun is blinding as it sinks lower in the sky and I head to the outskirts of the city where I remember being last night.

As I get closer, the sky begins to darken, but it's nothing to do with the time and everything to do with the smoke and dust that's billowing up from what's left of the building we were all in last night.

I gag just thinking about what I'm going to discover as I drive up the long driveway before the trees reveal what was a glamorous country club only twenty-four hours ago.

Blue and red flashing lights reflect in the smoke that's getting thicker every second. But it's not thick enough to hide the destruction.

"Holy shit," I cry as reality reveals itself.

The building has been reduced to nothing more than a pile of rubble. Rubble that is currently hiding, trapping, those I love.

I pull my car to an abrupt halt behind a fire engine and run toward the smouldering ruins.

"NICO," I scream, my eyes locked on my brother as I dart around another fire truck.

All eyes turn on me, but I pay them zero attention as I fly toward him.

He's dirty, bloody. His clothes are ripped, his eyes dark and haunted.

"Calli," he breathes in shock, and I don't stop until we've collided and I've got my arms around him.

"I thought you were dead, you arsehole," I wail as he holds me so tight I can barely breathe.

"I couldn't leave them, Cal. Fuck. We can't find Dad."

His entire body trembles as he holds me, and I can't help but wonder if looking up and seeing me just broke something inside him.

"We will. We'll find him."

Tucking his face into my neck, he drags in a shuddering breath. I sense that we're joined by others, but I don't move. I just cling to Nico like my life depends on it as grief and despair like I've never experienced before threatens to rip me to pieces.

Dad and Daemon have to be here, just waiting for us to free them.

They have to be. There can be no other option.

A hand lands on my back. I have no idea who it belongs to, but I drag as much strength from it as possible before arms circle both of us.

Ripping my eyes open, they immediately collide with Alex's. The girls are gathered behind him, but I can't focus on them. Alex's despair draws me in.

My breath catches in my throat, because the darkness, the pain swimming in his grey depths is all I need to tell me that they have no news on Daemon.

I didn't think it was possible, but my heart rips apart all over again.

Desperate to get to him, my arms slip from Nico's, and the second everyone around us backs away, I release him and fall into Alex.

Just like Nico, he's barely holding it together. And the second I feel the heat of his tears on my neck, a pained sob rips from my throat.

"I'm so sorry, Cal. I can't find him." His voice is rough and choked with emotion, and it guts me.

I hold him tighter, falling apart right alongside him.

"It's not your fault," I whisper.

He nods, sucking in shaky breaths, his fingers twisting in the back of my hoodie.

"He won't go down this easy, Alex. He won't. He's

the stubbornest motherfucker out there. It's going to take more than this. He's here somewhere. He is."

"I know," he says with a wrecked laugh. "He's here. I know he is. I'd feel it if he were… if he were gone, I'd…"

We stand there, lost in those words. Both hoping, praying that they're true.

After a few more minutes, Alex's grip loosens and his arms fall away from me. Lifting his hands, he wipes his face before tipping it up to the sky, I can only assume sending up a prayer.

I watch him with a lump of emotion the size of a basketball lodged in my throat, my eyes burning from all the tears I've cried.

After letting out a long, calming breath, he looks back at me.

I gasp as his pain collides with mine. The connection between us is stronger than ever as we share this… this grief, this desperation.

"You shouldn't be here," he whispers.

"I need to be. I need to help. I need to…" My words trail off as I look over his shoulder to the giant pile of rubble.

"He knew this was going to be a disaster," Alex confesses absently. "He knew we shouldn't have agreed to it. He was so worried about you getting hurt that—" A sob rips up his throat, cutting off the end of his sentence.

"They were confident it was the right thing to do. We have to trust them," I say, my eyes on Uncle Damien as he stands amongst his capos, digging through the rubble to find his men. His brother.

"Come on, A. We're gonna keep searching," Nico says, wrapping his arm around Alex's shoulders.

Not willing to let him, either of them, out of my sight, I reach for their hands.

I gasp when their ripped and battered skin collides with mine and stare at their bloody and dirty fingers.

"You need to sto—"

"Not until we find them," Nico says, his voice low and deadly as he snatches his hand back. "Dad's too good to die here."

He's gone before I get a chance to respond, and I watch as he climbs over some of the rubble and begins heaving pieces of what I assume is roof out of the way, digging down in the hope of finding someone.

"Don't do anything stupid, baby C," Alex breathes in my ear before he marches toward Nico. Theo, Seb, and Toby follow behind.

Arms wrap around me once more, but I don't move my eyes from the guys as they all start working together to clear the area they're in.

All four of them are dirty, their hands wrecked from searching, and guilt floods me that I've been at home sleeping while they've been here helping.

"How many are they missing?" I ask.

"We don't know for sure. At least five more, from what the guys have figured out."

I scan the scene before me. There are soldiers, firefighters, Reapers, and Wolves everywhere, working their way through the ruins.

"More?" I ask, bile rushing up my throat at what that could mean.

"They've pulled four out already."

I nod, swallowing down the rush of emotion that bubbles up.

Squeezing my eyes closed, I take a step forward.

"What are we waiting for then?"

"You sure you want to do this?" Jodie asks, and as I look over at her, my eyes catch on Bri's concerned ones.

"Yes. I'm sure. We'll get them out quicker with more of us."

The four of them nod in agreement, and together we join the boys and start working.

2

CALLI

"Fuck. Over here," someone yells, stopping us all immediately in favour of looking over to see what—or who—he's found.

It's late. The sun set a while ago, leaving us with only the silvery hue of the moon and the spotlights the firefighters have set up to aid the search.

My heart is in my throat as Stella and Emmie take my hands and help me walk over the rubble. Everyone is beginning to congregate as more men focus on that one area to discover what's been seen.

"Oh shit," Stella gasps when a dark figure emerges beneath the rubble.

"Oh my God." My stomach knots, tightening so violently that I have to fight not to puke right there as I freeze and watch as the men gently pull the body free.

Everyone is shouting and barking orders, but it's all a blur. There's nothing but white noise in my ears as I watch this nightmare play out before me.

Paramedics rush over, jumping into action, and my heart tries to crash right out of my chest.

The grip on my hands tightens, but I barely register what I'm seeing as my sheer panic overrules everything.

But then a voice breaks through it all, and reality crashes down around my feet.

"Dad," Nico cries, pushing through the crowd until Uncle Damien grabs him, stopping him from getting in the paramedic's way. "DAD," he bellows, his voice cracked with pain and fear.

Silence ripples around all of us as the paramedics do their thing, but the second they start CPR, I know. I feel it right to the depths of my soul.

"Dad," I whimper as Stella and Emmie push in tighter, practically holding me up.

"It's going to be okay, Cal. It's—"

"NO," Nico roars, finally breaking free of Uncle Damien's hold and rushing toward the stretcher they've got Dad on. "Dad, please. We need you."

Tears track down my dirty and dusty cheeks as I stand there shattering all over again while my brother falls apart.

Nico doesn't break. Ever. So the sight of his slumped shoulders and trembling body wrecks me.

Hushed words are said, but as the paramedics take a step back and Uncle Damien once again steps up to Nico, I have all the answers I need.

Stella and Emmie's concerned stares burn into me, but I don't look at them. I can't take my eyes away from Nico as he kneels beside our lifeless father.

Darkness descends around me, numbing everything until I swear my body is made up of nothing but rock and ice.

I watch everything happening around me as if I'm watching a movie, not my own life.

Hands hold me up, but I lose track of who they belong to as Theo, Seb, and Toby surround Nico and attempt to keep him together.

I don't notice the person who's absent from their little group until another set of hands lands on my hips and I'm spun away from the scene before me.

Alex stares down at me with terrified eyes, and it makes everything slam into me like a truck.

My knees give out as pain rocks through me.

But he doesn't let me fall. He never would.

He catches me and drags me into his chest, wrapping his arms around me and holding me tight.

"I'm so fucking sorry, Calli," he breathes in my ear, and the realisation of what he's telling me, even though I already knew, completely breaks me.

Warmth surrounds me as my girls comfort me, doing anything they can to make this any more bearable.

But none of it works. The pain is too raw, too brutal. And the fear... Fuck, the fear of this only being the first of the agony is just as overwhelming as the grief.

"Where is he, Alex?" I whimper.

"Fuck, Cal." His grip on me tightens and it does little for my fragile state. "I don't know."

Tucking my face into the crook of his neck, I sob for

everything I've lost, and everything I can feel slipping away from me.

Voices carry in the air around me, but I don't hear a word. People move, engines rumble, and rubble continues to be moved. The only constant is the arms banded around me.

Alex's support never falters, despite the fact that he's in as much pain as I am.

"Do you want to go and see him?" he asks, his voice strong, giving me something to latch onto.

"Um..." My head spins with the magnitude of that question. I squeeze my eyes tight, trying to decide if I want my last memory of my father to be one of him smiling tonight as he celebrated Mum's birthday, or lying on that stretcher probably battered, bruised, and broken.

"Nico is still over there."

I nod into Alex's chest and suck in a huge breath.

This isn't just about me. I'm not the only one who's lost someone here. Nico, he's—

A sob rips through my throat.

My brother has just lost his hero.

"N-Nico needs me."

Alex's lips part to respond, but I don't give him a chance. I slip around him and walk toward where my brother is still kneeling on the ground in front of our father.

I drop down beside him with my heart in my throat and my eyes on his profile.

Nico's expression is blank, his mask firmly in place.

But the second I reach for him and wrap my arm around his shoulder, everything changes. It's like my touch crumbles the shattered foundations that are holding him up and he falls into me, squeezing me so tight I struggle to breathe.

He says nothing and makes no sound as we just hold each other. Our pain collides, our grief only growing as the seconds and minutes pass.

It's not until a shadow falls over me sometime later that I finally look up from the crook of his neck.

I find Theo staring down at us with a wrecked expression.

"The boss has gone to see your mum," he tells us, his voice all business, but I understand why.

Nico nods as he finally releases me and looks back to where Dad lies peacefully, and before I know what I'm doing, I follow.

My breath catches as I take in his dirty face.

"Dad," I whisper, moving forward and reaching for his hand resting on his chest.

It's still warm, and I cling to it as if it's a lifeline despite the fact that I know it's fake.

He's gone. I know that. And worse than that? I feel it.

"You deserved better than this," I tell him. "I-I'm sorry that you're not going to g-get t-to me—" The lump in my throat cuts off the rest of my words as my hand comes to rest on my stomach. A move that I'm hoping everyone will miss. Everyone but Alex, it seems, as his hand lands on my shoulder, squeezing gently.

"You should go home, Calli. It's late and—" Nico swallows and lets out a long sigh. "We need to keep digging." He hangs his head for a beat before he pushes to his feet and walks back to where some of the guys are still working.

"N-no, I can't—"

"He's right, baby C. It's late, you haven't eaten and —" Alex's words cut off when I glare at him.

"He needs us, Alex. He needs us to find him."

He nods, understanding passing through his grey eyes, but there's more, and before he even opens his mouth, I know what's about to come next is going to wreck me.

"And he needs me to look after you." His eyes drop to my stomach as the pain of our current situation threatens to floor me once more.

"B-but, Dad," I say, looking back over my shoulder.

"The guys will take care of him. You don't need to worry." I glance up, my eyes catching on the paramedics who are watching us from the sidelines, waiting to do whatever it is they need to do. They both give me sympathetic smiles and I nod in appreciation for allowing Nico this time. I'm sure it's not actually a part of their job description.

"Let him look after you, Calli," Stella says from somewhere behind me.

My brows pinch, wondering why she's not demanding that she does it herself. But equally, I don't argue, because the only other person I want holding me right now isn't here. Or he is, he's just…

"Okay," I concede.

Before I even have a chance to move, Alex pulls me into his side and begins walking me toward my car.

Driving here feels like a lifetime ago now. Being here at the party last night almost feels like a dream, or a nightmare. Yet it was only twenty-four hours ago.

"You should stay. You're the most likely to find him," I argue when he drops into my driver's seat.

He reaches for my hand and squeezes. "I'm doing the right thing," he assures me, although his eyes don't move from the pile of rubble.

"But what if—"

"They'll find him. They have to."

"And what if—"

"Not possible. He's in there somewhere, just waiting, I know he is."

"Then you should be—"

"Looking after you. It is what he'd want, I assure you."

I stare at his profile, focusing on the hard set of his jaw as my vision blurs with tears.

"Thank you," I whisper.

Slowly, he rips his eyes away and turns to me. The darkness and pain reflecting back at me is like a physical blow to my chest.

"He'll come back to us, Calli."

"And if he doesn't?" I ask, my voice cracking with every word.

"Then I'll be right here every step of the way with you."

I blow out a shaky breath as my emotions threaten to get the better of me once again, the weight of his promise settling around me.

"No, I can't ask you to—"

"One step at a time, yeah?"

His thumb brushes over my scratched knuckles, his love and support seeping through my skin.

"Y-yeah. Okay," I whisper, unable to do anything but follow his lead. I'm running on empty and I'm going to fall apart in my car if he doesn't get me back fast.

With a nod, he starts the car. With one lingering look at where my father is lying with the paramedics beside him, then at Nico who's refusing to stop, I close my eyes and allow Alex to take me away from this nightmare.

Neither of us speaks on the way home. There are no words to say. Nothing is going to fix this. Nothing is going to bring my dad back, and nothing is going to turn back time and stop the events of yesterday changing the course of all of our lives.

By the time we pull up at the house, I've entirely shut down.

I've somehow managed to push the pain and grief into an impenetrable box, and I've pulled on my own mask that I'm sure Daemon would be proud of.

I don't feel strong as I step out of the car. I feel... nothing.

My body moves as if it knows what it needs without instruction from my brain, and I just let it do its thing.

Loud cries come from the direction of the living

room, but I don't move in that direction. The last thing I want to witness right now is Mum falling apart.

"Calli, wait," Alex calls from behind me. But I don't stop as I bolt for my basement.

A shadow fills the living room doorway a beat before I pass, and when I look up, I find Jocelyn standing there. For the first time ever, her hair is a mess, her make-up running down her face.

Lifting my hand, I cut her off before she can say anything and continue forward, heavy footsteps following me the entire time.

"Calli, wait," Alex calls as I run down the stairs, the solitude of my basement too inviting to ignore.

I need the silence, the darkness, then—another sob erupts.

"You should go back," I say, my voice stronger than I was expecting as my insides crumble to nothing but ash.

I storm through to the bathroom, turning the bath on and pouring in some bubbles.

Alex is still standing in the middle of my space when I return, but I refuse to look at him. I can't.

"Calli, please. Just stop," he begs, reaching for me. I dart out of the way before he gets a chance to pull me into him. If I stop while he's watching, then he's going to be forced to witness me break, and he's more use out there searching than he is drying my tears right now. My heart aches at just the thought of sending him away, but I know it's the right thing to do. Daemon needs him more than I do right now.

"Go back and find him, Alex. Please, I'm b-begging y-you."

Kicking my shoes off, I drag my dirty hoodie over my head and shove my ruined leggings to my ankles.

I don't lose his stare, and I hate that any kind of heat that I'd usually experience from it just standing here in my underwear is absent. Just concern and grief in its wake.

"I'm going to wash all this dirt off me. Then I'm going to bed."

I take off once more, his eyes tracking my every movement across the room until I get to the bathroom and swing the door shut behind me.

The second I'm alone in the dark, the tears come as pain rips through me so fiercely, I've no idea how I remain standing.

I stumble toward the tub, somehow managing to shed my underwear and step into it.

I don't feel the temperature of the water as I sink beneath the layer of bubbles. I don't feel anything but pain as my tears come faster and my cries get louder.

"Calli?" Alex calls. "Don't do this." The agony in his voice cuts through me.

"Just go," I sob. I have no idea if it's loud enough for him to hear me.

"I won't let you shut me out like this."

"Just go, please. I need—"

The door swings open, the shock of the loud bang making me forget my words.

He reaches behind him and drags his dirty and

ripped shirt off. His hands and forearms are covered in dirt and blood, and it quickly becomes obvious that the rest of him is just as battered from hours of moving rubble.

"What the hell are you doing?" I gasp, dragging my eyes from the cuts and bruises littering his body.

"Being what you need, and taking what I need in return."

I'm too shocked to do anything but watch with wide, tear-filled eyes as he kicks his shoes off, shoves his trousers down his legs and steps up to the bath in just his boxers.

"Shift forward."

"Alex, I'm naked. You can't just—"

"Fuck, Cal. This is freezing," he gasps when he dips his toes in.

I shrug. "Can't feel it."

"Jesus."

Reaching in, he pulls the plug, letting half the cold water drain before putting the hot tap back on.

I might not have felt the cold, but I sure as hell feel the warmth of the water as it surrounds me.

With my legs pulled up to my chest, I scoot forward, finally doing what he asked of me and allowing him to step in behind.

Thankfully, the bathtub is huge, allowing for his long-arse legs to encase my body. His arms wrap around mine, which are hugging my legs.

"I'm so fucking sorry, Cal," he whispers in my ear as the water continues to swallow both of us.

I nod, twisting my head to the side so I can rest it against his shoulder.

I blow out a shaky breath, but I don't say anything. I don't have any words. How could I? Nico might be okay, but Dad's gone, and Daemon is—

A pained cry rips from my throat.

"I've got you," Alex murmurs, holding me tighter. "And I swear I won't fucking let go."

Twisting around, I curl myself up against him and let the grief I've been trying to hold back engulf me.

3

CALLI

I wake to the sound of soft female voices and the scent of coffee. The warmth of someone's hand on my calf is equally as comforting as it is painful.

For the briefest of seconds when I come to, I hope, pray that it was all one big joke. But the ache in my chest, the soreness of my eyes even before opening them tells me that all of this is very, very real.

"Tell me I dreamed it all," I whisper, my voice hoarse from both sleep and the hours I spent crying on Alex last night.

The bed dips, and when I crack my eyes open, I find Emmie and Stella on either side of me. Both of their faces are covered in dirt, their hair is a mess, and their eyes are ringed with dark circles from lack of sleep.

"How are you doing?" Stella asks, although from the way she winces, I think she realises what a stupid question it is the second it rolls off her tongue.

"I need coffee."

"Lucky for you, I have impeccable timing," a comforting voice says before Jocelyn appears at the end of my bed with a tray full of coffee, orange juice, and fresh pastries.

She doesn't look much better than Emmie and Stella, and when her eyes collide with mine, her face falls as pain flickers through her features.

"Oh, my sweet girl," she breathes, abandoning the tray on the end of the bed and walking around so she can pull me into her arms.

I suck in deep breaths as I fight to keep my emotions in check. I have no idea how long I cried last night, but I need to get it together. I've got people who need me. Falling apart right now isn't an option.

"It's decaf," she whispers before she finally pulls away.

My brows pinch for a moment as I try to decipher what she's telling me. The second realisation hits me, I want to curl back up under the duvet and never emerge.

How the hell did my life turn into this shitshow?

Silence falls around us as Jocelyn pulls up a chair after handing us all a mug. Emmie and Stella look at her in confusion. She's never hung out with us before, but right now, I need it. I need all of their strength and support, and Jocelyn seems to know that better than anyone.

"Thanks for this, J," Emmie says with a soft smile. "Is there whisky in it, by any chance?"

"Sorry, just caffeine."

"I'll take it."

"Have you two had any sleep?" I ask, looking between my two best friends.

They both shake their heads. "We've been out searching with the guys."

"Where are they? Where's Alex?"

"Alex went back as soon as we got here to keep you company."

Guilt washes through me that he left Daemon because of me. He should have been there. He could have sensed something the others couldn't.

I nod as memories of my time with Daemon in the past couple of weeks flicker through my mind like a movie.

"I've been seeing Daemon," I blurt.

Silence.

Looking up, I meet Jocelyn's kind eyes and she nods in encouragement. She's more than aware of the huge secrets I've been keeping.

It's more than time for me to start confessing. At least to some of it.

"Y-you... uh..." Stella starts.

"You've been fucking Daemon?" Emmie gasps, realisation hitting her upside the head. "Daemon? Daemon Deimos? Twin of the guy who follows you around like a lost puppy, Daemon?"

"Yeah we all know who she's talking about, Em," Stella snaps, anger and disappointment that I hoped I wouldn't hear evident in her voice.

"I'm sorry I didn't tell you, I just... the whole thing has been insane, and now he—"

"Oh shit," Stella breathes, abandoning her coffee mug on my bedside table before stealing mine and throwing herself at me.

"I'm okay," I whisper unconvincingly.

"They'll find him. He's better than being buried beneath a building."

"I thought that about my dad, but look where that landed me."

Another set of arms surrounds me until I'm in the middle of them, being damn near crushed to death.

"I'm going to leave you girls to it," Jocelyn says now I've confessed my first sin. "Call me if you need me."

By the time Stella and Emmie release me, she's already vanished.

"Okay, so..." Emmie starts as Stella passes me back my coffee. "Let's focus on the most important elements of this revelation. How big is his cock?"

"Emmie," Stella chastises.

"What?" she says with a shrug. "We're knee-deep in hell right now, we're allowed a little dick talk, right?" Emmie glances at me, an almost pleading look in her eyes.

Christ knows what the pair of them have seen during their hours digging through that devastation. Just like Alex, their hands and arms are scratched and bloody, their clothing ruined. I figure the least I can do right now is help them through this as much as I know they're going to help me.

"He's pierced," I confess quietly.

"Oh my fucking God. I knew that boy was a freak," Emmie laughs, although her usual humour is pointedly lacking.

Silence falls once more and I let out a heavy sigh, pain and loss filling every inch of my body.

"How long have you two been..." Stella prompts.

"It started at Halloween," I confess with a wince.

"Shit," she whispers, hurt showing plainly on her face.

"I'm sorry," I breathe, reaching for her hand. "It... it was this one-time thing. I wasn't even meant to know it was him. He never took his mask off and—"

"It's okay, Cal. You don't have to do this. It's a shock, sure. But we're here for you, no matter what," Emmie assures me.

"Thank you."

"What about Alex? He likes you, he—"

"He knows. Has done the whole time, although we didn't know that until recently. He was pushing us to confess by being... himself." A sad laugh falls from my lips.

"I guess that kinda makes sense."

"When I was away last week," I confess, "I was with Daemon."

"Oh, wow. Okay." Stella pushes her wild hair from her face as she processes everything.

"There's more."

"Jesus, Calli. Have you been living two entirely different lives or something?" Emmie asks.

"Kinda." I look at Stella. "You remember Ant and Enzo?"

"The Italians? Of course. They were ho—"

"I didn't stop seeing Ant. Nothing happened between Daemon and me after that one night at Halloween. But then a few weeks ago, the night they raided the Italians, I was in Ant's room. Daemon stormed it, and well... safe to say I wasn't here doing homework that weekend."

"You were having a sex-fest with the devil?" Emmie guesses.

"Yes and no." I drop my head into my hands. "God, all of this is such a mess."

"It's going to be okay, Calli. They'll find him and he'll—"

I look up, my eyes colliding with hers, begging her to stop with the false hope.

"How long has it been?"

"Um..."

"Like thirty-six hours," Emmie answers.

"And how many survivors have they pulled out?" My heart rips in two asking that question, but I refuse to allow myself to believe something that just isn't going to happen.

"Two, but that was almost immediately. Everyone else has been..."

"This isn't going to be okay, Stel. Nothing about this is going to be okay."

"But it has to be," she argues, refusing to believe the inevitable.

"But what if it's not?"

Hidden under my duvet, my hand slides to my belly once more, the harsh reality of all of this pressing down on me. But despite my confessions, that one life-changing truth stays locked inside me.

I'm nowhere near ready to attempt to come to terms with the result that stared back at me the night before last.

"I know you're trying to be realistic here, Cal. I get it, I do. But this isn't the end for Daemon. It can't be. I fucking refuse to believe it," Emmie says fiercely, her eyes holding mine, giving me just a little bit of the strength she manages to cling on to.

Despite both looking utterly wrecked and in desperate need of a shower, both Emmie and Stella sit with me while I try to process everything that has happened since Saturday night. On one hand, our day at the spa and getting ready at the Prestige seems like a million years ago. But then I remember the explosions, the gunfire, people's screams of fear as the Italians unleashed fury on us, and a spike of adrenaline shoots down my spine as if it happened only minutes ago.

Ant.

He should be the last of my worries right now, but it doesn't stop me from being concerned for his safety.

When he told me he'd get them out, I believed him.

It was probably naïve of me. But I can't help it.

He's never been anything but trustworthy and honest with me.

"Shit," I hiss, attempting to scramble from the bed to find my phone. I find my best friends passed out on either side of me.

Without waking them, I find it still in my clutch from Saturday night, next to the pregnancy test.

My hands tremble as I stare at the result again.

Shouldn't this be the happiest time of my life? Shouldn't we be celebrating.

I catch my sob before it breaks free and wake my phone up.

It has two percent battery, so I make quick work of firing off a message to Ant.

If he kept at least part of his secret, then he might know something.

Might.

It's not until a soft knock comes from the door at the top of the stairs that I'm forced to move from my position, staring down at the message I just sent in the hope it gets read.

The door opens and I silently move across the room, trying not to wake them. And when I look up at the stairs, I find Jerome hobbling down.

Memories of him with blood pouring from his thigh come back to me, and I rush over to help him.

"You probably shouldn't be doing that," I point out as I wrap my arm around his waist and guide him toward my sofa.

"I needed to see how you were doing," he admits with a sad smile. "I'm so sorry about your dad."

"Thanks," I mutter, a fresh wave of grief and despair rolling through me. I hadn't forgotten, not by a long stretch, but it was a little easier to bear while the girls avoided mentioning it.

"How's it feeling?" I ask, glancing down at his leg despite the fact that it's covered by what I assume are Nico's sweats.

"Yeah, Gianna worked her magic. I'll be good as new in a week or so."

"You lost a lot of blood."

"Yeah, I think I was pretty lucky. If you didn't get me out of there as fast as you did then... Thank you."

I shake my head. "I didn't do anything," I whisper.

"Calli, you were a bad-arse. You didn't show an ounce of fear. You should be proud of yourself. I know your dad would be."

Tears burn the backs of my eyes as a lump the size of a freaking football climbs up my throat.

"Daemon too," he adds, just to rip that wound a little wider.

I drop my head into my hands and fight to keep it together.

After a few deep breaths, I look back up at him. I can see all the assurances that both Stella and Emmie gave me flickering through his eyes. But I don't want to hear them. I don't need false hope. It'll only make all of this worse when the inevitable happens.

We live in a dangerous world full of pain and death.

Something like this is always just around the corner. It's something I've been all too aware of my entire life, even as I was kept on the sidelines.

"Your dad, is he..." I wince, feeling awkward that I don't already know the answer to that.

"He's okay. He's been out searching with the others."

I nod. If I was more with it, then I probably would have noticed when I was out there doing the same. But honestly, everything since that first round of gunfire has been nothing but a blur. The only bit that sticks in my mind as clearly as if it happened only seconds ago is staring down at Dad.

"Good. That's good."

"Mum is looking after yours."

"Shit," I breathe, remembering that I refused to even consider going to see her when Alex brought me back last night.

"Take your time. Mum, Jocelyn, and the others have it in hand."

Shit, Gianna.

I push from the sofa. "I need to go and show my face."

"Calli, right now, you don't need to do anything."

"I do. Mum's lost her... Gianna..." I can't even finish the sentences, but I don't need to. Everyone is more than aware of the situation.

With a heavy heart and my world in tatters, I head for the stairs.

When I look back, I find Jerome slumped on my sofa, clearly exhausted from his trip down here.

"Hang out, yeah? Rest," I instruct, but I don't think my words are needed. He's not going anywhere for a while yet.

The house is eerily silent as I make my way through the kitchen. All the downstairs rooms are deserted.

With each step, the dark pit of despair that opened up the second the gunfire started on that country club gets bigger, threatening to drag me under.

I push thoughts of Mum being so consumed by her own grief that she hasn't even tried to come and comfort me aside. Now isn't the time for bitterness, although it's really freaking hard to ignore it.

I trudge up the stairs, my exhausted body making each movement harder than it should be. I might have slept for a few hours but it was fitful and full of nightmares, which quickly turned back into reality when I opened my eyes.

Movement ahead of me slows my movements, and my breath catches when Gianna slips out of Mum's room.

Her eyes collide with mine a beat later and she runs full speed toward me.

She gathers me up in her arms and holds me tight against her chest. It's a move I've always craved from my own mother, but the walls she built around herself don't seem to crumble for her kids even in times of need.

Despite my attempts to keep it together, tears once

again spring from my eyes as I think of Dad, of Daemon, and all the guys still out there searching.

"Come on, sweetie," Gianna whispers, guiding me toward my old bedroom. "I've given your mum something to help her sleep. Clio and Iris are still with her."

I stare at her, my blank expression obviously enough to clue her in as to how I feel about Mum right now. Obviously, I'm devastated for her that she's lost her husband, but equally, that's not a reason to forget you have two kids.

"I'm so sorry, sweetie," Gianna says softly as she sits beside me on my old bed.

I suck in a deep breath, my eyes dropping from hers for a beat as I drag up whatever strength I have left. "Gianna, Daemon and I—"

"I know," she says, squeezing my hand in support. "I know."

My brow creases. "H-he told you?"

A sad smile plays on her lips. "No, sweetie. That boy never tells me anything. But he's been enamoured with you for as long as I can remember. I knew it was only a matter of time before you found your way to each other."

My lips open and close like a fish as I continue to stare into her exhausted and devastated eyes.

She's been here since everything kicked off, taking care of everyone else. Yet, she's lost just as much as we have in all of this.

"He loved you before he even knew the feeling existed, Calli. The way you helped him, the way you saw who he really was."

My bottom lip trembles as her words flow through me.

"For him, there was always something so magical about you. I just always prayed that you saw the same in him and that one day, he'd get everything he deserved."

"Oh my God," I whimper, losing the battle with my tears. "I see it," I whimper. "He's... incredible."

She nods, holding me tighter.

"I hated watching both of my boys step into this life, Calli. My biggest fear when I fell in love with Stefanos was having boys and having to endure both of them doing the kinds of things I knew he did for the Family. And then when I discovered I was having identical twins." She shakes her head. "I've never felt fear like it.

"When it became clear early on that Daemon was going to have some health issues, I selfishly hoped that it would mean he wasn't cut out for this life. That maybe fate had a different path for him in mind. But the second I saw him, saw the fight and determination in his eyes, even in those early days while he was hooked up to more machines and equipment than any newborn baby should be... I knew. I felt it deep within my soul that this was where he belonged.

"If I had any doubt, I never would have left them here with Stefanos when we parted."

"The Family is his life," I breathe.

"Yeah. Despite my fears, I gave birth to two fierce soldiers."

"They're both so much more than that," I tell her, pulling from her embrace and looking her in the eyes.

Her cheeks are stained with tears just like mine, but there's a softness there as she thinks about her babies.

"They are. I must be honest, I feared they would end up falling out over you."

I can't help but laugh.

"They're different in so many ways, but both of them watch you as if you're this magical creature they don't quite believe exists."

"Stop, that's not—"

"How's Alex doing?" she asks, changing the subject. "I saw him briefly on his way out of the house a few hours ago, but he wasn't exactly forthcoming."

"He's..." My stomach knots uncomfortably. "I don't know," I confess. "He's been so set on looking after me that I d-don't—"

"It's okay. That's how he is. Those he loves always come first."

"He's so loyal and supportive. I wish I could make it better. I wish he didn't get that look in his eyes when he watches Daemon and me together."

"Do you remember what I used to call him when he was a kid?" Gianna asks me.

"Pup?"

A smile breaks across her face. "He was always my little puppy. So loyal, dependable, lovable."

"Tell me more about them as kids," I ask, desperate

to lose myself in happier times, of a time when I'm sure Daemon didn't see quite so much ugliness in the world.

Gianna gets this faraway look in her eye as she reminisces before she indulges me in story after story about her boys. And I soak up every single one, my heart full of love for both of them but in such different ways.

4

CALLI

It's late by the time the front door opens and heavy footsteps pound down toward the kitchen, where I'm sitting with Jocelyn, Jerome, Iris, and Clio, picking at the food Jocelyn has laid out.

I'd sent Stella and Emmie home after my heart-to-heart with Gianna. They were both exhausted and dirty as hell. Despite their protests, they needed showers and their own beds.

Gianna was called by Stefanos to go and help out with some injuries at the destruction site, and she jumped at the chance to help. I'm not sure if she needed the distraction from the inevitable, or if she was just glad to get away from my mother.

She still hasn't appeared. I've also not ventured to see her. Whatever Gianna has given her has knocked her right out, and for now, I'm happy with that.

I've got all the people I need. Well, kind of.

The footsteps get louder and my heart jumps into

my throat that they might be here with some good news. But as Alex, Theo, Nico, Seb, and Toby appear in the doorway, it quickly vanishes once more, morphing into the indescribable pain I've been battling with all day.

Pushing to my feet, I walk toward Nico.

He is wrecked. His face is black with dirt and soot from the devastation of the fallen building. He's got smudges of blood everywhere. I have no idea if it's his or someone else's.

"Nic—"

"Don't," he growls, taking a step back.

"Please, don't do this. Don't shut me out."

He swallows harshly, the agony written across his face making it hard for me to breathe.

"I'm not, Calli. I just..." He reaches out, resting his dirty hand on the wall as if he needs it to keep him on his feet.

"Get him up to bed," I instruct, my voice coming out shockingly authoritative.

"You got it, baby C," Theo agrees, his deep voice etched with anguish. He and Toby wrap their arms around my brother and guide him toward the stairs. I watch them until they're out of sight, my eyes then falling to the dark handprint he left behind on Mum's perfectly white wall.

"The sheets are clean, and there are fresh towels," Jocelyn calls, doing her bit to be useful in these desperate times. "Shout if you need anything."

"Thank you, Jocelyn," Toby calls politely before their steps disappear.

"How are you doing?" Seb asks, stepping closer to me.

"I'm..." Dragging my eyes to him, I swallow the lie that was about to fall from my lips. "Lost."

His arms lift as if he's about to hug me, but his gaze catches on his dirty skin and he thinks better of it.

"You gonna be good if I head home?" he asks, his brow pinched in uncertainty.

"Of course. Go and check on Stella. Get clean. Get some sleep."

"There are guys still out there digging. But we haven't found anyone a... alive for a while."

I nod, hearing the words he's not saying loud and clear.

A groan rumbles deep in Alex's throat and I step closer to him, threading my fingers through his in silent support.

"Stella told me. She said she wasn't meant to, but—"

"It's okay, Seb."

"Shit, I'm so fucking sorry, Calli." This time he gives in to his need for a hug and drags me into his body. "I know how much this fucking hurts and I wouldn't wish it on anyone. If you need anything, you know where we are, yeah?"

"Thank you," I force out.

"Anything." He drops a kiss on the top of my head before handing me over to Alex, who doesn't waste any time in dragging me into his body now I'm thoroughly dirtied up.

DARK LEGACY

"Get some rest," Seb tells Alex. "We'll be back at it when the sun rises, yeah?"

"Yeah, man. Go find your girl."

Sadness washes through Seb's face before he turns and takes off, running out of the house at full speed despite the fact he hasn't slept in... a long fucking time.

Alex turns to me, his battered hand coming up to cup my cheek.

His lips part to speak, but I beat him to it.

"You need to go and rest too. You look exhausted."

"Damn," he breathes, just a flash of his usual cheeky twinkle lightening up his eyes. "And here I was thinking I looked all hot and shit."

"He thinks he's so smooth," Jocelyn deadpans from across the room.

"I am and you know it, Ms. J."

Jocelyn smiles compassionately at him. "My girl has a point, Alexander," she says, her brow quirked.

"I know," he agrees. "Wanna lend me your bed, baby C? Company is appreciated."

As inappropriate as his words are, I can't help but be grateful for his attempt to be normal in such a depressing situation.

"Actually," I confess, "I had something else in mind."

"Oh? Do tell. I'm up for all your wild plans."

"You're a nightmare. Come on." I tug his hand, ready to drag him down to my basement, but Jocelyn stops us.

"Wait. Take this. You look like you need it." She

passes over two cans of Coke, a sandwich that could be used as a doorstop it's so huge, and a sharing bag of crisps.

Alex takes them all eagerly before following me down to the basement.

"I should probably shower before you have your wicked way with me, baby C. Can't say I'm all that fresh."

The second we both hit the ground, I spin on him and pull everything from his hands—much to his disappointment as he watches the sandwich go like I just stole his puppy—and place them all on the side before wrapping my arms around him and holding tight.

"You don't need to do that with me."

"Do what?" he asks innocently as his arms return the embrace.

"Put on a front to hide your pain." It hits me right there and then as I listen to his heart racing beneath my ear that really, deep down, Alex and Daemon aren't all that different. While Daemon hides his pain in his darkness, cutting himself off from everyone, Alex uses his humour to mask it.

Lifting my head from his chest, I stare up at him and take his cheeks in my hands.

"We're in this together now. Let me in."

His eyes shutter and my heart fractures—not that I'm sure it was whole enough to break again.

"Alex, you know my secrets. Trust me with yours," I beg.

"My secrets aren't your burden to bear, Calli.

You've taken on Daemon's. That's more than enough for one person."

I shake my head. "That's bullshit and you know it."

"Fuck, Calli," he breathes, resting his brow against mine. He stares down into my eyes, his pain mingling with mine, but as much as it hurts seeing it, it gives me some strength. I know without a doubt that he's going to be standing right beside me through this, and it might be selfish of me to allow it. But right now, I need it. I need it so fucking much. "It hurts so fucking bad, and I know it's nothing compared to what you're going through and—"

"No. Don't compare. We're not playing that game."

"But—"

"No, Alex. I mean it."

He nods and whispers, "Okay."

Releasing him, I force myself to take a step back.

"So did you want to shower or..." I look around my room, the emptiness inside me only carving deeper despite Alex being here.

"Or..."

"Can we go to your place? I—" I sigh. "I need to get out of here."

"You want to come sleep in my bed, baby C?" Alex asks with an exhausted twinkle in his eye.

"You can say no, I just—"

"Shut up, Cal. Pack some stuff. I told you, whatever you need."

He smiles at me, but while his lips might curl up, it never meets his eyes. He's trying. He's really fucking trying to put a brave face on all of this, but he's losing the fight. I can see the cracks showing. And I have every intention of being there when he finally loses his grip. He caught me when I fell, and I'm determined to do the same for him.

I race around my room, grabbing the few things I might need before coming to stop in front of him again.

He eyes my bag with suspicion.

"You moving in?"

"Maybe. Anything has got to be better than being here right now."

"I'm pretty sure there's an insult in there somewhere, but I'm too tired to find it. Or care."

Reaching down, he lifts my bag and throws it over his shoulder.

"You okay to drive?"

We swing by the kitchen to let Jocelyn know where we're going. She looks at me with concerned eyes, but she doesn't say anything, just lets Alex lead me out of the house with his hand supportively placed on the small of my back.

That little bit of heat gives me strength, keeps me moving forward instead of just crumbling to a pile on the floor.

The drive across town toward the boys' building is in silence. Alex's face is set in a stone mask, his battered hands clenched tightly in his lap, and despite his exhaustion, his leg bounces anxiously.

It hits me as I descend to the underground car park

that he's probably not been back here since it all went down.

I hesitate before parking, but in the end, I pull my car into the same spot I would if the situation were different. Right between Alex and Daemon's cars. Daemon's bike is parked on the other side, and pain rips through me as I think about the one time I rode on it with him.

I thought that journey held some of the worst moments of my life. If only I knew what was going to be thrown at me only a few days later. I might just have held on a little tighter.

"Was this a mistake?" I ask after killing the engine and turning to look at Alex.

He hasn't moved. Not an inch.

"We can go back if you're not rea—"

"It's okay, Cal. I'm going to have to be here eventually. May as well just get it over with, right?"

"Fuck," I breathe, pushing my hands into my hair. "This is so fucking hard."

I squeeze my eyes closed, desperately trying to keep the rush of tears in as I allow myself to drown in reality.

I startle when a warm hand lands on my stomach, his thumb brushing over me gently.

My pulse spikes and my eyes pop open.

"It's time to show the world that strength you've been hiding inside you all this time, baby C."

His eyes remain locked on my stomach, the intensity of his stare making everything feel a little too real.

"I'm pretty sure it was all a myth."

"Nah." His eyes find mine. "It's there. I've seen it time and time again. So did Daemon." His voice cracks as he says his brother's name.

I nod, unable to speak through the lump in my throat.

"Come on, I really need a shower and to pass out."

"Shit, yeah." Shoving down my pain, I focus on Alex and being what he needs right now.

He grabs my hand as he rounds the car. My bag is thrown over his shoulder, and I hold on tight as we walk into the lift.

His grip tightens with every floor we climb, and I step a little closer, desperately wanting to give him some strength.

A pained sigh falls from his lips as the doors open, revealing an empty hallway. We turn toward their flats, my limbs heavy with grief as we approach Daemon's door.

The thought of him hiding behind fills my mind, but as much as I might wish for it to be true, I know it's not. He might be cold, ruthless, and dark. But he wouldn't do something so cruel to either of us. He might not want the world to see it, but he cares. Really cares.

"He told me he loved me," I blurt. Our steps falter until we stop right outside his flat.

"He did?" Alex asks, a deep frown marring his brow.

"At the party, when he cornered me in the bathroom."

"Did you tell him about..." His eyes drop, right along with my heart.

I shake my head. "No. I didn't know then. The first time I saw that result... it was with you."

"Fucking hell."

Alex combs his fingers through his dirty hair, agony etched into his features. He looks older, wiser. And not in a good way.

"Come on, you need to get clean." His brow quirks. "What? I don't think you need me to tell you that you stink."

"No, I'm aware. I just..."

He looks from Daemon's front door and then down to his, as if he doesn't know which one he wants more.

Making the decision for him, I tug him toward his flat.

We're going to have to deal with going inside and being surrounded by him soon enough. Right now, he just needs sleep.

I have no choice but to stop so he can press his hand to the biometric scanner, but the second the door swings open, I continue forward until I'm standing in the middle of his bedroom.

I release his hand and just look around.

"What?" he asks, hesitating behind me.

"Nothing. It's just so... normal."

He barks out a laugh that lightens my soul a little. "Christ, Cal. What were you expecting?"

"I dunno. But a mirrored ceiling at the very least."

"What kind of image have you painted of me in that head of yours, huh?"

"One where you spend most of your time talking about sex. There's not even a blow-up doll," I quip.

"Okay, now that is insulting. I don't need an inflatable to get laid."

"Is that right?" I mutter, walking toward the window to look out at the illuminated city below us. "When was the last time you saw any action?"

He scoffs behind me before fabric begins rustling as I assume he starts stripping out of his disgusting clothes.

"Are we really going there, baby C?"

"It was just a simple question," I breathe, getting lost in the moving lights of the cars and buses.

My skin prickles with awareness as he steps up behind me and presses his palms to the glass, caging me in.

"You don't need to worry about me," he whispers before dropping a kiss on my cheek and disappearing as fast as he appeared.

Spinning around, I catch a glimpse of his bare arse as he slips into the bathroom.

He leaves the door open, and only a few minutes later, steam billows out from inside.

Kicking my trainers off, I drop my hoodie to the chair in his room. Well, I assume there's a chair and it's not just an epic pile of clothes, and I shove my leggings down my legs before walking over to his bed and pulling the covers back.

The coolness of the sheets calls to me, my body instantly begging me to curl up and get some rest. But movement in the mirror on the wall beside me catches my attention and stops me from sliding down.

My breath catches as I watch Alex in the reflection. His palms are pressed against the tiles, his head hanging defeatedly between them as the water rains down on his back.

"Shit," I hiss, aware of just how much he's struggling to keep it together.

He refused to let me fall last night, and there's no way I can't return that favour.

I'm at the end of the bed, my legs ready to take me to him when the shower suddenly cuts off.

He emerges a beat later with a towel wrapped around his waist and water running down his freshly cleaned skin. But none of that is what really captures my attention. It's the darkness in his eyes.

That along with his wet hair laying against his brow, his jaw covered in scruff, he looks more like his other half than I've ever seen.

He pauses when he finds me obviously on my way to rescue him.

His jaw clenches as he studies me, but no words fall from his mouth. Instead, he just shakes his head, rips his eyes from mine and walks toward his drawers.

I sit there frozen as he tugs the towel from his waist and runs it over his body, collecting up the lingering water before scrubbing it over his hair and dropping it to the floor. Dragging a drawer open, he pulls on a pair of boxers and finally turns back toward me.

"You're welcome," he quips, finding me blatantly

watching the show. But there's none of the Alex I know and love in those two words. They're empty, just like the look in his eyes.

"I-I wasn't—"

"I know." He throws back the covers on his side of the bed and slips in.

"Do you need anything? Are you hungry or—"

With his eyes already closed, he reaches for me, wraps his hand around my forearm and drags me up the bed.

I melt into his side, resting my head against his chest and listening to the steady beat of his heart.

He tugs the covers up over both of us as I wrap my arm around his waist and twist our legs together.

"Tell me that tomorrow will be easier," he begs, the pain in his voice turning the air to ice around us and making it hard to suck in a breath.

I sigh, holding him tighter, unable to give him the reassurance he so desperately craves.

He falls asleep faster than I thought possible.

But the escape of sleep doesn't claim me quite as quickly, and I lie there for what feels like hours with the steady beat of his heart keeping me grounded, his firm hold on me, even in his slumber, tight enough to keep me together.

Thoughts of my Batman float around my head, and I think of all the things I should have said to him, all the confessions I should have made before everything went so wrong.

"I love you," I whisper, the need to get the words out

in the hope he somehow might hear them too much to deny.

Alex's fingers tighten on my waist, and I still in fear of waking him up.

"He knows," Alex whispers, making my heart shatter into a million pieces.

5

DAEMON

"Sharp scratch," a deep voice rumbles as I fight my way out of the darkness that's consumed me for... fuck knows how long.

The realisation that I'm in the hospital is somewhat of a relief as the scratch I was warned about hits my upper arm before a rush of cold liquid floods my veins.

Everything hurts, every-fucking-thing.

All I can hope is that whatever was just pumped into my body was some serious fucking painkiller.

There's movement around me, and I start to drift off once more, letting the darkness where pain doesn't exist drag me into its clutches again before the scent of the room stops me.

I didn't notice it when I first came to, but the more air I suck in through my nose, the more it begins to become obvious that I'm not actually in a hospital.

My surroundings aren't sterile, and something tells

me that the liquid I was just injected with isn't something that's going to help me.

Digging deep, I summon up some strength and move my arm.

It's heavy, every single one of my limbs is, but it's not my exhaustion and whatever is flowing through my veins that stops my arm from shifting an inch. That would be the bindings strapping me to the bed.

A loud grunt of pain fills the room, and I finally crack one of my eyes open.

It barely works, and I have to assume that some of the pain I'm battling with is courtesy of a serious beating.

The last thing I remember was the bone-chilling crash as the building above me collapsed with one final, ground-shaking explosion.

The last thing I remember thinking about was her and sending a silent prayer up that Alex would take care of her should the worst happen.

The thought of leaving her when we'd barely even started wrecked me, but I knew she'd be okay. I just had to hope that the others got out too.

The girls were safe. I saw that for myself as Calli ran toward the car waiting to take them to safety.

But what about my brother, Theo, Nico—

Another cry sounds out, and after focusing on the dark, dirty ceiling above me, I glance to my right.

My breath catches when a shadowed figure emerges as my vision clears.

Crack.

The sound of the whip makes my entire body jolt as memories flood me.

Without permission from my brain, my eye falls closed and I'm dragged into the darkness of the past.

I'm just a little boy in his grandfather's shed. The place where almost all my nightmares are set.

A whimper falls from my lips as I look around at the dark space.

I have no idea how long I've been in here this time. It's always bad when he decides it's time to teach us a lesson, turn us into the men, the soldiers we were born to be. But today is worse, because I'm alone.

Alex is at a football tournament with the others. Dad's with them too, cheering them on, supporting them, all the while leaving me here to have 'fun'.

Mum's at work. She promised to pick me up once her shift was over, and all I can do as I sit here in the dark is hope that that shift is due to be finished sometime soon. Or that the hospital is overstaffed—unlikely I know, but a boy can dream, right?—and she gets sent home early. It's not going to happen, I know that, but if I don't have some kind of hope, then what do I have?

Heavy footsteps sound out from beyond this small slice of hell, and my entire body trembles as I wait to discover if he's just taunting me, or if he's actually going to come back and 'train' me.

He hasn't even put the TV on today. I'm starting to wonder if it's because he's realised I've started to enjoy watching the torture he gifts us with.

Alex hates it. He closes his eyes and does his best to

turn away. Not that the pained cries of the men in the videos don't flow through his entire body, poisoning him bit my bit like they do me. But he doesn't lose himself in them like I do.

I use them to fuel my need for vengeance. My desire to get myself out of these situations and prove that I'm already the man, the soldier that Grandad wants me to be.

I don't need this... this torture.

I startle when there's a loud bang outside, but I don't make a noise—not so much as a squeak.

I learned a long time ago that if I showed fear, it made whatever is due to come next worse.

I had to swallow down my pain, my disgust, my hatred, otherwise it would get worse. It always got worse if I showed any kind of weakness.

It's what he feeds on. And when he sees it, he digs his knife in and twists until there's nothing left but pain.

Fear runs down my spine like ice water as the door is pulled open, allowing the warmth of the summer day outside to rush in, taunting me with what my day could be like. If I were into football, I could be running around with Alex and our friends. Friends I never really feel like I fit in with.

I'm different. I always have been. But it's never stopped them trying to include me.

Sometimes I humour them because they try so hard, but I can't help feeling like a round peg trying to fit into a square hole when I hang out with them.

There's only one person—Alex aside—who makes me

feel like I might actually have a place in the world. And she's someone I really shouldn't be tainting with my kind of darkness. But every now and then, I cave. Just like when she invites herself into my room and forces me to do homework with her.

I make out like it's the worst torture in the world. I mean, yeah, doing homework almost sucks as much as this right now, but being with her... it makes it worth it.

A smile twitches at my lips as I think about her smooth blonde hair, her light blue eyes that sparkle every time she looks at me. Her non-judgemental smile and the way her face lights up every time I make her laugh. I have no idea how I do it. I'm the least funny person in the world—she's probably just humouring me, feeling sorry for me. But hell, it makes me feel like the king of the world every time she does it.

My back is to the door, but I'm sitting backward on the chair with my legs spread and my arms tied around the backrest.

It hurts, and it's really uncomfortable now I've been in this position for... I have no idea how long.

I can't see what he does as he shifts about behind me, and I refuse to even try and look despite the need to know, to be prepared, that burns through me.

"You've impressed me today, boy," he growls after the longest time.

To many, it might sound like praise. I guess it is, in a way. But I know not to take it like any child should from their grandfather. I know he's not done yet.

He has me alone, and that means only one thing.

Pain.

A lot of pain.

The sharp crack of the leather cuts through the air a second before it connects with my back.

I'm wearing a sweatshirt, but it does little to protect my skin and pain erupts across my shoulder blades. My eyes water and a cry of pain lodges itself in my throat. I fight it with everything I have, because I can't let it out.

It will only get worse if I do.

Crack.

The next time I wake, I'm covered in a cold sweat and my body is trembling, the lingering images of my nightmare refusing to leave my brain, the pain of them mixing with the very real agony that's still burning through every inch of my body.

I have no idea what's happened to me during the time I was out, but it's more than obvious that someone or multiple people have had some fun.

I've got a good clue as to who that might be. But to be fair, I've unleashed my silent brand of torture on more than a few deserving individuals over the years, so really, it could be a number of people.

The room is in silence this time, and I risk dragging both of my eyes open in an attempt to assess the situation.

I'm yet to find myself in a place I've not been able to escape from. But I'm not an idiot, I know I'm not fucking Houdini. At some point, my luck is going to come to an end, and as much as I like to believe the fact that I'm alive now and not buried beneath that building like I'm sure plenty of others are means I lucked out, although I doubt my captives are going to let me think that way for long.

My head spins when I open my eyes, the blinding light immediately making them water so everything blurs around me. My stomach turns over, bile rising up my throat, making my mouth even more disgusting than it already was from how long I've been out of it.

Sucking in a deep breath, I squeeze my eyes closed again for a moment, begging my body to comply. I need it on fucking board if we're gonna figure a way out of this.

Calli.

The image of her sitting on the beach in her bikini, the light breeze blowing her dark hair, and her skin sparkling in the warm sun plays out in my mind.

Need floods my veins.

Fuck. I need to get out of here and get back to my girl.

My eyes spring open once more, determination for what I need to do burning through me.

I scan the dirty walls. Dark stains cover them, stains I recognise because I've caused similar ones many, many times over the last few years. The stench is familiar too. Only I'm not usually the one festering in the scent of death, I'm usually the one causing it.

Oh, how the tables have turned, Nikolas Deimos.

My grandfather's belittling tone fills my ears and a shiver of fear races down my spine. But I never gave into that back then, and I'm certainly not going to now either.

One single spotlight illuminates the room, but it's not pointed at me. Instead, I've been thankfully left in the shadowed corner while all the focus is on someone else.

My muscles scream as I lift my head from the hard surface I've been strapped to to find out who I'm in here with.

My heart races, poison and the need to do anything to protect my boys dripping through me as my eyes narrow on the sight before me.

A male body hangs from a hook in the ceiling, rope bindings cutting into his wrists, causing blood to drip down his arms.

His body is covered in welts, cuts, and bruises. Whoever it is, they've really gone to fucking town on him.

He's alive, though.

His shallow breathing fills the silence, and if I really focus on him, I can see the rise and fall of his shoulders which I can only assume is unbearably painful with his injuries.

Suddenly, a whirring starts from somewhere behind me and a rush of ice-cold air blows over my sweat-slick body.

A violent shiver rips down my spine, and when I glance down at myself, I find I'm strapped here in just my boxers. My body, although better than the guy hanging from the ceiling, has seen better days. No wonder everything fucking hurts so much.

It's nothing I can't handle, though. I'd walk through hell if it got me back to my girl. And something tells me that getting out of this place is going to be akin to that.

The pain in my neck from holding my head up eventually gets the better of me, and I have no choice but to rest back as the cold from the fan seeps through my skin.

Another starts up a few minutes later, but I don't feel the impact of that one.

My cell buddy sure does though, and I flinch when he suddenly screams, "You motherfuckers. You're going to die for this."

His voice is familiar, enough to know it doesn't belong to any of my boys, and I breathe a sigh of relief that it's not one of them. But not enough for my drug-filled brain to register who it does belong to.

"Hey," I hiss, that one slurred word ripping my dry throat to shreds.

But he doesn't reply. I have no idea if that's because he's ignoring me, or if he's just passed out. From the state of him, it could quite easily be either.

6

CALLI

Despite Alex's wish for things to get better the next day, unsurprisingly, when I open my eyes the pain hasn't lessened and the world doesn't appear any brighter despite the morning sun spilling through the window at the other side of the room.

Stretching my legs, I discover that I'm still very much entangled with Alex and heat rushes to my cheeks at how intimately we're lying.

We've slept together a few times now. I've woken up in his embrace more than once. But not like this. Not with him clinging onto me as if I'm the only thing stopping him from drowning, like I'm the only ray of light in his otherwise dark life.

Lifting my head, I peel my cheek from his chest, my skin damp with what I hope is sweat and not drool, but after how deeply I slept, I can't really rule the latter out.

Releasing my hold on his waist, I lift my hand to my

mouth, praying I don't find a little river of saliva running from the corner of my lips.

Thankfully, I don't, and I breathe just a small sigh of relief.

Lifting my eyes, I don't find Alex sleeping like I thought he was, and instead he's staring down at me, deep in thought.

One side of his mouth kicks up in a smile as our eyes collide, and I can't help but give him a sad one in return.

"Hey," he breathes, his voice rough with sleep.

"Sorry, did I wake you?"

"No, I've been awake a while."

"Have you been watching me sleep like a creep?"

A sad laugh falls from him. "Guilty. You were talking."

"I was?" My blush from when I first woke deepens.

"Yeah. You were calling his name."

I swallow thickly as reality hits me full force.

I shrug. "I miss him."

"Same, baby C."

We fall silent, our minds running over everything we've lost in the past few days.

His fingers twitch and our current situation comes back to me.

"You're aware your hand is on my arse, right?"

"Of course. I always sleep better when I've got something to hold."

"I bet the guys love that when you crash with them."

He throws his head back and barks out a laugh.

"I'm still breathing. None of them have caught me yet."

"Okay, well. I need to pee, so if you could let go, that would be great."

"Jeez, you're no fun."

"Not what your brother says." The words roll off my tongue before I've engaged my brain, and I cringe hard when I hear them.

Alex flinches beneath me and I push myself so I'm sitting and hang my head.

"I'm sorry. I—"

"Don't apologise for talking about him, Cal. The last thing I want right now is to forget him."

"Fuck. This is so fucking hard."

His hand lands on my back in support.

"I'm glad you're here. That we can do this together."

I squeeze his thigh, hoping like hell he gets the same kind of strength from my touch as I do his.

I allow myself to drown in my pain for a few silent moments before my need for the bathroom finally gets the better of me and I slide off the bed and stalk toward the bathroom.

"See," Alex mutters behind me. "It's a good arse. I'd be a fool not to make the most of it."

"You are a fool," I laugh, kicking the door closed.

"Yeah, and you love me for it."

"I do," I whisper. It might not be in the same heart-stopping, knee-weakening, all-consuming way I love his brother. But I do love him, and having him standing by my side right now, and being able to do the same for him, is everything to me.

I pee, then splash my face with water, hoping it'll be enough to wash the grief away that's etched into my skin, before pulling open Alex's bathroom cabinet in hope of finding a spare toothbrush.

But before I do my eyes land on the massive—and I mean massive—box of condoms.

"Jesus," I mutter, unsure if I'm terrified or impressed by the amount of action he's expecting before these go out of date.

But as my amusement ebbs away, I'm still staring at them like a weirdo and my hand drifts to my belly.

Maybe Daemon should have borrowed some.

I stumble back until my legs find the toilet once more.

My heart races and my head spins as the reality of my situation hits me full force.

I haven't really had a chance to think about it since Alex and I both stared down at the positive test result a few days ago.

But the reality is there in the form of another freaking person growing inside me.

Holy shit.

I lift my hand to my chest as my heart continues to race to the point I struggle to catch my breath.

Everything around me begins to blur. The only thing I can focus on is how my life is about to spiral utterly out of control.

A crash somewhere near me barely even registers

before the door flies open, revealing Alex with a panic-stricken expression on his face.

"Calli, what's wrong?"

But I can't respond, the grip of my panic attack too much to break free from.

"Shit. Shit. It's okay, Cal. Everything is going to be okay."

He drops to his knees before me and wraps his hands around my thighs, staring up into my eyes.

"Breathe, Calli. In." He sucks in a deep breath with me, mimicking what he wants me to do. "Out... in... out... in..."

Eventually, with his voice in my ears and the heat of his hands soothing me, everything begins to return to normal. My heart stops beating dangerously fast and the room comes back to me.

"Fuck," I gasp, my chest heaving still as if I've just run a marathon. "I'm sorry."

"No, Calli. You've got nothing to apologise for."

I nod, but shame still burns through me at what he just witnessed.

"What do you need?" he asks, his eyes finally moving from mine in favour of the cupboard I left open.

"Toothbrush," I whisper.

Getting to his feet, he leans forward and presses his lips to my brow.

"I've got you, Calli." His hand wraps around the side of my neck, and I melt into him, soaking up his strength.

"I don't deserve you right now."

"You deserve everything I can give you and more. But first... toothbrush. It's probably a good idea, your breath is rank."

"Hey," I argue as he releases me and steps back. "You're not so fresh right now either."

He chuckles as he opens a lower cabinet that I never noticed, and in only a few seconds he has a new toothbrush in his hand and is offering it to me.

"Thank you," I say, pushing to stand and then accepting the blob of toothpaste he squeezes out.

We stand side by side, brushing our teeth like an old married couple. It's weirdly soothing.

"Should I be worried that I slept in a sex addict's bed last night?" I ask after putting my brush in the holder, my eyes catching on the box of condoms again.

Alex barks out a laugh.

"These are what gave you a panic attack?" he asks in confusion, pulling the box from the cupboard and holding it up.

"Well, not them exactly. Just what the lack of them has resulted in."

He stares at me, his eyes soft and compassionate. It makes something shatter inside me just as much as it helps rebuild some of the broken bits.

Not wanting to burst into tears and have another meltdown on him in less than ten minutes, I glance down at the box. Or more specifically at the tape that's holding the lid closed.

"Wait... you haven't even opened them," I gasp.

"They were a house warming gift from Nico," Alex

confesses, throwing them back in the cupboard and walking toward the toilet, pushing his hand into his boxers ready to take a piss.

Jesus. Boy has zero shame.

"I'm just gonna..." I rush out of the room to give him some privacy while the sound of his laughter follows me.

"You're too cute, Cal," he calls as I walk through the bedroom on a quest to escape.

"You're not," I shout back.

"I know. I'm too sexy to be cute."

"Give me strength," I mutter, turning toward the kitchen, or more specifically the coffee machine.

When Alex joins me, he's pulled on a pair of sweats and is carrying one of his hoodies and my bag.

"Here," he offers as I stand resting back against the counter in just my vest and knickers.

"Thanks," I mutter, dragging it over my head and covering myself up. "Coffee?"

"Hell yes. But go sit down, I can do it."

My lips part to argue, but he reaches up into the cupboard for two mugs and my words fall away in favour of backing up toward his sofa.

I curl myself into the corner as the scent of coffee fills the air around me, making my mouth water, and pull my phone out. I've got messages from Emmie, Stella, Jodie, and Jerome, checking in. But my heart sinks when I discover that there's still nothing from Ant. And when I look at our chat, it only gets worse when I realise he hasn't even read it.

Please, for the love of God, don't let him be somewhere in the middle of all that rubble too.

"Here," he says, passing a steaming mug over, dragging me from my morose thoughts. "Found these too, in case you're hungry."

He places a new packet of shortbread on the cushion next to me before dropping onto the sofa opposite.

I'm not overly fond of his distance, but I let it go. The last thing I need right now is to become dependent on Daemon's twin brother.

Somehow, and sometime soon, I'm going to have to figure out how to stand on my own two feet and embrace what my future is going to look like. Just... not yet. We need to get out of this current shitshow before any of us can think about tomorrow.

"H-how are you feeling?" Alex asks. "About the..." he trails off, clueing me in to where he's taking the direction of this conversation when his eyes drop.

"Baby?" I ask, the word sounding alien on my tongue. It's the first time I've said anything about its existence out loud, and I've got to say, it doesn't help my lingering panic all that much.

"Yeah. I know shit is crazy, b-but are you going to..."

"Keep it?"

"Shit. I'm sorry. That's totally the wrong question to ask right now and entirely unthoughtful."

"It's okay," I say in a rush, hating the way he internally berates himself for the question. "And yes. No matter how fucked up my life might be, there's no way I could put an end to this. Fate obviously had a plan for me so..."

"You believe in all that stuff?" he asks, a deep V forming between his brows.

"Right now, I don't believe in much of anything."

"I get that," he says on a sigh as he studies me. I have no idea what he's trying to find in my eyes, but I'm pretty sure he fails at whatever he wanted. "I have no idea about any of this shit, Cal. Do you need to see a doctor? Do anything to keep him healthy?"

"Him?" I ask, a smile twitching at my lips.

He throws his hands up. "I don't fucking know. My knowledge on this shit ends at how to do everything possible to stop it happening, something my brother clearly never paid any fucking attention to."

"I'm just as much to blame."

"You're on the pill though, right?"

"Jesus, how do you all know the intimate details of my life?" I mutter. "Don't tell me, you pulled my medical records too?"

Alex's eyes widen in surprise. "Uh... no. I saw them in your make-up bag while we were away."

"Okay, good. That's less weird and possessive."

"I wanna be here for you, for this if... if the worst happens," he confesses quietly.

"Alex," I sigh, my heart swelling for the selfless guy before me. "I can't ask you to do that. I'm not your responsibility."

"You're not a responsibility, Cal. You're one of my best friends, and you're carrying my b-brother's ba—"

He swallows down the word as emotion overcomes him.

"Even still. You have your own life to lead, Alex. You can't make these kinds of promises." *Especially when you're wracked with grief and sorrow.* Although, I don't say those words out loud.

Emotions are running high right now, and we're all feeling things more extremely than we usually would, thinking differently from usual. I refuse to allow him to make such life-changing promises when he's exhausted and drowning. It's just not going to happen.

"But I want to," he pleads.

"I know you do, and you have no idea how much that means to me, Alex. But right now, we need to take one step at a time. Life isn't going to be normal again for a—"

"Ever. It's never ever going to be the same again."

I stare at him as his eyes fill with tears. He blinks them back, fighting them, and I do the same right alongside him.

"What's happening today? Are you heading back out on the search?"

He nods, a dark expression crossing his face.

"Theo's gonna come and get me. Emmie and Stella are going to come hang out with you."

"I told them about me and Daemon," I blurt. Although he surely figured that out when I briefly spoke to Seb.

"What did they say?"

"Honestly, I think they were too exhausted and delirious to really register any of it."

"I get that," he agrees, lifting his scratched-up and bruised arm to push his hair back from his brow. "I'm fucking struggling to compute anything right now."

"Tell me about it," I mutter as his phone pings in his pocket.

He slides it free, frowning at whatever stares back at him.

"They're on their way down," he sighs, dropping forward and resting his elbows on his knees and hanging his head.

"You might find him." There's a hopeful lilt to my voice that I don't really feel.

He looks up, his dark eyes holding mine.

"I—" He swallows, not wanting to say the words that are on the tip of his tongue. "We haven't pulled anyone out alive for... d-days."

"I know. Fuck, I know. But there's still a chance, right? When things like this are on the news, they find people days later, shocking everyone."

"Sometimes, yeah," Alex confesses. "But the chances are slim."

"What if he got out?" I ask, knowing it's stupid and hopeful, but I can't help stop my fickle heart from coming up with these wild scenarios where this could be okay.

I've lost Dad. I know that, and while it doesn't feel real, I know it's going to fully hit me at some point in the coming days, but I'm not ready to give up hope. I can't.

He deserves for us to have more faith in him than that. After everything he's been through, everything he's endured in his short life, he needs us to keep hope. To believe in him. To believe in the unthinkable.

"Calli," Alex sighs, conflict warring in his eyes.

"But there is a chance. There's always a chance, right?"

"I guess. But please... don't get your hopes up, because that chance is—"

"Small, I know. But I need him, Alex." My hand slides to my flat stomach as my insides knot.

I'm terrified. Fucking petrified at the thought of having to do this alone.

My hand trembles as Alex slides to the edge of the sofa.

"I'll do anything I fucking can, Calli. But I need you to be realistic."

"I am. I just also need hope right now, because otherwise, I have no idea how the hell I'm meant to keep going."

"I know. But you've got us. All of us are here to keep you together, yeah?"

"I haven't told them about... about the baby, and I'd prefer it—"

"Whatever you want," he promises.

"Just for a while. Until I've had a chance to come to terms with it and I'm further in."

"You don't have to explain yourself to me. You want it to be just between us, then that's how it'll be."

"Brianna got me the test. She's going to be demanding answers soon. But she's trustworthy."

"Just tell me what you need me to do."

The door knocks a second before the locks disengage and voices float down to us.

"I asked Theo to give you access to everything in this building so you can come and go from here as you wish. You're welcome to stay as long as you want."

My heart jumps into my throat at his generosity, but then thoughts of another flat in this building pops into my head, and my eyes fly to the wall that divides the two.

"C-can I get in there?" I whisper, as footsteps and voices get closer.

"Yes."

"Calli," Theo breathes, racing around the sofa and dragging me up to wrap me in his arms.

"Hey cous, how's it going?" I mutter into his chest.

"Fucking shit. I'm so fucking sorry."

"It's not your fault."

"Daemon knew this was going to happen." My body tenses at the mention of his name, but Theo doesn't react. I can only assume Emmie told him and that he's aware of the situation. "He fucking warned us it was a stupid thing to do, but we stood by my dad, by Uncle Evan, and walked straight into that ambush."

"You couldn't have known," I assure him, pulling back. "Your dad and mine will have planned everything as best they could. They'd have been convinced they'd covered all angles. But as much as we might like to wish they are, they're not—they weren't—God. This kind of thing is a risk anytime you guys step outside the house." I hate saying it, being so frank when all I really want to do is crumble, but it's the truth. A truth we've lived with all our lives.

"I should have questioned them more, like Daemon did. He could see it. And look where that landed him."

A sob rips through me as I think of him under all that rubble. I just have to hope he's hanging on, that he can hear the guys trying to get to him, not giving up on him.

"It's gonna be okay, Calli. We're gonna get him. We're gonna bring him back to you."

"So you can kill him yourself?"

"Something like that," he mutters, staring down at me with more understanding in his eyes than I think I've ever seen.

Emmie has done that. She's softened him. Showed him that there's more to life than just being a cold, detached soldier, future boss.

"We're gonna get through this, Calli. All of us." He pulls me back into his chest once more and drops a kiss to the top of my head.

"Have you spoken to Nico?" I ask as he releases me once more.

"No. He's not answering his phone." Something dark flickers through Theo's eyes at the mention of my brother that makes my insides twist up into a painful knot.

"What aren't you telling me? I swear to God, if you're still keeping shit from me then—"

"I'm not, Cal. I don't know anything. I'm just worried about him. Since we discovered your dad, it's like something inside him just... broke."

7

DAEMON

I have no idea how much time has passed. Every time I shut my eyes, I can't help but feel like the world is whizzing by outside of these four walls. And it terrifies me.

How's Calli coping? Is she okay? Are Alex and the girls taking care of her?

Did everyone get out of that building?

It collapsed so hard and fast, I find it hard to believe that everyone got out. The thought of losing any member of the Family makes my chest ache, but the fear of losing one of the boys, the girls, or any of our parents turns my blood to ice.

Have faith, a little voice rings in my ear.

But while I remain here, strapped to whatever this slab beneath me is, I'm finding it harder and harder to hold onto anything.

They could all be out there looking for me or... they could all be dying in that rubble of destruction.

The locks on the door to this cell clang and my body tenses a beat before light floods the room once more.

At some point, I woke to find that the spotlight had been turned off, plunging us into total darkness in favour of pumping white noise through hidden speakers instead.

All I could make out was the outline of his body. But still, he said nothing and he continued hanging there, accepting his fate.

And while I stared, desperately trying to figure all this out with my fuzzy, drug-laced mind, all I could think about was why he was up there and not me.

"Good morning, campers," a deep voice drawls as he and two Italians step into the room.

I squint, trying to focus on them, but everything is hazy and I find it hard to focus on anything as the room and the people in it spin.

The chains that are hanging from the ceiling rattle as the guy hanging there fights, proving to me that he is actually alive.

"Now, now, kid. That's no way to greet your owners, is it?" another of them growls when the guy tries to fight him off with his legs.

"Thought you'd have lost your fight by now."

"Fuck you," whoever it is snarls. Once again, a flicker of familiarity washes through me at his voice.

"Seems like we've got some more work on our hands."

A loud grunt of pain fills the air as one of the guys holding us here throws his fist into his victim's ribs. And

I swear to God it's so hard I hear a crack before his wail of pain echoes off the concrete walls around us.

The attack is brutal, and I have no choice but to watch every hit they land on his body.

It's surreal. After spending more hours than I should probably ever admit to in their position, hurting our enemies, torturing them until they talk, you'd think that the beating wouldn't affect me.

But not knowing who it is, not knowing if he deserves it or not makes something twist up inside me.

Everyone I've ever tortured deserved it. They wronged us, worked against us, played us.

Is that what that guy did?

I don't know. And I don't like the way that feels.

Everyone thinks I'm nothing but a cold-blooded monster, and on most days, I'll wear that badge with pride. It's what earns me my respect, the reason anyone with half a brain fears me in this city. Although something tells me that those Italians really don't give a fuck. And why should they? While I'm strapped to a bed, I'm hardly a fucking threat to them. Even more so when I have no idea if anyone knows I'm even here.

They could all be at home mourning—maybe—the loss of me. Yet here I am, in desperate need of them to fight for me.

They could bring the door down at any minute, storm in here, overpower our captives and get us out. I've no doubt they could do it.

But they'd need to know first. And while I'm pinned here, I have zero fucking clue as to how I can make sure they know I'm alive, that they know to come and search for me anywhere but in all that rubble.

"Argh." The pain in his cry sends a shiver down my spine and makes my pulse pick up.

It's obvious from the pain that aches through every inch of me and the blood that covers my skin that they've had some fun with me. But it must have been like child's play compared to what they're doing to that guy.

I wince as one of the men picks up a bat that was propped up in the corner and takes it to the guy's ribs, leaving no doubt in my mind that more than a few are broken right now.

The crunch is sickening, and it affects me in a way I've never experienced before. Bile rushes up my throat, burning until the disgusting taste fills my mouth.

I have no choice but to spit it out, and the moment I do, all eyes turn on me.

I still, feeling the weight of the unspoken threats in their eyes. But I refuse to cower down, to beg for them to leave me alone.

For one, I know it'll never happen. These men are soldiers, and they've been sent in here with one mission. There is nothing that will stop them from following orders. I should know—I'm one of them.

"Looks like your friend here has just let you off the hook," one of them quips, looking the battered and broken guy dead in the eyes.

The only sound that comes from him is a pained

whimper as two of the men reach up and unhook him from the ceiling.

I can only imagine how much his arms and shoulders hurt right now. As far as I know, he's been up there since we were first brought in... hours... days... fuck knows ago.

He tries to fight the pain, I feel it deep in my soul, but as one of the men forces his arms down in front of him, stretching the muscles the opposite way from how they have probably fused into place, but it's futile and his cry of agony rips through the air.

I wince, feeling it almost as keenly as he is.

I have no idea who he is, but there's some deep-seated connection there. A connection I can't even begin to explain. But it's there nonetheless.

And only a few seconds later, I find out why.

The two men holding him up finally turn him toward me.

My mouth goes dry and my entire body goes rigid with realisation.

Holy fuck.

My eyes scan his face, his hardly recognisable face, and my heart sinks into my motherfucking feet.

No.

His pained gaze collides with mine. But I don't see any of the shock that's rocking my usually very solid foundations.

He knew I was here.

My eyes follow their movements, holding him firm in the hope he finds something to give him some strength in my eyes. Hell knows he fucking needs some right now.

They throw him into the corner of the room and he lands with a grunt of pain before curling up into a ball.

To my surprise, they allow him to do so, but not before they reach for the chains secured to the wall and cuff both his wrists and ankles to stop him from going anywhere.

My heart races as I watch each of their movements, because I know what's going to happen next.

They're coming for me.

They've broken one of their little toys. Now, it's time to start on the other.

As if they can hear my thoughts, the three of them share a look before turning to me.

I don't so much as flinch as they glare pure hatred at me.

I narrow my eyes at them.

Bring it on, motherfuckers.

It'll take a lot to break me down. And I'm twistedly excited about watching them try.

"Daemon Deimos," one of them taunts as they close in on me. "The Cirillos' very own bogeyman. Aren't we lucky?"

I sneer at him, causing the split in my lip to crack open.

My shackles are released and I'm hauled to my feet. If they're expecting me to fight, then they're going to be disappointed. I'm more calculated than that.

When I turn on them and fuck them over, they won't see it fucking coming.

Of course, right now, I have no fucking clue how that's going to happen.

But it will. I have that much faith in myself at least.

Even if I never get to see daylight again after this ordeal, I'm gonna make damn well sure I take these motherfuckers to hell with me.

"Compliant little shit, aren't you?" the older of the men points out, a smirk playing on his lips.

"And here we were, thinking we'd scored ourselves the ultimate little pet."

My arms are wrenched above my head, bound with rope, and I'm hung up like a piece of fucking meat ready to go to the slaughter.

They circle me as if they're lions waiting to take down their prey. But none of them make a move.

Refusing to show any fear, I hold each of their eyes in turn.

Clearly, they're familiar with my reputation, and I'd hate to disappoint them by showing them anything other than the cold, detached motherfucker they all think I am.

"Some pretty little scars you got there, boy," the older one taunts again.

He pulls a knife from inside his sock and holds the point to the very top of my longest scar.

"Maybe we should open you back up again. See what they replaced your heart with when you were just a babe in arms, huh? Rumour has it, your granddaddy sold your soul to the devil long before you were born and that left you with nothing but a cold, rotting piece of meat in its place." The mention of my evil shit of a grandfather almost makes me react, but I stuff it right down into the lockbox I keep inside for all that shit.

He presses the knife harder into my scar, the sharpness of it easily slicing through my skin.

Glancing down, I watch as blood immediately pools around the blade.

"Truly thought you'd bleed black," the guy, who wears an ugly scar across his cheek like a medal, mutters.

I've no idea who these motherfuckers are—not by face, anyway. But then, the Italians are good at keeping their secret weapons well hidden. If one of them were to spill a name though, I've no doubt I'd know every single thing about them from the intel I've heard over the years.

"Disappointed," the third, who's rocking a scraggly beard, agrees while the one with the knife continues slicing down my chest.

It's not actually that deep, but fuck, it stings like a motherfucker. Not that I'm going to let them see that.

Blood runs down my abs before soaking into the waistband of my boxers.

Beard watches and his eyes flare with excitement, clueing me into what's next.

His scarred fingers twist in the elastic, and he tugs hard enough to rip through the fabric which leaves me swinging, my toes barely scraping the rough floor beneath me.

"I wasn't fucking finished," the old one complains, staring at my half-sliced-open scar.

With smirks playing on their lips and excitement in their eyes, they watch me until I've fallen still once more before they continue, making each touch, hit, and slice through my skin more painful than the last.

My anger and need for retribution burn red hot within me as I watch them, learning their weaknesses and trying to somehow get the upper hand, all the while hanging broken, bloody, and naked from the fucking ceiling.

By the time they decide to give up, the darkness of this pitiful situation is starting to get the better of me.

"Put him out," Scar instructs, and only a second later, that familiar feeling of drugs running into my system hits me before everything goes black and I'm forced to enter a whole other kind of hell.

8

CALLI

The guys leave not long after Emmie and Stella get themselves comfortable on Alex's sofa.

We each receive a kiss before they disappear, although the one I get from Alex is much more PG than the one they both get from their boys.

Emmie and Stella both cling to them as if they never want to let them out of their sight. But we all know they need to go. And there is no way they'd ever stop either of them from doing what they needed to do.

The second the front door closes, they both turn their compassionate yet intrigued eyes on me.

"Don't," I breathe, knowing exactly what they're going to say. I hug my warm mug closer and take a sip.

"Judgement free zone, baby C. You do whatever you need to do right now to help. But just know—"

"We're going to want details," Emmie finishes as if they're one freaking person.

"I love you two, you know that, right?" I ask, feeling

their support, even if it comes in their own brand of teasing and fucked-up-ness.

"We love you too, Calli," they both say in unison.

"So... how comfortable is Alex's bed?" Emmie adds with a smirk.

A sad laugh falls from my lips. "It's what I needed. He's... fuck," I sigh, lowering my mug. "He's just the sweetest, most supportive person I think I've ever met."

"Rude," Stella mutters lightly.

"I know he's doing it because of the whole me and Daemon thing, and if that hadn't happened then I'm sure things would be very different right now. Being with him makes me feel closer to Daemon, and I kinda think he feels the same."

"You really are a cute little throuple, aren't you?" Emmie asks with a smile.

"A thro... what?"

"Ignore her. She's just teasing." I glare at the two of them. "She's suggesting you're hooking up with both of them."

"Uh..." The look on my face is apparently enough to give them the answer they already knew, because they both laugh at me. "There's nothing like that with Alex."

"We know. We're just teasing."

"I'm so glad he's being what you need."

"I just hope I'm returning the favour, because I can't even imagine what he's going through right now."

"Has he said anything?" Emmie asks, suddenly sounding serious.

"Like what?"

She shrugs. "I dunno, but you hear those stories all the time about twins. About them feeling pain for the other, knowing when they're ill and all that weird shit. I just wondered if..."

"I don't think they're those kind of twins," I say sadly. "Although he has said that he doesn't feel like he's gone. But what does that even mean? It's probably just hope talking."

"It might not be. It's proven that twins know these things. Alex could be onto something."

As much as I want to latch onto that train of thought and run with it until it's all I can think about, I know I can't. Hope right now is a dangerous thing. I need to keep my head on straight.

"I can't afford to let myself believe that."

"I understand that, Cal. I really do."

Silence falls as we get lost in our own heads.

"I thought you promised me coffee and breakfast," Emmie eventually pipes up.

"You're as bad as the guys," Stella mutters.

"We're ordering in, yeah?" I ask in a rush. The strength of the fear that slams into me at just the thought of walking outside of this building and facing the world is almost crippling.

Seeing it consume me, Stella rushes to my side, wraps her arm around my shoulders and takes my free hand in hers.

"Whatever you need, Calli," she whispers.

"I-I'm just not ready to—"

"Shh. You don't need to explain anything to us,

okay? We're happy following your lead and just being what you need."

What I need right now is to be in Daemon's arms, or get a hug from my dad.

But neither of those are going to be happening.

That realisation causes a sob to erupt from my throat as a wave of grief so strong washes through me, I have no chance of fighting it, so I just allow myself to drown in its darkness.

The mug is taken from my hand before Emmie's warmth spreads down my other side, leaving me sandwiched between the two of them.

I lose myself in my grief and sob on Stella's shoulder, soaking her hoodie and clinging to both of them like they're going to be able to stop me from drowning.

At some point, my sobs subside, and my exhaustion sets in.

I drift off with them still holding me, and my traitorous dreams take me right back to Daemon's grandparents' house, where the sun is beating down and my boy is lounging beside me shirtless and with a wide smile on his face.

I have no idea how long I'm out for, or realise that I've been moved so I'm lying on the sofa with Alex's duvet covering me. His scent surrounds me, helping ground me and give me some strength.

"I hate feeling this helpless. There's got to be something we can do," Emmie says, her voice hushed somewhere in the room.

"We just need to be here. Or if you want to go and do some more digging, I can stay," Stella offers.

"Do you really think they're going to find anyone else alive? Theo said it's been days."

"I know. I just... we can't give up hope."

There's no movement, but I feel their eyes on me. My skin tingles, my blood heating.

But I don't open my eyes or let them know that I'm awake.

"I'm worried about her," Stella whispers.

"She'll be okay. She's so much stronger than everyone thinks she is."

"Well, she managed to tame the devil," Stella quips, trying to lighten the mood.

"It makes a lot of sense, you know. The way Alex used to shamelessly flirt with her... it was all to get a rise out of him."

"Didn't work though, did it? That stubborn fuck is like a rock with his emotions."

I can't help but let my heart soar as Stella talks about him as if he's still here. It feeds that bit of hope I'm trying to keep suppressed.

"Something tells me he's very different with her."

"Fuck, I want to get the chance to see it."

"Yeah," Emmie sighs. "Do you really think there's a chance?"

Stella's response is silent, and it shatters what she said before.

"She doesn't deserve this. Losing Evan is bad enough. But if she loses him too..."

"I know. But she'll be okay. She's got us, Alex, all the others."

"Did Theo manage to speak to Nico this morning?"

"Nope. His phone was still going straight to voicemail."

"Shit," Stella hisses. "What the hell is going to happen now? He's next in line for Evan's job, right?"

"I guess, yeah."

"Would they give it to him, though? He's so young and—"

"Stupid?" I offer, finally letting them know that I'm awake.

Emmie barks a laugh.

"I was going to be more sympathetic than that and say inexperienced, but I guess if the shoe fits..." Stella adds.

Swinging my legs off the sofa, I sit up, keeping the duvet clutched to me as if it's a comfort blanket.

"How are you feeling?" Emmie asks, both of them studying me as if I'm about to shatter into a million pieces right before them.

"Groggy," I mumble, ignoring the incessant ache in my chest.

"You missed the coffee and breakfast," Stella points out, and I glance at the empty wrappers in front of them.

"Missed it? It's been hours, I'm hungry again."

We both stare at Emmie in amusement.

"Of course you are. What do you fancy, Calli?"

"Uh..." I hesitate. I have no idea when I last ate, but

doing so is the furthest thing on my mind right now. I should probably be starving, but I can't feel anything but pain.

"Chinese?" Emmie suggests, knowing it's my favourite, but I'm not sure I can stomach it.

I shake my head, trying to come up with something I could pick at. I need to eat, hell knows I do. Somehow, I've got to figure out a way to push past all this grief and misery and give my body the fuel it needs.

Guilt knots up my stomach tight as I think about the huge secret I'm keeping from my closest friends. But I know it's the right thing to do.

I need the secret right now. I need this little connection to Daemon that only Alex is aware of. In some way, it's helping keep him alive.

"Nachos," I blurt. "I could eat nachos."

"Mexican sounds like a winner to me." Emmie grabs her phone from the side to find somewhere to order from. "Margaritas?" she asks, a smile lighting up her face.

Shit.

"You two can. I'm not sure drinking is a good idea for me right now," I say, praying they don't see through my statement.

"You sure? It might help take the edge off," Stella asks.

"I'm sure. I'll just have water or something in Alex's fridge," I say, pushing from the sofa and padding down toward his room to use the bathroom.

I pee before standing in front of the basin and staring at myself in the mirror.

My face is pale, so pale it's bordering on grey, and the skin beneath my eyes is so dark it almost looks like I've been punched. But it's the brokenness in my usually bright blues that makes my breath catch.

"Get it together, Callista. Everyone needs you to be strong. Your baby needs you to be strong."

Tears fill my eyes as I whisper those words to myself.

It's so surreal. As if I'm living someone else's life right now.

Sadly though, this is very much reality.

I need to do something about that positive test. Book a doctor's appointment. Google what the hell I should be doing. Something. Anything. But the prospect of thinking ahead, to a future where he might not be in it, where this baby might not only be missing a grandfather but a father too?

Fuck.

I bend over, the pain cutting through me too much to bear as I think about what could be.

I give myself two minutes to wallow before I splash my face, brush my teeth once again, attempt to widen my shoulders, and hold my head up high.

It's hard. Really fucking hard.

But I have to do it.

For Dad.

For Daemon.

For the little bean that's growing inside me.

My hand splays across my flat belly.

No matter what happens, this little one is their legacy. He will walk in their footsteps and be proud of where he came from.

Forcing down the lump of emotion that clogs my throat once more, I throw the door open and walk out.

Both Emmie and Stella watch me with concerned eyes as I continue to battle with the tears pooling in my eyes. But at least with my entire life falling apart around me, they have no reason to ask what these specific tears are for.

"Dude is five minutes away. You can go this time," Stella tells Emmie after checking the phone sitting between them.

"I'll go," I blurt.

"No, it's okay."

"I'm serious," I say, taking a step toward the front door. My need for some fresh air is too much to deny.

"Uh, okay. Do you want us to come?"

I look between the two of them, hating how much they're struggling with how to help me right now.

"I'm okay. I just want some air. I'll grab the food and come straight back up."

"You should probably put some more clothes on," Emmie suggests, looking down at my bare legs that are poking out of the bottom of Alex's hoodie.

"I'll only be a minute," I say, tugging down the hem and heading for the door.

"Take this. Just in case," Stella urges, holding out my phone for me.

"Sure thing, Mum," I tease. She shrugs, not caring

one bit that she's being a little overbearing. And honestly, I don't either.

"Love you, Calli."

"Love you too," I say, my heart twisting up with the words I wish I'd said to Daemon Saturday night.

With a sigh, I leave them behind in search of just a few minutes of solitude.

As I expected, the hallways are deathly silent, and in only seconds I'm standing in front of the lift, waiting for it to rise through the building.

But as I stand there, memories begin playing out in my mind.

The night I ran from him—the night I drugged him—comes back to me, and I stumble back against the wall as the weight of that rash and reckless decision hits me full force.

I could have killed him that day. I had no idea what I was doing when I crushed those pills into his Fanta.

"Daemon," I breathe, feeling his loss even more potently in these few minutes.

But despite the threat of another panic attack, I manage to get ahold of my breathing before it spirals. And instead of locking myself in a metal box without enough air, I head for the stairs.

The second I push through the double doors at the entrance, I suck in a deep breath of air and lift my face to the sun, letting it warm my skin for a few minutes.

I want to say it makes me feel better, but right now, I'm not sure anything has the capability of doing that.

The sound of an approaching moped drags me back

to reality, and when I lower my head, I find he's pulled up in front of me.

"For Emmie?" he asks, casting a curious glance at my outfit, but he quickly pulls himself together and opens up the little pack on his bike to reveal our giant bag of food. My eyes widen at the sight of it, but I can't deny the rumble of my belly just thinking about what's inside.

I mutter my thanks before heading back into the building, and this time, I hit the button for the lift, unwilling to hike it all the way back up to the penultimate floor.

Voices hit my ears a beat before the doors open, not giving me the chance to run—not that I really need to run from anyone in this building anymore, but it still gets my hackles up. That is, until the two people inside smile sadly at me and step back to let me join them.

I smile at Jodie, but it's Bri who really steals my attention. Curiosity burns through her. And I understand why. It's been days since she got me that test, and she still doesn't know the result. It must be killing her.

"How are you doing?"

"Yeah, you know," I mutter, joining them.

"I do," Jodie mutters. And the fact that she really does after everything she's been through recently gives me a connection with her that I've never felt before. "I know it seems hopeless right now, but it will get better. I promise you that."

"Thanks. I'm hanging out in Alex's flat with Emmie

and Stella. We've got Mexican," I say, holding up the bag. "You guys wanna join?"

"Great minds, huh?" Bri says, holding up a matching bag.

"Sounds good to us," Jodie says with a smile.

No one says anything else until the doors open once more and Jodie steps out first, leaving me to trail behind Bri, but she slows her pace to put some space between us.

"How's Nico?" she asks, genuine concern in her eyes which warms something inside me.

I knew she cared, but when the pair of them spend most of their time at each other's throats, it's easy to forget that.

"Honestly, I have no idea. I've barely spoken to him, but the guys are worried."

"Do you... do you think he'd see me if I tried to talk to him?"

"There's only one way to find out."

"You think he'll come back here tonight? He crashed at your parent's place last night, right?"

I shrug. I have no idea what's going through my brother's head right now, and honestly, I'd hate to even try to figure it out.

"I'm sure the guys will let us know."

She nods, glancing over her shoulder to check that Jodie has moved far enough away.

"How are you holding up really?" she asks.

"I'm a mess." It comes out on an awkward laugh that just makes me cringe.

She nods in understanding. "For what it's worth, I think he's going to surprise you all and just turn up one day like nothing happened. Maybe with an Italian head or two as prizes."

"We can only hope, right?" I mutter sadly, wishing once more that I could latch onto that hope.

"Calli, what was... what did it say?"

I sigh, dropping my eyes from hers for a beat.

"It was positive, Bri.

She gasps at my confession. "Oh shit."

"Pretty much sums it up. But listen, only Alex and you have any clue about this, and I'd really like it if—"

"Your secret is safe with me, Calli. And if you need anything, a friend to visit the doctors, someone to talk to. Anything. I'm right here, okay?" She reaches out for my hand and squeezes it softly. The move seems to have a direct line to my tear ducts. Before I know what's happening, I'm in floods of tears and falling apart all over again.

9

DAEMON

"**M**otherfucker." The loud grunt of pain drags me from the darkness I'd drifted off to.

Even here, with the drugs they keep pumping me full of, I can't get any rest.

Every time I close my eyes, all I see is her.

Alone.

And it fucking wrecks me.

I know that's not true. I know she's going to have all the others supporting her, but it doesn't stop my fear.

I have no idea how much time—how many days—might have passed since we've been in here. But with every second that passes, and the short amount of time I get as the drugs leave my body, my memory of that night begins to clear. The events that led me here are emerging, helped by the guy groaning in pain chained up in the opposite corner of the room.

"Fuck. Shit."

My eyes move to my cellmate. For once, my view of him is clear as whoever was in here when I was last passed out left us some food and water—and the lights on.

It would be easy to think that one of them might be going soft on us. But I know that really, it's just a way to extend their time with us. They don't want us dying yet, and the mouldy bread and lukewarm water will help with that.

His eyes meet mine, and I see the pain I feel in every inch of my body as I stare back at him.

Any fear I had about him not being genuine, about him not caring about Calli, or lying to me the day he risked his life to tell me that she was in trouble has been obliterated.

Because since the moment I discovered who my cellmate was, I've seen nothing but genuine loyalty to her—to us—which is a head fuck at best, but I'm not exactly in a place where I want to dive too deep into that.

One thing I know for sure though is that Antonio Santoro is one loyal, yet stupid motherfucker.

He didn't have to end up here. He could have walked away from the destruction that night when the rest of the Marianos did. But the stupid shit decided he needed to honour the promise he apparently made to Calli as she ran, and tried to drag me out just seconds before the roof came down on both of us.

He might have been successful, but we ran straight into his uncle. And that motherfucker was not happy, although he couldn't also mask the satisfaction at having a Cirillo in his grasp that blazed in his eyes.

The last thing I remember was a blinding pain exploding on the side of my head before the world around me went black.

"You make that sound like it hurts," I mutter, my voice rough, pain ripping up my throat from lack of water.

"Fuck you, man," he grunts back, but he doesn't give up. He keeps punishing himself until he finally manages to sit upright on the cold concrete floor.

He blows out a long slow breath, his eyes closed tight as he fights his way through the pain.

We haven't really spoken. This is one of only a few times that he's been awake or lucid enough to say anything that makes any sense.

After what must be a good few minutes of silence, he finally opens his eyes again.

"I hate you, you know."

A smile kicks up at the corner of my mouth, splitting my lip open and filling my mouth with blood.

"Yeah, feeling's mutual."

His shoulders shake once before his ribs must hurt so much that he quickly stills again.

"Why'd you do it?"

"You know why," he states.

"You're a real stupid motherfucker, you know that, right?"

"I promised her, man."

"But your Family. Your loyalties should be with them."

"With my corrupt, blood-thirsty uncle, you mean? Nah, I'm fucking good."

"You're lucky to still be alive," I mutter, not that it really needs saying.

"Am I, though? Something tells me being dead would be easier right now."

Pain darkens his eyes, but it's not just from his physical injuries, and that twists me up on the inside.

"You really care about her, don't you?"

"Does it matter?"

"No, she's mine," I say fiercely.

"I know. It was right there the second I saw the two of you together. You're the only lucky motherfucker in this room."

"Pretty sure we're both failing at life right now. Now, did you want the last chunk of green bread or can I have it?" I deadpan.

Stretching my leg out, I kick the tray toward him with my toe.

It was a rhetorical question. From the look of him, it's clear to say he needs it more than me.

Those guys might be brutal with me. But it's nothing compared to how they treat him.

I'm the enemy. But Ant is worse. He's a traitor.

"Yum... my favourite," he mutters, not arguing with me over it and reaching forward, albeit slowly.

Each chew looks painful, but I sit there and watch, my brain racing as fast as it's capable of right now, trying to come up with a way to get out of this. But there aren't all that many fucking options in the concrete box we've been locked in.

"We're gonna have to go out through the door," Ant says as if he can read my thoughts.

"Yeah, I wasn't thinking about digging a fucking hole."

"We just need to be patient." I glare at him, seriously un-fucking-impressed with that suggestion. "My uncle will send different guys at some point."

"How is that going to help? I can't see them just opening the fucking door and wishing us well."

"Well, no. It's never going to be that easy, but there will be a chance."

I study him, trying to read his unspoken words.

"You've already got a get-out plan, haven't you?"

"Yes and no. But as you should be well aware, you dance with the devil, you need a way to get the fuck away from him as fast as you can."

I nod, seeing a whole new side to Antonio Santoro.

Time moves on, but other than painful visits from our captors and the odd food delivery, nothing changes.

Our wounds never heal, because they ensure they deliver more agonising blows to guarantee the pain never lessens.

They never utter a word about their plans for us, if

and when they plan to kill us or how long they want to continue torturing us.

The longer it goes on, the more chance they might have of being discovered—assuming of course that everyone hasn't just assumed I'm dead.

Hell, they could all be at my funeral right now.

The thought of Calli standing there mourning me knots up my gut and makes my heart ache.

I hate the idea of her hurting because of these Italian cunts.

But if they're out there looking for me, then every day is a day closer to them finding me.

It's a big if right now, but it's all I've got. That along with the hope that whatever Ant has planned that he's refusing to give me details on.

I let out a sigh, resting my head back against the wall and closing my eyes.

The only thing I guess I can be grateful for right now is that neither of us have been hung from the ceiling for what I assume is a few days, instead left chained up in our corners. At least we can move our aching limbs, although finding any kind of comfort is impossible.

My stomach growls loudly, but just like every other time it's happened, I ignore it, using its pain to give me strength.

My thoughts shift to my girl, to our time together at my grandparents'. I think about her smile, her laugh, her gentle touch and quick wit.

I drown in my memories, in the lightness she brings into my life.

But before long, my memories morph and the guy she's touching, kissing, smiling at like he is literally her whole life isn't me.

It's Alex.

Pain rips through my chest.

I made him promise me that he'd look after her. And I've no doubt he will.

He loves her. Maybe not in exactly the same way I do, but his feelings for her are powerful enough that he'd do right by her.

But just how far will that lead...

I've seen the way she looks at him. I mean, we're identical twins, it would be weird if she wasn't attracted to him, right?

As my body caves to its exhaustion, the images playing out in my mind of the two of them continue, their relationship growing, their bond strengthening until I'm nothing but a memory. Everything plays out in my mind, them together, kissing, fucking, him putting a motherfucking ring on her finger and her belly swollen with his baby.

"NO," I cry, sitting up so fast that pain shoots through every inch of my body.

I find Ant staring back at me with wide eyes before the lock on the door clicks, the hinges groaning under its weight as it's opened.

Even more dread seeps into my bones as I wait for the inevitable. It feels like it's been a while since they laid into us, although that could all just be a figment of my imagination and the hallucinations I've been suffering with from whatever that drug they like to use on us is.

The old guy and Scar step into the room, but the third guy is different.

He's younger, less... scary. Not that I'm actually scared of these motherfuckers.

I glance at Ant, who's laid out on his side of the room, pretending that he's equally as unfazed by their arrival as I am, all the while silently hoping that this new guy is a part of his plan.

I'm more than fucking ready to get out of this shithole and find my girl.

"Get him up," Oldie barks, pointing toward me, and my heart sinks, although I can't deny the promise of more pain makes something blaze inside me.

The second the new guy turns toward me, recognition flickers at the back of my mind.

I know him.

He's Ant's friend. Cousin.

Fuck. *Fuck.*

Is this it? Is this the beginning of his escape plan?

"Well, well, well, the rumour is fucking true," Enzo mutters, his eyes running over every broken, bruised, and dirty inch of my naked body. "We caught ourselves the Cirillo bogeyman."

My jaw tics in irritation as he looks at me as if I'm nothing. All the while, all I can do is hope and fucking pray that this is all an act.

He steps closer to me and drops to his haunches.

"How the mighty fall, huh, Deimos? I think this is what they call karma." His top lip peels back as he makes a show of sniffing the air around me.

Yeah, dickhead, I know I smell like a half-rotting corpse. I have to live with the stench every second of every fucking day.

"I heard what you did to our guys. I heard the pain you caused, the torture you delivered. It only seems fair that we get to deliver payback in the form of blood and broken bones, right?" Lifting his foot from the ground, I swallow down a grunt of agony as it collides with my already bruised ribs.

"Fucking. Greek. Fucking. Cunt," he growls with every blow he lands on me.

Fuck. If this is an act, then he's fucking convincing. His eyes are dark and full of malice, nothing but hate and the need to settle the score etched into his every feature.

When he's finished, he grabs the key for my shackles off Oldie, and with Scar holding me should I be stupid enough to try and fight, I'm hauled to my feet, my wrists bound in rope once more and my arms wrenched above my head so I can return to the hook in the ceiling.

Like always, I don't say a fucking word.

I keep all my threats for their long and painful deaths locked down. I'll wait to have my say when I've got them strapped to a fucking chair, my own vials full of hallucinogenic drugs and every weapon I can get my hands on to cause as much pain as physically possible.

And it's those dark thoughts that help transport me out of this shitty, hopeless situation.

"Good, now your little friend over there," Oldie instructs, turning Enzo's hatred on the guy he used to call a friend.

"He's not a friend of mine," Enzo spits. There's so much bitterness and distrust in his voice that I start to wonder if he's nothing to do with Ant's plan.

But he has to be, right?

Ant's beating is even more brutal than mine, and when he's finally hooked up to the ceiling so that his back is pressed against mine, I'm pretty sure he's passed out.

"This one's still conscious," Oldie says before swinging his fist toward me. The blow is so hard that everything instantly goes black.

10

CALLI

I gasp when a pair of hands slides around my waist. Arms wrap around me, holding me tight.

I didn't see him coming, despite standing in front of a mirror having a serious discussion with myself about being strong enough to handle today.

He drops his face into the crook of my neck and breathes me in.

"How are you holding up?" Alex whispers, his rush of air sending goosebumps racing over my skin.

"Badly," I confess.

"Anytime you want to get out of there, all you've got to do is say the word."

I nod in agreement. It's not the first time he's made me those promises, but I know it's not something I can take him up on.

"I need to be there, Alex. Nico needs me." My thoughts flicker briefly to Mum. I want to feel guilty for the little time I've seen her since we lost Dad. But I just don't. My heart is consumed by too much pain and grief to allow anything in for the woman who obviously doesn't care about how I'm getting on.

I've come back here a couple of times over the past few days, mostly because I needed to pick some things up. School work mainly, in the hope it might have been something of a distraction, but while I might have sat and stared at my textbooks, the reality was that nothing went in. The words just swirled around in front of me, leaving me no better off than when I started.

The only thing I've been able to read and actually soak up is the early pregnancy stuff that Alex and I have been reading together.

Butterflies flutter in my belly as I remember just how sweet he was, lying with me while I read through what to expect in the early weeks out loud so he could learn with me.

"He does. But he's got all of us too. And Bri is coming, right?"

"Yeah, although I'm not sure he's going to be all that impressed when he discovers that."

Just like she promised, Bri has tried to see Nico since we spoke the other day, but each time, he's point-blank refused. At first, he had the excuse of being busy still searching for survivors in the rubble, but since the authorities have called off their search, and then Uncle Damien had little choice but to do the same after not finding anyone, dead or alive, for days he didn't have a leg to stand on.

Now, he's just being a prick.

I mean, I get it. I don't exactly want to open myself up to the world right now. I'd happily hide in Alex's flat forever if it meant I never had to face my new reality.

With no sign of Daemon amongst the remains of the country club, and no other clues that some kind of miracle might have happened and he might have got out—which everyone loves to keep teasing me with and giving me false hope—the only serious conclusion to all of this is that he was buried too deep and that we're never going to find him. The prospect of that, of having to watch my belly grow, to have our child, to live without him rips me in two. It's a kind of deep-rooted pain that I'm not sure I'm ever going to be free of.

"At least it will give him something else to think about," Alex mutters lightly.

He lifts his head, resting his chin on my shoulder, studying me in the mirror. My black dress fits me like a second skin, and his eyes darken as he appreciates it.

"You look hot, baby C."

"Not exactly the look I was going for to attend my father's funeral."

"No, I know. But you should still be able to feel good about yourself while everything is falling apart."

"Not sure that's possible."

Unwrapping his arms from me, he places both of his giant hands on my belly.

"You've got to focus on the good," he whispers. "Both of them are going to be so proud of you, and even though they're not here, you just know that they're going to love this little one so hard."

"Seriously?" I bark as my eyes fill with tears. My mascara might be waterproof, but I don't think even the most expensive brand in the world is capable of holding steady when Alex says words like that.

"You know it's true."

When his eyes lift to mine once more, his own grief shines as bright as mine.

Twisting in his embrace, I throw my arms around his shoulders and hold him tight.

"Thank you," I whisper in his ear. "I couldn't have done any of this without you."

"Sure you could, Cal. You're a Cirillo, you can handle anything."

Dread sits heavy in my stomach for what I'm going to have to handle today.

There's a knock on the door at the top of the stairs before it's pulled open. Alex and I part as Jocelyn calls down for us. "The cars are here."

"We'll be right there," Alex says back, obviously able to tell that there's no chance I'm going to be able to force words past the giant, messy ball of emotion in my throat.

He steps back from me, takes my cheeks in his hands and holds my eyes.

"You've got this, Calli. Walk out there with your head held high and let everyone know what a kick-arse motherfucker your dad was."

I nod, it's the only response I'm able to give as the grief threatens to swallow me up and never spit me back out.

Alex takes my hand and pulls me toward the stairs.

Jocelyn gives me a soft, sympathetic smile as we pass her. She's dressed as flawlessly as ever, but her white shirt has been replaced by a black one as she mourns right alongside us.

Voices float down from the formal living room and when we appear in the doorway, all eyes turn on us.

Mum is sitting in the centre of the sofa with Aunt Selene and Iris on either side of her. But she doesn't look like she needs their support. Her make-up and hair are flawless, and her designer dress screams money and pretence.

Her eyes find mine and something akin to hate crackles between us.

We've spoken barely ten words to each other since discovering that Dad died, but they were enough for me to know that she doesn't approve of the fact I've basically moved in with Alex. I mean, nothing official has happened or anything, but he's been my rock this week. And the last place I wanted to be, even if it's surrounded by comforting memories of my dad, is here, with her.

She's devastated, of course she is. But... I don't know. Something about the way she's acting just doesn't sit right with me. Although, I could probably say that about the way she's acted most of my life, so there's really not much new there.

"Hey," Emmie says, stepping up to me and severing the weird tension between me and my mother.

"Hey, thank you for coming."

"Oh shush. You know there isn't anywhere we'd be other than supporting you right now." I look over her shoulder, finding Theo standing there, and then to Uncle Damien standing with Christos. Jerome is on the other sofa with his leg awkwardly stretched out before him.

He's assured me in the last few days that he's fine, but that it's going to take a little time to be able to use it properly again.

I smile at him, needing him to know that I appreciate his support.

"Are we all ready to go?" Uncle Damien asks, his voice unusually rough as he takes a step toward his wife and holds his hand out for her. She smiles at him, staring him dead in the eye, and I'm sure she sees way more pain in his depths than he'll ever allow us to see.

"Yes," Mum says, getting to her feet. A flash of white catches my eye, and I find that she's clutching a white handkerchief in her fingers. Seems a little pointless when there's no evidence of her shedding a single tear today, but whatever. I've got enough of my own issues right now to worry about her.

She's ushered to the door between Iris and Christos and the rest of us fall into step behind.

"Where the hell is Nico?" I whisper to Emmie in the hope she's overheard something.

"No idea. He didn't answer when we knocked for him. He's not answering his phone. But he should be here for this."

The sight of the black funeral cars parked in our driveway rocks me to my very core, but it's nothing compared to the moment my eyes land on the coffin in the back of the hearse and then the flowers in front of it that spell dad.

"Oh my God. This is really happening, isn't it?"

My entire body trembles as the grief bubbles up inside me, desperately trying to find an outlet.

"You can do this, Calli. We'll be right behind you, okay?"

Alex presses a kiss to my temple as an arm threads around my shoulder and I'm pulled into another body.

"He's right, baby C. We've got you," Theo promises, leading me forward and toward the car directly behind the hearse where Uncle Damien and Aunt Selene are just slipping inside.

Sucking in a deep breath, I drag my eyes away from Dad's black and copper coffin and focus on putting one foot in front of the other.

The funeral and then the wake that, thankfully, Uncle Damien and Aunt Selene organised to save Mum from having to lift a perfectly manicured finger, has been the most exhausting thing I've ever experienced.

The emotions, the tears, the pain... all of it has been utterly draining. Not to mention the worry over Nico.

He turned up. Thankfully. But not until the very last minute.

We were all being ushered into the church for the service to commence when his car came tearing into the car park. He tumbled out in his black suit, looking as suave as the rest of the boys, but I barely paid attention to that because the dark look in his eyes terrified me.

He's not coping, that much is more than obvious. I was worried before, but seeing his pain bleeding from him only shredded my heart even more than it already was.

I want to help him, hold him, try and convince him that things will one day be okay. But he's put a barrier up around him so high that I'm not even sure I'm going to be able to scale it.

Before I even had a chance to get close to him, Jocelyn wrapped her hand around my upper arm, and I had no choice but to walk into the church, leaving Nico, Uncle Damien, Charon, Galen, Stefanos, Christos, and Michail to carry Dad's coffin inside.

"Calli," a soft voice says, dragging me from the clutches of sleep before a large warm hand lands on my thigh. I told myself that I would keep my eyes open until we got back and I could get changed, but the second Alex pulled away from the hotel, my eyelids turned into something resembling lead weights and I immediately lost my fight. "We're home."

Home...

A lump crawls up my throat as I think about the two men in my life who were those things to me.

My dad, the quiet strength around our house. His calming nature was the tonic Mum's personality needed, and without him, I have no idea what's going to happen.

And Daemon. Every single thing about my dark boy signified home to me. The second he wrapped his arms around me, something settled inside me. I relaxed, knowing that I'd found my place. Discovered where I was meant to be all this time.

But with both of them gone, I'm not sure I'll ever replace everything they gave me.

Alex is doing his best. So is Theo, the girls, and Jocelyn. But it's not the same. And it never will be.

"Y-yeah, okay," I whisper, my voice cracking with emotion.

He smiles sadly at me, but unable to find any words that might come anywhere close to making me feel better about life right now, he kills the engine and pushes the door open.

I move at a snail's pace, my entire body heavy with tiredness, and by the time I curl my fingers around the handle, the door opens and I find Alex staring down at me.

"Come on, baby C."

Slipping my hand into his, I let him pull me to my feet, drag me into his side and wrap his arm around me.

I sink into his warmth, his support as my body moves without instruction from my brain.

In only seconds, we're inside the lift and heading toward his floor.

Just like every time I walk down the hallway toward his flat, my eyes linger on Daemon's door. Despite knowing that I can let myself in anytime I want, I haven't done it yet. The urge to do so is there, but the thought of being surrounded by his scent, by him, has been too terrifying to even really consider.

Right now though... it's different.

I need it.

Him.

My steps falter, forcing Alex to stop with me.

"You want to..." His words trail off, clueing me in to the fact that he's been putting off going inside too. We've not talked about it. But it's been an elephant in the room for days.

"Y-yeah. I think... I think I need it. After today, I need to feel close to him. Is that okay? Can you..." I swallow nervously, hating the thought of him feeling like he has to do this with me if he's not ready.

"Y-yeah, it's totally fine. Whatever you need."

"This isn't just about me, Alex."

"Right now it is. What you've done today... Hell, Calli. I don't know how you've held it all together. I'm in fucking awe of your strength."

"I don't feel all that strong right now," I confess.

"I know. I know the pain you're hiding. Your dad would have been so fucking proud of you today. You're fierce, Cal."

A smile curls at my lips.

All I've wanted all my life was to break through the image of the perfect, pretty little princess they all painted me as. And I can't help feeling that I might finally be doing it.

I want to be seen as a strong woman who can stand on her own two feet. Who can handle all the shit this life throws at her and keep her head held high through it all. I want to be seen in the same way Stella and Emmie are.

I want to be fierce.

I'm Callista Cirillo, Evan Cirillo's daughter. This shit literally runs through my veins, and I want to own it. Stand up and claim my place as more than an heir producer. Okay, so that might be slightly ironic, seeing as I'm standing here growing one right now, but still.

Unable to respond to that comment, I lift my hand to the biometric scanner and wait for the light to turn green.

The second it does, I twist the handle and push the door open.

My entire body jolts and I barely get over the threshold before his scent surrounds me, rendering me utterly useless.

Maybe this was a really, really bad idea.

Memories of my time with him swamp me as I stand there frozen, my surroundings blur and the only thing I can focus on is him and everything I've lost.

"Calli?" Alex's voice breaks through my pain. "You sure you want to do this?"

"Y-yeah," I say, taking an unsteady step forward.

Kicking my heels off beside a pair of trainers

Daemon had left next to the cabinet in the hallway, I place my bag on the top before taking off toward the living room.

Images from the last, and only, time I was here play out in my mind.

I see myself perched on the kitchen counter as he cooked us breakfast, sitting on his lap at the table as he fed me, laid out on the top as he ate me.

My cheeks burn as I picture how we looked.

So much happened between us in such a short amount of time. Yet no one knew. It's a travesty that I couldn't share all of it with anyone. It's now this beautifully broken secret that's destined just to be ours.

Lifting my hand to my chest, I press my palm over my heart, hoping to squash the hurt that has taken up residence there.

"This place suits you, know you," Alex says quietly somewhere behind me.

"I was so shocked by this place when I first saw it. It's so—"

"Normal?" he asks with amusement.

"Yeah. I expected it to be like Theo's house of horrors."

"I think you know as well as I do that Daemon isn't like that, not really. Yes, he's dark and tortured and full of pain that he doesn't know what to do with, but deep down, he just wants to be normal. And this is it. This is where he gets to do that."

"I love it. It's so homely, so comforting."

"Yeah," he agrees. "And it's his. No one can hurt him here."

"I did," I blurt.

"You don't count, Cal. You could never really hurt him, not like others have."

"Thank God for that," I mutter. "You think he would mind if I borrow some clothes?"

Alex chuckles as he walks around me. "I think he'd love it."

With a nod, I take off toward his bedroom, needing to get out of my dress and be surrounded by nothing but the boy I never got to keep for myself.

"Can you?" I ask, aware that Alex has followed me down here.

Pulling my hair from my neck, I give him access to the zip running down my back.

A shiver runs down my spine as his fingers brush over my skin and goosebumps erupt over every inch of my body.

It's wrong. I know it is. But his touch makes me feel alive in a way that I haven't felt in so long. It holds a promise of something more than pain and grief, and right now I need an escape from it more than I need my next breath.

My heart begins to race as his knuckles brush over the small of my back, grazing the top of my underwear before he pulls his hand back.

Sucking in a breath, I try and force everything from my head as I turn around and find his eyes.

They're dark, telling me that that simple act had an effect on him too.

My breathing increases as our gaze holds. Something that isn't usually there—okay, so maybe it is, but it's never as intense as it is right now—crackles between us.

Desire like I've not felt since being in the bathroom with Daemon at the country club sits heavy in my lower stomach. But as much as I might try to convince myself it's the same, it's not. It's full of desperation, and not the if-I-don't-get-my-hands-on-you-now-I-might-die kind, but the if-you-don't-drag-me-out-of-this-pit-of-misery-by-making-me-feel-something-else-then-I-might-drown kind of way. It's way less sexy, but it feels just as necessary at the moment.

I take a small step forward, giving Alex enough clues as to where my head is at right now.

Is it too early to blame my libido on pregnancy?

"Calli, don't look at me like that," Alex warns, his voice rough with his own less-than-pure thoughts.

"Why?" I breathe, more than prepared to push him right now if it's going to result in getting out of my own head. Hell knows I can't turn to alcohol to do it, so I need the next best thing.

"You know why. We can't cross this line, Cal. It'll change everything and—"

"It doesn't have to." Taking a massive risk, I let my dress fall from my shoulders. It pools at my feet, leaving me standing in nothing but my strapless bra and my lace knickers.

It pains him to do so, I see it in his eyes, but his gaze never drops and he shakes his head.

"You're not thinking straight right now." He takes a step forward as anger surges through me. I reach out and wrap my fingers around his upper arm, stopping him from reaching the wardrobe.

"Don't tell me how I am right now. You have no idea how I'm feeling or what I need."

My vicious tone forces him to suck in a breath before he responds.

"You're right. I'm sorry. I have no idea what you're going through. But I do know that this," he says, glancing down at where I'm touching him, "isn't the answer."

I stand there in my underwear, feeling stripped bare as my battered emotions war within me.

"Y-you don't want me?" I don't mean to sound like a whiny little brat, but I can't help it.

My head is a mess and I don't know which way is up. But I do know that when he's touching me, everything feels more possible.

"Calli," he says, moving back in front of me again and dipping his head until our brows are touching. "What have I ever done to make you think I don't want you? You're beautiful, sexy, smart, strong. You're so much more than everyone else sees, and I'm totally in awe of you. But this isn't about what I want. It's about what you need, and that isn't me."

I stare up into his eyes, our breaths mingling as the heat of his body seeps into my skin.

"But he's not here. What I need is gone, Alex. And I don't know what I'm meant to do to banish this pain."

He smiles at me sadly. "I can assure you, fucking me won't help. I need you just as much as I think you need me right now," he confesses, cupping my cheek and sending warmth racing down my neck. "And I can't lose that too, Calli. I'd never forgive myself."

He shifts his head, pressing his lips there instead and drawing me in for a hug.

The second he releases me, I crave his touch even more. But I've had time to cool my libido, and I know he's right.

Allowing something to happen would be reckless, and it would risk everything we've built in the past few days.

"Here," he says, holding out one of Daemon's black hoodies for me to wear.

I hesitate to take it, unsure if it's going to be too much. But in the end, my fingers wrap around the soft fabric and I draw it closer, lifting it to my nose to breathe him in.

"I'll leave you to it. Do you want me to order any food or—"

"No, I'm fine thank you," I whisper while drowning in everything that is the boy who stole my heart and took it with him when he left me.

By the time I rejoin him, I'm wearing just Daemon's hoodie and my underwear, loving how the brushed fleece inside feels against my skin.

"His clothes look better on you," Alex mutters, ripping his eyes away from whatever he's watching on the TV and dropping them to my legs. "Come and sit down, you look wiped."

Unable to argue, I pad over to the sofa he's sitting on, drop right beside him, and cuddle into his side.

No words are said between us as our grief collides once more. They're not needed. Our pain speaks for itself.

After a few minutes, he lies down and drags me with him.

Snuggling back against him, he wraps his arm around my waist and holds me tight, his hand splayed on my stomach possessively.

"Relax, Calli. I'm not going anywhere."

With his thumb brushing back and forth over my stomach and his shallow breathing in my ear, I soon drift off into a fitful sleep.

I startle sometime later when a loud bang rocks through the flat.

My eyes fly open, expecting to find Alex in the kitchen, breaking something, but it quickly becomes obvious that he's still behind me and still holding me.

There's another thud before what I'm sure is footsteps somewhere close, but that's not possible, because only the two of us have access. Alex made sure of it a few days ago.

My brows draw together as my heart rate picks up and the shuffling steps come closer.

A shadow appears and my lips part to scream to wake Alex up when the person the shadow belongs to stumbles around the corner.

11

DAEMON

The door slams shut on our cell, and I slump back into the corner of the room as pain screams through my weak, battered body.

I'll never submit to these arseholes. I'll never break and give them any intel on my Family, on my brothers. But fuck if the idea isn't tempting.

Ant is hanging from the hook once again, blood trickling from his wounds as he fights to drag in pained, rattling breaths.

Honestly, I don't know how much time he's got left. His body is wrecked. And while I might want to try to save him after what he's done for me, for Calli, right now, I'm pretty fucking useless to do anything but wallow in my own self-pity.

His eyes fall closed as he loses his battle against his body, and mine get heavy, the threat of darkness sweeping over me.

I fight it, not wanting the nightmares, the vivid

images of my past hell and the promise of a future that will never be mine.

"*Hey, is that you?*" *Calli calls, her soft voice washing through me and instantly making me relax.*

My girl.

My fucking girl.

I race toward her voice, barely noticing my surroundings. I'm too focused on seeing her face again, holding her tight to me, feeling the softness of her lips against mine.

But when I get to her, I watch as she walks straight into the arms of another.

Alex.

My heart begins to race, my blood pumping through my veins at an alarming rate as I watch the two of them.

He holds her as if she's the most precious thing in the world—which of course, she is. But she's my precious thing. Not his.

Pain slices through my chest as he nuzzles her neck, soaking up her sweet scent, drowning in it before he pulls back to look at her.

Everything around me blurs. My only focus is them as Alex stares down into her light blue eyes.

Why can't they see me?

"*Calli?*" *I try to call, but no noise leaves my lips.*

"*Calli?*" *I try again, only louder this time. But again. I'm mute.*

Alex's hand cups her cheeks, his thumbs brushing her soft skin, and his head dips.

"No," I cry, seeing what he's going to do, but it's pointless.

They can't hear me, they can't see me.

It's as if... it's as if I'm not even here.

But I am.

The pain is too real. The way my heart bleeds for her, my body aches for her, it has to be real.

"No," I breathe, my entire world falling out from beneath me as his lips meet hers.

She dives head first into the kiss just like he does, and I'm forced to stand there and watch as he steals away what is mine.

I try to move, but my legs won't work. I try to scream, to stop them, but no noise leaves me.

The only thing I can do is stand there and watch as my world crumbles around me and I lose the one good thing in my life.

It's how it should be. I've known that for a long, long time.

Alex would be better for her. Kinder, sweeter, more romantic. He's loyal and honest, smart. Everything I'm not and—

My body startles as a bang rocks through me and I rip my eyes open, instinctively curling into the corner.

My breathing is ragged as the image that was just playing out so vividly in my mind remains.

I told him to look after her. I trusted him to ensure she can move on from me if I fail to ever get back to her.

But fuck. Seeing them together, even if it was fictional, almost fucking broke me.

DARK LEGACY

It takes me a few seconds to drag myself from my torment to realise that no one came through the door. That those Italian cunts aren't bored sitting out there and decided that today is the day they deliver one too many brutal blows on their captives and put an end to all this bullshit.

"W-what's go—"

"You need to get me down," a weak voice says from a few feet away.

"Uh..."

"D-Daemon." He pauses, as if just talking causes him so much pain he can barely survive it. "Th-they're not coming. That w-was a signal."

"A-a-a s-s-signal?" I stutter, hating myself for it but too weak to try and fight it.

"Enzo. He's—"

"Fuck," All the air rushes from my lungs.

"He's hel-ping us."

The first bit of real hope I've felt in... what feels like a lifetime that we've been locked up in here floods through my veins.

"Well, he could have been a bit nicer about it," I mutter, pathetically rolling onto my hands and knees as I breathe through the agony that tears through my body. The chains attached to my ankles rattle ominously, pointing out one major flaw in his plan. "How exactly is that going to work?" I ask, looking at the heavy-duty locks keeping me attached to the wall.

I have every confidence that I could pick them if I

could find something to use, but this concrete cell is nothing but floor, walls and ceiling.

"I've got the keys. Just... get me down."

My legs tremble as I get to my feet, the grey, depressing room around me spinning as I try to find my balance.

My ribs scream, my muscles burn and my head pounds. But I can't let that stop me. If Ant is right and we have any kind of chance, then we have to take it.

"H-how a-a-am I-I-I—" The thought of lifting his weight sends a ripple of fear down my spine. But I know I have little choice.

I shuffle forward, my legs beginning to feel a little more useful as the seconds pass until my chain is pulled tight.

"Where is the key?" I ask with a wince. We're both still naked. Surely there are only a few options as to where it could be hidden.

"Tucked in the rope," Ant wheezes, and my eyes shoot to his bound wrists.

I know it's futile, but I still reach out to see if I can get to it. My fingertips are nowhere near, but I can reach his body. And if I can lift him, then I can unhook him and we can get it.

My heart pounds a steady beat in my chest as hope and fear meld. If we get caught, it's going to be the end of both of us. But if we get out...

"You need... you need to lift me off," he says, fear already glittering in his eyes.

The second I wrap my arm around him, it's going to

hurt like a bitch, because there is no way that more than a few of his ribs aren't broken.

I nod, trying to dig up some inner strength from somewhere.

My body is weaker than I've ever known. The repeated beatings, the lack of food and water, it's all seriously taking its toll. But I can't let them win. I refuse to.

We have a chance—I have a chance to get back to my girl—and there's no fucking way I'm not making the best of it. Even if it does end with both of us dying at those motherfucker's hands. At least I'll know I tried.

"You're sure about this?" I ask, needing the assurance that Enzo really is on our side.

"He's my ride or die, man. He just... he's out there trying to prove he's not."

I nod, aware that I'd do the exact same thing for Alex or any of the guys.

It's just a means to an end. And I have no choice but to believe everything Ant says. Hell, he's yet to prove he's anything but trustworthy.

"Okay. You're gonna need to try and swing a little closer then."

He sucks in a deep breath which makes him wince in pain, but something tells me that's just the tip of the iceberg when it comes to what tonight is going to hold, whichever way it goes.

He manages to get momentum, and the second he's close enough, I reach out, wrapping my arms around him.

A yelp of pain rips through the air as I crush his busted ribs, but other than that, he holds it together as I force my body to lift him.

My muscles strain and tremble with the exertion I'm forcing on them.

I don't feel like I'm achieving anything other than taking his weight from the hook and probably causing him more pain than he's ever experienced in his life. But after a few seconds, his weight gets heavier and the pair of us go crashing to the unforgiving floor in a heap of quivering limbs and pained groans.

"Fuck," I grunt, rolling Ant's body from on top of mine as gently as I can, while my hip smarts from where I landed on it.

His moan rips through the air.

"You okay, man?"

His eyes open, holding mine as he breathes in and out slowly.

"You're gonna be able to go through with this, right?" The thought of following through with whatever this plan is without him sends a wave of panic through me. I'm not leaving him behind after all this.

He nods slowly. "Yeah. Got this."

Crawling to where his bound hands are resting on his stomach, I make quick work of untying them and pulling two silver keys from where they were tucked between his skin and the rope.

My heart races at the sight.

So, so many things could have gone wrong with this.

If they had come back and unbound him and found that...

I shudder. The thought doesn't bear thinking about.

I hold those two keys in my hand as if they're the most precious things in the world. They're not, but they could lead me to the person who is.

I make quick work of freeing myself from my bindings with one of the keys before kicking the chain into the corner.

After another few seconds, Ant finally manages to push himself from the floor, and with my help, he gets to his feet. Although, he looks unsteady as fuck.

"What now?"

"There's a back exit. Leads into trees. I've got a..." Lifting his hand, he presses it to his ribs. "A car hidden."

"A car?" I ask, impressed by his level of planning. But as much as I might want to discuss exactly what he's set up, I'm aware that we don't have all the time in the world.

He nods. "Everything we need."

"The only thing I need is my girl, not gonna lie," I mutter. "So we just unlock that door and walk out?"

"Pretty much," he agrees.

It all seems too easy, and I can't deny that suspicion flows through my veins. He's an Italian, it's ingrained in me not to trust him.

But he protected Calli.

He pulled me from impending death in that building.

I have to trust him.

"Enzo will make sure they stay away."

"What the fuck are we waiting for then?"

Selecting one of the keys, I push it into the lock.

My heart sinks when it doesn't fit. But before I allow myself to think the worst, I try the other.

"Yes," I hiss when it slides in perfectly.

The clunk of the lock rocks through me just as it has every time they've come for us. But this time, there is hope that follows the sound, not just blood-freezing fear.

My hand trembles as I pull the door open, and listen for voices, anything on the other side.

"Clear?" Ant whispers behind me.

"Yeah. Come on, before we miss our chance."

We slip out of the door, and I pull it closed, quickly locking it behind us before I follow Ant out the back of the building. He uses the wall for support, and I swear each of his steps is slower than the last, but before I know it, we're spilling out and into darkness that rivals being stuck in that cell.

I squint as the rain blows the ice-cold drizzle into my eyes and a violent shiver rips down my spine.

"Which way?" I ask, unable to see anything.

Thankfully, Ant seems to have a better sense for where we are before he takes off, his feet crunching on the dead leaves and sticks beneath us.

"Daemon," he hisses the second he realises that I'm not following, and I quickly—well, as quickly as either of us is really able to move—follow him.

Each step is painful. The sticks and stones dig into the bottom of my feet every time I put them down, but the cold, biting wind makes every one of my injuries hurt even more than they did inside.

"Shit," I bark when Ant stumbles on something before crashing to the ground before me.

It takes everything I have to help him to his feet.

I can barely make out his features, it's so dark out here, but that doesn't mean I can't see the pain in his eyes.

"How much farther?" I ask, my body quickly giving up, and the last thing we need is to pass out here. We're so close to safety.

I'm so close to Calli.

"Th-the other side of the woods," he says, voice deep with agony and exhaustion.

Wrapping my arm around his waist, I give him little choice but to continue forward.

"We're getting out of here tonight," I promise him.

We stumble a few more feet before he goes down again.

"I can't. My legs... my body..."

"Motherfucker," I grunt, staring down at him. "I'm not fucking leaving you here."

"Just go," he whispers. "Go and get your girl."

"Nah, fuck that, man. Not after everything."

With thoughts of Calli filling my head, I channel every ounce of strength and determination I have and get him up.

I can barely move with his weight hanging over my shoulder, but there is no other way for this to end.

We are getting out of this together.

Despite the cold and the rain, when I finally break through the tree cover and spot an old black car parked at the end of a gravel track, sweat is rolling down my back. Each breath is agony.

"We did it," I tell Ant, but there is no response. "Ant?"

Nothing.

"Fuck."

If the situation were different, I might breathe a sigh of relief when I finally lower him onto the back seat of the car, but as it is, he's passed out, his chest barely moving and his entire body trembling.

He's going into shock.

"Fuck. Fuck."

I take a step back, desperately trying to think, but my head is fuzzy as fuck. My skin is burning up and my heart is racing.

He planned this, I tell myself. He said everything was here.

Shuffling around to the boot, I pop it open and almost sob at the sight of a duffel bag sitting there.

In a rush, I unzip it, finding a whole heap of clothes and blankets.

Grabbing two pairs of sweats and the blankets, I head back to Ant, putting his needs first.

Trying to drag the trousers up his legs is harder than I expected it to be, but before too long I have him wrapped up, and hopefully a little warmer. But he needs help. And he needs it fast.

Dragging on the other pair of sweats, I pull open the

driver's door and begin the hunt for the key, which I eventually find in a little cubby hole beneath the air vent.

"We're getting out of here, Ant. I'm gonna get you help. And then we're going to come back and slaughter those motherfuckers for what they did to us."

Rainwater, sweat, and blood run from my skin, soaking the waistband of my borrowed trousers, but I don't give any of it a second thought.

My focus is on the guy in the back who deserves every bit of my help right now, and my girl.

I'm coming, Calli. I'm fucking coming.

12

CALLI

"Daemon," I breathe, barely able to believe what I'm seeing.

My heart slams against my ribs as I just stare at him, my body moving of its own accord as I shove Alex's arm from around my waist and place my feet on the floor.

"Ange—"

It all happens so fast. One minute he's standing there, covered in blood and looking like he's been dragged back from hell, and then he's reaching out for something, anything before he collapses to the floor.

"DAEMON," I scream, surging forward. I dive over the coffee table and drop to my knees beside him. "Daemon, Daemon. Wake up." I cup his face in my trembling hands, my eyes tracking every single cut and bruises.

"Wha's going on?" Alex mumbles sleepily from the sofa before me.

"Alex, get up. He needs you," I shout, panic flooding my entire body as Daemon remains terrifyingly still before me.

"He? He who needs what?"

"ALEX."

Finally, the sheer terror in my body breaks through his sleep haze.

"Holy fuck, what the— Daemon, Bro. What the fuck, man?" he barks, dropping beside me and staring down at his twin in utter disbelief.

"H-he just... he just walked in. I woke up and he was standing there. I don't... I... What's wrong with him?"

"Jesus fucking Christ. I'm gonna call Mum, then we need to get him to bed. Check he's still breathing," Alex demands, appearing as calm as ever as he pulls his phone from his pocket.

"W-what?" I blurt, a whole new wave of panic hitting me.

"Just do it. Mum will ask."

"Holy shit. Yeah. Okay. Fuck."

My entire body trembles as I lean over Daemon's bare chest and rest my ear just above his lips.

The tickle of his shallow breath might just be the best thing I've ever felt in my life.

"Yeah, he is."

"You need to come to Daemon's flat now," he barks the second the call connects. "He... he's here, and he's a mess, Mum. You need to hurry."

Alex paces back and forth for a few seconds before he pauses and stares down at his brother.

"I don't know. He's passed out. Blood and bruises everywhere, but he got up here so it can't be that bad, right?"

He listens for a beat as my eyes search for all the wounds. Bleeding cuts on his chest and stomach, the dark bruising around his ribs. It's hard to see everything with the amount of dried blood and dirt that clings to every inch of his body.

"On the living room floor. Yeah. Yeah. Okay. See you soon."

"What did she say?" I ask in a rush the second he hangs up.

"As long as we don't think there's anything too serious, we should get him to bed."

"He was standing there, Alex. He walked in. There can't be anything t-too—" My words are cut off when a sob rips from my throat.

Alex sucks in a deep breath, staring down at Daemon as if he can't believe he's really here.

"This isn't a dream, is it?"

I sniffle as tears silently track down my cheeks, dripping from my chin.

"He's here, Alex. He's here. He's..." I want to say that he's okay. Which he clearly isn't. But he's alive. "Fuck."

With one hand resting gently on Daemon's stomach, I drop my head into the other and sob big, fat, ugly tears of relief.

He's here. He's...

Alex's hand lands on my back as even more emotions slam into me.

"Come on, he needs you, Cal. Now isn't the time to break."

I sniff and try to pull myself together.

"Go pull the sheets back, I've got him."

"Are you sur—" But before I've even spoken, Alex has scooped Daemon into his arms and staggers toward me. "Calli," he grunts as Daemon's weight gets the better of him.

"Shit, yeah."

I rush forward, pulling the duvet back and quickly fluffing the pillow before Alex lowers him down.

"What do we do now?" I ask, sounding and feeling completely useless.

"Sit with him. Hold his hand. Let him know you're with him. He's going to need you," he says firmly before he hightails it out of the room.

My lips part to call for him, but no sound leaves my throat.

Instead, I turn back to the broken boy before me.

I swallow down another sob as I take him in.

"Where have you been, devil boy?" I whisper, gently brushing my fingertips against his cheek. "I really hope you gave them hell."

The sound of Alex crashing about somewhere else in the flat, and then his voice as he must speak to someone on the phone again helps to keep me grounded as I categorise each of Daemon's wounds.

I need to get up and find something to clean them with. Most, I hope, are superficial and will heal up with a few days' rest. But others, like the fresh slices down his chest and the deep cut through his bicep with its steady bleeding look a little more serious. But something tells me that all of these injuries are nothing compared to the pain on the inside.

Daemon wouldn't have stayed away this long unless he didn't have a choice. He wouldn't have allowed us to believe he was dead. He just wouldn't. So whatever this is. It's serious. And that thought twists up my stomach until I find it hard to breathe.

"Here." Alex's voice startles me before he rounds the bed with a tray full of supplies. "Should be enough to get us started."

I study the bowl of water and the first aid supplies he's brought in. "Shouldn't we wait for your mum?" I ask.

"I've patched him up enough times to be able to clean up a few cuts, Cal."

"His blood doesn't send you funny then?" I ask.

"Thankfully not, or he'd have been fucked all these years from the number of times he's come home looking like he's done ten rounds with the devil."

"What do you think happened to him?" I ask quietly.

"I've got a few ideas."

Silence falls between us as Alex dips a cotton ball into the warm water and begins cleaning up Daemon's battered face.

My body trembles as I try to stave off the sobs that want to rock through me at the sight of them.

"You can help. I'm pretty sure he'd rather you be doing this than me anyway."

Hesitantly, I reach over him and grab a cotton ball.

I brush it against his cheekbone so lightly it barely does anything. But the thought of hurting him more than he already is terrifies me.

"He's not going to break, Calli. Nothing you can do to him now will hurt him, I swear to you."

I nod and use a little more pressure to clean up the blood.

All too quickly, the cotton ball is stained with both old and fresh blood, and I'm reaching for a second when Alex's phone starts ringing.

"It's Mum," he explains, climbing off the bed to answer it. "I'm gonna go open the door for her," he explains before disappearing.

The sound of his footsteps gets softer, leaving me alone with my boy once more.

My heart feels like it weighs ten tonnes in my chest as I continue working. I'm so happy to have him back, but I'm struggling to feel it as fear for what he's been forced to endure engulfs everything.

"CALLI." The tone of Alex's shout sends a shiver down my spine. "CALLI, you need to come here right now."

"Shit. I'll be right back," I whisper to Daemon as something in Alex's voice tells me that his words weren't a suggestion.

"CALLI," he booms again, forcing me to move faster.

I look over my shoulder before I slip out of the room, hating that I'm being dragged away from him when I've only just got him back.

I rush toward the front door but come to a grinding halt as I round the corner, my eyes landing on another body.

My gasp of shock rips through the air as my hand lifts to cover my gawping mouth.

"Ant?" I breathe, barely able to recognise him with the state of his face. But it's him, I know it is.

Alex looks up at me from where he's kneeling beside Ant's lifeless body with his fingers pressed against his neck.

"T-tell me h-he's—"

"He's got a pulse," Alex confirms.

"Why the hell is he..." I look back over my shoulder, although I can't see Daemon from here. "They were together." It's not a question, it's a fact.

"I'll get them out, all of them. I fucking promise you."

His words from that night come back to me.

Confusion wars within me.

What does all this mean?

How did they even get here in this state?

Question after question flickers through my head as I stand there staring.

"What is happening right now?"

I back up a few steps, torn between running back to Daemon and staying with Ant, because as bad as Daemon might look right now, Ant looks a hell of a lot worse.

"Get the guest room ready, Calli. Looks like we're going to need it."

I nod, glad to be given a job to stop me drowning in all the questions and fears rattling around in my head.

In a move identical to when he scooped Daemon up, Alex heaves Ant from the floor and I turn, ready to run toward the hallway, but Gianna's voice cuts through the air.

"That's not my son," she says, and when I look up, I find her staring down at Ant with her brow knitted in confusion.

"His name is Antonio," I say.

"He's a Mariano," Alex continues.

"Daemon is in his room," I say. "Come on."

With one more look at Ant, I turn and head down toward the guest room, looking in on Daemon as I pass to make sure he's still there. I don't quite believe this is all real right now, so I need all the assurances I can get.

Gianna's gasp of shock as her eyes land on her son doesn't make the situation any better, but I force my legs to keep moving. Daemon isn't the only one who needs me right now.

I repeat my actions from earlier before Alex emerges and lays Ant down on the bed.

He moans in pain as he lands on the soft mattress,

but his eyes remain closed and he shows no other sign of coming to.

"Get out of the way," Gianna demands, physically shoving Alex aside to inspect her patient.

"Daemon?" he asks, watching as she quickly runs her eyes over Ant. He doesn't have as much blood covering him, but his bruising is extensive. I can't even imagine how much he must be hurting.

Anger surges through me as I run my eyes over his ribs.

I don't realise I make a noise until Alex wraps his arm around my shoulder and pulls me into his side.

"It's okay, Cal. We've got them. They're going to be okay."

His mum glances up and locks eyes with her son, but I can't read the unspoken words in them like he can.

"Let's leave Mum to it and go sit with Daemon."

"Is he okay?" I ask Gianna as Alex tries to lead me from the room.

"On first inspection, it's all superficial."

I have to bite my tongue to stop me from spitting back a response about any kind of wound on Daemon always being more than superficial.

She already knows, I see it in the depths of her eyes. I see her concern, her fear for her son. But right now, she's in nurse mode, and it would take an idiot not to see that Ant needs her more.

"Keep the pressure on the cut on his arm, yeah?"

"Anything else?" I ask.

"Just carry on with cleaning him up. I'll be through in a minute or two."

Alex guides me from the room, and in a heartbeat, we're standing in the doorway of Daemon's room, staring at another person who must have arrived with Gianna.

"My sweet girl," Jocelyn breathes, her eyes full of unshed tears as she presses wadding to Daemon's arm. "He needs you." She nods toward the bandages, encouraging me to take over. "I'll go and make coffee," she says, rushing out of the room.

I watch her go in a complete daze.

"Who would do this, Alex? Who would hurt them like this?" I whisper.

"Do you really need me to answer that?" He asks, dragging a chair over to his brother's side, taking over the pressure on Daemon's arm and allowing me to crawl on the bed with him.

"It's my fault," I confess, staring down at Daemon's bruised and swollen face.

"Don't talk shit, Cal. This has nothing to do with you."

I glare at him. "It has everything to do with me. If I didn't try to escape from my sheltered life and break all the rules with Ant, then we never would have ended up like this."

"What's that got to do with anything?"

I sigh, pushing my hair out of my face.

"After Daemon got us out of the country club, I ran into Ant. He..."

"It's okay, Cal."

"He promised me that he'd do anything he could to get them out for me. H-he did this. He... he rescued Daemon for me, and he got caught. The Marianos have turned on him. Ant is a traitor, and Daemon is his enemy."

"Fuck. Do you really think—"

"Ant is a good guy, Alex. He would have done this."

"Well, if he did, we fucking owe him everything."

All I can do is nod as I reach for another cotton ball and continue cleaning up my broken boy's face.

I work in silence, my skin tingling as Alex's eyes flick between me and his brother.

Jocelyn returns with coffees and glasses of water before rushing away again.

It's not until Gianna rejoins us that I shift back and Alex moves to the corner of the room to give her some space.

"So?" Alex asks impatiently when his mum has finished and stepped back from Daemon.

"Until they wake, it's hard to tell."

"Well then, wake them up," he demands.

"Alex," I breathe, resting my hand on his upper arm.

"I can't. Their bodies are exhausted. They'll wake when they're ready."

I stare at the line Gianna has put in the back of Daemon's hand and trace it all the way to the bag of liquid she's attached to it.

"He's dehydrated," she explains, in case that wasn't obvious. "I can't feel any obvious breaks, but that doesn't mean there aren't any. We may need to take them both to the hospital in the morning."

"No," Alex barks. "No," he repeats, a little softer when his mum startles at his fierce tone. "No one can know they're here. They've escaped and—"

His words cut off, not wanting to guess what they've been through.

"Then you might want to get rid of the car that's been abandoned in the middle of the car park," Gianna suggests.

"Shit. I need to call Theo. The boss is going to have a fucking field day with this."

With one more look at Daemon, and after placing a kiss on my temple, Alex heads for the door. But the sound of his mother's voice stops him in the doorway.

"Make sure they pay for this. No one hurts either of my boys and gets away with it."

"You got it. Everyone who dared laid a finger on him is as good as dead."

A surge of determination goes through the room, and I can't help but wish Daemon was awake to see it, to experience those who love him fighting for him.

Alex takes off, the sound of his voice rumbling in the living room as Theo must answer his phone despite it being the middle of the night.

"What time is it?" I ask.

"Uh... nearly two AM."

I nod, fidgeting as I stand in the corner of the room like a spare part.

"Calli, you can come closer. You can lie with him,"

she encourages softly. "He'll probably be aware of your presence."

"I... uh..." I look between the two of them, my stomach knotting with anxiety, fear, and so much relief I don't know what to do with myself.

"He's here, Calli. He came back to you. He fought to come back to you."

My sob rips through the air as I move closer to the bed.

I run my eyes over him, the fierce protectiveness that floods through my veins rocking my foundations. "I want to go out there and hurt people, Gianna. I want to go and do things no human should ever want to do to another," I confess quietly.

"Sweetie, you are not the only one."

"He deserves so much better than this."

"That's what he's fighting for. For better. For you."

More tears fall at her words.

"You know," I sniffle. "You're really not helping this situation," I say, pointing to my face.

Gianna chuckles as she pushes from the chair.

"Lie with him. Talk to him. I'm going to check on Ant and see how Alex is doing. If you need anything, just shout. Jocelyn and I are here for you. For all of you."

"Thank you," I whisper as I crawl onto the bed once more, being as gentle as I can not to rock him before I lie down at his side, sliding as close as possible. "And thank you for calling Jocelyn."

Gianna watches us from the doorway for a beat, but

I don't pay her any attention. I'm too focused on Daemon being laid beside me to think about anything else.

The second she's gone, I rest my hand on top of his.

"You came back," I whisper. "You came back for us."

13

DAEMON

"Calli," Alex's moan rips through the air as I watch him back her into his bedroom, his face tucked into her neck, getting a taste of everything I want, everything I need.

My blood turns to lava as Alex wraps his fingers around the bottom of Calli's dress and peels it up her body, leaving her in nothing but her lace underwear.

"Oh God," she breathes when his head descends toward her breasts. "Yes."

Fury, jealousy and desperation burns through me as I watch them.

If that is what death is like, then I can only assume that I have been sent straight to hell, because even after everything I've been through, watching Alex take my girl is the worst kind of torture. After all the bad shit I've done in my life, I guess it's exactly what I deserve.

His shirt goes next, then his jeans as he teases her through her underwear. Touching her as if she's the most precious thing in the world, building her up until she's begging for him to take her.

My cock aches, but I can't reach for it.

I can't move, my arms hanging like lead at my sides, which only makes the torture that much more unbearable.

My breath catches when he lifts her off her feet, wrapping her legs around his waist.

A gasp rips through the air, and it's not until reality slams back into me and my eyes fly open that I realise it came from me.

I stare up at a perfectly white ceiling and my brows knit together as confusion rains down.

My heart pounds, and despite everything, desire still licks at my veins from seeing my girl like that, even if it was all in my head.

I blink a couple of times, desperately trying to get my brain to clear.

Images of running through the woods, the memory of having Ant thrown over my shoulder and my bone-deep exhaustion play out in my mind and make my muscles ache.

We escaped. We...

I lift my head from whatever I'm resting on and look around.

The room spins and blurs, but recognition still hits me.

I'm...

I'm home.

A relieved sob catches at the back of my throat and

my head falls back onto the pillow.

Suddenly, everything begins to make sense.

The soft bed I'm lying on. The fact the air around me doesn't smell like death. Instead, it smells like—

I twist my head to the side and my breath catches as I find my angel curled up beside me, fast asleep.

I stare at her in complete awe, unable to do anything but drink in the sight of her beautiful face.

Her eyelids flicker as she dreams. Her cheeks are flushed a soft pink, and her full lips are parted and entirely too tempting after being locked away with no kind of soft touch for who knows how long.

I ache for her. Every single inch of me craves her touch, her kiss, her... her anything.

Movement behind her catches my attention, and when I drag my eyes from her, I find Alex crushed in behind her, the three of us once again in the same bed.

He moans in his sleep, curls into Calli and wraps his arm around her waist, holding her tight.

Jealousy threatens to swallow me up, and it takes everything in me to fight it.

Sucking in deep lungfuls of fresh air, I lift my hand from my side, but when a pinching pain shoots up my arm, I have no choice but to look over.

I discover a cannula vanishing in the back of my hand, and when I follow the small plastic tube, I find an almost empty bag of liquid hanging from a little hook on my bedside table.

Mum's here.

The urge to pull it free and fight the treatment I've

no doubt she's going to try to enforce on me burns through me, but I refrain. Something tells me that if I don't do exactly what I'm told, I'm going to disappoint the girl next to me, and I don't ever want to do that again in my life.

Turning back to her, I suck in a deep breath and attempt to roll onto my side.

Everything hurts, but it's not as bad as I remember, so I can only assume that Mum has already pumped me full of painkillers.

Unable to resist touching her, I reach out and brush my dirty, bloody knuckles down her cheek.

To begin with, she doesn't react to my touch, all the while the softness and warmth of her skin send sparks of electricity shooting down my arm.

Being able to do this, to be close to her once again, is the only thing I've been able to think about since I woke up locked in the Italians' cell.

And now she's here.

I'm pretty fucking sure I'm never going to let her out of my sight again. Ever.

My eyes study every inch of her face, and my heart sinks when I spot the lingering dark make-up that looks like it's been washed away with tears.

"I'm sorry," I whisper. "I'm sorry I scared you. I'm sorry that I didn't come back to you. I'm sorry I caused you pain. I told you I wasn't worthy of you, Angel." My voice is rough, and each word burns down my throat as if I'm trying to swallow rusty nails, but each one needs to be said. I can't even begin to imagine what she might have been through in the past few days—hell, weeks.

Resting my hand on her cheek and wrapping my fingers around her slender neck, she finally rouses from sleep.

A little guilt ripples through me as her eyelids open, but then her blues land on me, and I forget everything as my heart pounds like it's just been jump-started.

She gasps the second she realises I'm staring back at her.

"Hey," I force out. A smile twitches at my lips for what feels like the first time in forever.

"Daemon," she sobs, her eyes filling with tears. "You're really here." Her bottom lip trembles as her hand comes up to cover mine where I'm holding her.

"I'd have moved heaven and earth to get back to you, beautiful."

"W-we... we thought..." She squeezes her eyes closed for a beat before they fly back open again as if she regrets not being able to see me. "We thought you were dead."

"It's going to take more than that to rip me from you, Calli." My fingers tighten on her neck, hopefully emphasising the strength behind my words. "You're all I thought about. Having you in my arms again. It's the only thing that's kept me going," I confess, forcing her tears to spill. "I'm sorry. I don't want to make you cry."

"It's okay," she says, her voice cracked with emotion. "You're here, you can do anything as long as you stay."

"I'm going nowhere."

Silence falls between us as we just stare at each other, barely able to believe it's happening.

"I love you, Calli."

"Oh God," she sobs. "I love you too."

She scoots forward and wraps her arm around me, clinging to me as if she's afraid I might vanish into dust if she releases me.

A grunt falls from my lips as pain shoots through my body, but it's nowhere near enough to make me stop her.

"Shit, I'm sorry. I don't want to—"

"Don't you dare let me go, Angel," I warn, my voice hard and giving her little choice but to follow orders.

"Never. I'm never letting you go again."

We lie there holding each other, soaking up each other's warmth, strength, love. And it's fucking everything.

The unfamiliar darkness of sleep begins to come for me when she speaks again.

"Are you... are you okay?" she asks hesitantly, the tip of her nose touching mine as she stares into my eyes.

"Yeah, Angel. I am now."

She leans forward and brushes her lips against mine. It's the sweetest but most needed kiss of my whole life.

I desperately want to return it, but I lose my fight with my own body and instead sink back into the clutches of sleep.

The next time I wake, there are voices in the distance that make me instantly relax. Mum and Alex's voices float through my ears and wrap around me like a warm blanket. I can't make out their words, but I don't need to.

I really am home.

Soft snores come from beside me and I turn over so I can watch her sleep. Moving is easier now, and when I look up, I find that the bag of liquid is full once again.

Tucking my non-cannulated hand beneath my cheek, I just lie and watch her, soaking up her presence and allowing myself to remember the good times, all while believing that we might actually get some more.

The voices continue outside the door, but no one comes in to check on us as the seconds and minutes tick by.

It's the most peaceful I've felt since we were at my grandparents' beach house, and I appreciate every single fucking second.

Eventually, Calli begins to stir, and the second she opens her eyes, a wide, beaming smile spreads across her face when she finds me here.

"It was real," she whispers, her voice rough with sleep. "You really came back."

"Always."

"How are you feeling?"

"Never better."

Her brow wrinkles. "Don't lie to me, Nikolas," she

warns, the roughness of her voice causing my blood to heat.

"Fuck, I missed you so fucking much," I growl, leaning forward and brushing my lips against hers, finally claiming that kiss I was too exhausted to indulge in last night.

"All right, kids. Enough of that," Mum chastises, her voice suddenly right there. "He's got a lot of healing to do. There's not enough energy for... that."

"Mum," I groan while Calli's cheeks burn bright red.

"Sorry, Gianna," she mutters.

"Ignore her, she's just yanking your chain."

"Alex," I say, forcing myself to sit up. My eyes fall on him, and another of my dislodged pieces falls back into place when our eyes lock. "Fuck. I'm so—"

"Shut the fuck up, yeah?" he says, his voice cracking with each word before he dives at me, knocking me back to the bed with a cry of pain. "And never ever fucking do that to us again."

I can barely breathe with his weight on top of me, and it hurts like fuck, but there's no way I'm making him move.

"Missed you, Bro," I grunt in his ear.

"Fucking love you, man."

"As cute as this is," Calli says, "you're hurting him, Alex."

"Shit, I'm sorry. I just... fuck."

When Alex pulls back, his face is wet with tears that he quickly swipes away as if they never happened.

"Baby," Mum breathes, selflessly waiting until last to greet me. "You gave us quite a fright there, Son."

"Can't say it was intentional," I mutter as she cups my face. "How are you feeling?"

"I'm f—"

"Honestly," she warns. "If you think about lying to me about any of it, I'll have you admitted to hospital."

I nod, knowing damn well that she would too.

"Everything hurts, but I think I'm okay."

"What did they do to you?" Alex asks, anger and the promise of retribution clear in his tone.

My eyes find Calli, who's now sitting beside me with her hand in mine, and I swallow the words. She doesn't need to hear the truth, the cold, brutal truth of what I've endured the past—

"What day is it?"

"Tuesday," Mum offers.

I release a breath. "Oh."

"What is it?" Calli asks, coming closer and squeezing my hand in support.

"It's only been two days."

"Uh..."

"No, Bro. It's been a week and two days. We should have all gone back to school yesterday."

I look between the three of them, seeing nothing but the truth in their eyes and I nod. "Right, yeah. That makes more sense."

We all fall silent as the weight of everything that's happened presses down on us like a physical force.

"What did they do to you?" Alex asks again, his need for the truth burning through him.

I get it. I'd be the same if the situation were reversed and he was the one in my position.

I shake my head. "It doesn't matter right now. They didn't do anything that I can't heal or detox from."

"Detox?" Calli blurts.

"I'm okay, Angel. I promise you."

Her bottom lip trembles once more, but she doesn't say any more.

"Do you know what they gave you?" Mum asks.

"No, but it's been a while since my last dose. Things already feel clearer."

"I've taken bloods," she says. "I should get the results back later for both of you."

"Both of— Ant," I gasp, my eyes widening. "Where is he? Is he okay? Do not tell me you sent him back to them."

They all stare at me as if I've lost my mind.

When the answer I need doesn't come fast enough...

"I swear to God, if you've—"

"It's okay. He's in the guest room."

"Fuck." All the air in my lungs comes out in a rush. "It needs to stay that way. He can't go back. They'll kill him."

Both Mum and Alex move closer before dropping onto the end of the bed.

"He pulled me out of that building right before it fell on my head. I would have died there if it weren't for him, I know it."

Alex drops his head into his hands, as if just hearing me say the words is too painful to deal with.

"He promised me he would keep you safe."

"Well, he did, Angel. And he's been through hell for it."

"He's not in a good way," Mum confesses.

"I know. The way they laid into him..." A shudder runs down my spine as I remember some of his more brutal beatings. The fact I managed to get him here still breathing is a fucking miracle. "We need to do whatever we can to keep him away from them until we fix this shit."

"Boss wants to come talk to you," Alex says, his eyes holding mine. "I told him to wait until you're stronger but—"

"Let him come. This is too important to sit on."

"Okay, you got it. The others are desperate to come to see you too."

"Tomorrow, maybe, yeah? I just want to be with you all for a bit."

"Whatever you need, man."

Lifting Calli's hand, I press my lips to the back of her hand.

"I've got everything I need right here."

"You hungry?" Alex asks, looking between the two of us with happiness filling his eyes. And if I didn't know him as well as I do, then I might miss the jealousy that's also there.

"Starving for anything other than mouldy fucking bread."

"That's what they gave you?"

"Yeah, Angel. They didn't put us up in a five-star hotel," I quip.

"Any special requests?" Mum asks.

"Anything."

She slips away, I assume to order something, because I can't imagine there's anything edible in my kitchen after being away for over a week.

Fuck.

I knew it had been a while. But over a week.

I shake my head in disbelief.

"You okay, man?" Alex asks, his hand landing on my foot beneath the covers.

"Yeah. It's just a lot to get my head around."

"You're fucking telling us," he says, forcing a little laughter into his tone.

"Thank you," I say, cutting off his attempt to lighten the mood. "Thank you for looking after her. For being here for her when I couldn't." I glance at Calli, and a giant lump forms in my throat at the all-too-real fear I've lived with for the past week that I might never get to look at her, touch her again.

"I made you a promise, and you know I always keep my promises."

"I appreciate it. Knowing you had each other while I was in there made it more bearable."

"Alex has been amazing," Calli says, looking at my brother with so much love it makes my heart ache. But not in a jealous way, because despite my worst fears and the nightmares that plagued me while I was locked up, she doesn't love him the same way she does me. I can see it every time she so much as glances his way.

"You've been pretty awesome yourself. Your girl's fierce, D. So fucking fierce."

"I know," I agree, a wide smile spreading across my face. "She's fucking everything."

He looks between the two of us, sadness still lingering in his features.

"You two probably need to talk," he says, climbing from the bed.

"I'll call the boss. You okay if Dad comes with him?"

"Yeah, Theo too," I say, knowing that he's not going to take too kindly to being shut out. "But that's it until tomorrow."

"You got it." Alex salutes me before looking at Calli with a supportive smile before he pulls the door closed and leaves us alone.

14

CALLI

My heart pounds and my blood rushes back to my ears as I stare at Daemon.

I've got so much I need to tell him. But... how am I meant to?

He's just been through... hell, I don't even know what he's been through.

"D-do you need anything?" I ask instead of blurting out any of my truths.

"Uh, yeah. I could really do with a piss."

"Okay, yeah. Sure."

After a moment, I throw the covers back and climb from the bed.

"I can get Mum to help if—"

"I've got this. I'll be the best nurse you've ever had."

As I walk around the bed, his eyes drop to my bare legs that are sticking out the bottom of his hoodie that I'm still wearing.

"You don't seem to be appropriately dressed."

I roll my eyes at him as I pull the covers off him. My breath catches at the sight of his injuries. Gianna has dressed the worst of the cuts on his chest and stomach, but the bruising is angry and painful looking.

"Are you okay to walk?" I ask when he hesitantly plants his feet on the floor.

"Angel, anything is easier than what I've experienced in the last week." I nod at him, watching as he uses the bedside table to help him up. "I promise I'm not going to break."

"I-I know, I just... I want to fix everything."

"I'll be back to full working order in a few days once I've had some rest and decent food."

"Daemon," I breathe as a wave of grief and relief slams into me.

"I'm here, beautiful. And I'm not going anywhere, okay?"

He staggers forward and I rush to grab the drip so he doesn't end up ripping it from his hand.

His movements are slow, but the stubborn arsehole doesn't accept any help.

I hover in the doorway while he uses the toilet, not wanting to intrude while he does his thing, but equally not willing to take my eyes off him for a second.

When the toilet finally flushes, I peek my head back inside. I find him standing at the basin, staring into the mirror hanging in front of it.

After a beat, his eyes find mine in the reflection.

"I look a bit of a mess, huh?" he mutters.

"You look as hot as ever to me." I walk closer, the tether between us pulling tight.

"As much as I appreciate that, I do have eyes, Angel."

"Like you said, you'll be as good as new in a few days."

"Some of these are going to scar," he mutters, studying his body.

"Every mark on your body tells a story of your strength, Daemon. None of them are anything to be ashamed of," I tell him, putting as much conviction into my voice as I can.

"I'm not so sure about that," he says, looking down at his body. "I did some of them myself. I'll never be anything but ashamed of them."

My gasp of shock cuts through the air.

"Daemon, I—"

"It's okay, Angel. I didn't tell you that for sympathy. It's just the truth. I know I've only touched on my past, on the things that happened in my grandfather's shed. But I need you to know that it's not because I don't trust you, or because I don't want you to know. I want you to know everything, to understand me like no one else does. But the thought of tainting you with that ugliness—" He shakes his head.

"I can handle it," I say determinedly.

"I know you can. I'm more worried about me," he confesses quietly.

"Whenever you're ready," I tell him, needing him to know that I'm happy to take things at his pace. Well, at least where his past is concerned. The future is an entirely different story, because the second my own confession falls from my lips, it's going to be like hitting fast forward on both of our lives.

The words balance on the tip of my tongue, but I quickly swallow them back.

Now isn't the time.

He needs to get his head around all of this first. Heal. Learn the truth about what happened that night and meet with Uncle Damien to try to figure out where we go from here.

As much as I might agree with Daemon about having Ant here after what they've both obviously been through together, we can't harbour an Italian for all eternity.

Suddenly, he reaches for the vanity and my heart jumps into my throat.

"You need to get back in bed."

"Y-yeah. I just really need to brush my teeth. It's been... Well, you really shouldn't have kissed me, put it that way."

He turns back toward the basin and reaches for his toothbrush.

"It would take more than bad breath to stop me after the week I've had," I confess.

"I'm s—"

"Don't, Daemon. Don't say it."

He nods and wisely keeps this apology to himself. None of this is his fault.

He spends so long brushing his teeth and swilling

his mouth out with mouthwash, I start to worry his knees are going to buckle.

"I need a shower," he says, staring at it longingly.

"One thing at a time. As soon as we get the okay from your mum, I'll help you have one."

He turns toward me. "Oh?" His brow quirks in interest.

"Stop that, devil boy. You're resting, remember?"

His ability to bounce back from this despite the pain he must be in and the exhaustion that's causing those dark circles beneath his eyes is astounding. But then, I guess he's used to running on empty, seeing as he fell out with sleep all those years ago.

"Anything that involves having your hands on me will be healing, trust me."

"Sure. Now let's get back to bed."

"Can't argue with that, beautiful."

The return journey is even slower, but Daemon refuses to give up.

After fluffing his pillows, he lets me help him back into bed.

There's a soft knock on the door before Gianna pokes her head in, quickly followed by two mugs.

"Coffee?" she asks with a smile.

"Yes," Daemon says eagerly, making us both smile as he reaches out for it like a toddler would chocolate.

I expect Gianna to stay, but the second she's passed our mugs over, she slips back out of the room again.

"Oh my God, that's the best thing I've ever tasted," Daemon breathes after his first sip.

I smile at him, still trying to convince myself that he's really here.

The pain of losing Dad hasn't lessened in the slightest, but looking at Daemon, knowing that I haven't lost him too... Fuck, the relief is like nothing I've ever felt before.

"You keep looking at me like I might vanish in front of your eyes," he says once his mug is empty while mine remains in my hands untouched.

"Because I'm scared you might, that I'm dreaming."

Reaching out, he wraps his hand around my thigh, his skin burning mine, sending warmth through my entire body.

"Talk to me, Calli. Every time I look at you all, I feel like I'm being kept in the dark about something. What's happened? What have I missed?"

Ripping my eyes from his, I stare down at his hand and shake my head.

"Th-that night... shit, Daemon. It was the worst day of my life."

"I told them it was a bad idea. No one would listen to me, they were all so—"

"Stubborn?" I ask, looking up at him again.

"Yeah. Arrogant. Self-important. It's like Damien and your dad thought they were indestructible. They totally underestimated the Italians. They might as well have just waved a big red flag at them and invited them to our party. They walked us right into the middle of a blood bath."

"Yeah."

"How many men did we lose, do you know?"

"A-about ten, I think. I don't really have all the details. But—"

"Shit. What a fucking mess. If they'd just have—"

"Nikolas," I whisper, needing to get this out at least before I crack.

"Yeah, Angel?"

"M-my dad." I swallow thickly. "He... he was one of them."

His brows pinch. "One of who?"

"One of the..." I blow out a long breath. "One of the ten."

His lips part to question me again before reality slams into him.

"No."

Disbelief covers his face as his eyes urge me to tell him I'm joking.

Tears fill my eyes as I think of everything that's happened since Alex, Theo, Seb, and Toby returned to the house without Nico and Daemon.

"We had his funeral yesterday."

"Oh fuck. Calli. Shit. I'm so sorry."

Despite the injuries covering his body, he reaches for me and pulls me into his arms to hold me as I sob once more.

"I thought I'd lost both of you," I whisper. "It's been... it's been..."

"I'm here, beautiful. I'm right here," he says into my hair and holds me as tight as he can.

I cry into his chest for the longest time, my relief and

my grief pouring out of me until I exhaust myself once more.

"How's Nico doing? Your mum?"

"Fuck my mum," I spit venomously, making his eyes widen in shock. "But Nico... We're all really worried about him. He's not talking to anyone. He turned up last minute yesterday to carry the coffin in and then he bolted at the first chance he got."

"Shit."

"Yeah. It's a mess. Everything has just been—"

Deep, booming voices come from the other side of the door.

"Looks like the cavalry is here."

Not two seconds later is the door thrown open, and when I look up, I find Theo standing in the doorway with his eyes wide and his chest heaving as if he's just run here.

If he realises I'm even in the room, then he doesn't show any sign of it as a smile spreads across his face and he starts laughing like a freaking psycho.

"Uh... bro, you okay?" Daemon asks, sounding as bemused as I feel.

"Fucking knew no one could take you down that easily."

With a shake of his head, he marches into the room and claps his hand on Daemon's shoulder. Something tells me that he wants to do more, but unlike Alex earlier, Theo is able to restrain himself.

"Fuck, man," he breathes, dragging the chair over and falling into it, staring at Daemon in disbelief.

"And I never thought I'd say it, but she looks good on you."

"Shut the hell up, cous," I groan, rolling my eyes at him.

"Safe to say that everyone knows about us then, Angel?"

"Yeah. Sorry, I couldn't keep that a secret anymore."

"So something good has come out of all of this, then. Theo is clearly okay with it. He's just sitting there with a smile instead of trying to kill me for real this time."

Lightly, I slap his shoulder.

"Too soon for jokes?" I ask.

"It will forever be too soon for jokes."

"From what I've heard, you're not a complete cunt when she's around, and you might even crack a smile once in a while. How could I possibly have an issue with something like that?" Theo says, his eyes twinkling with mischief. "Plus, it goes without saying that if you ever hurt one single hair on her head, then I will put you in the ground myself." Theo's smile is all malice despite his joking tone.

"You don't need to worry, man. If I fuck this up, I'll save you the work and put myself in that hole."

"Can we please stop talking about him dying?" I beg. The reality of all of this is too fresh to listen to them joking about it so soon.

"Sorry," Theo says with a wince before another shadow darkens the doorway.

"Dad," Daemon greets coolly, as if he hasn't basically just returned from the dead.

"It's good to see you in one piece, Son," Stefanos says, studying Daemon from a distance.

Before Daemon gets to respond, Uncle Damien joins us.

Unable to bear the level of testosterone that's suddenly filling the room, I squeeze Daemon's hand and whisper, "I'm gonna go see your mum and check in on Ant." I have no idea if Jocelyn is still here, but hell, I could use a hug from her right now.

Three sets of eyes burn into my skin as I lean forward and press a kiss to the corner of Daemon's mouth, but fuck them.

With a nod at Uncle Damien, I slip out of the room and practically run straight into Alex.

"What the hell did they say to make you move that fast?" he asks, grasping my shoulder.

"N-nothing. I don't need to be told to know I'm not invited to business meetings." I step aside and gesture for him to join them.

"You're one of us, Calli. If you want to stay in there, then you need to stand your ground."

"It's fine. I want to go and check in on Ant anyway."

"He's still out of it," Alex says before dipping his head and lowering his voice. "Did you tell him?"

I shake my head. "No, not yet. I think he needs a few days to get over this before I throw the next curveball, don't you? I told him about Dad."

"Calli," Alex warns. "You need to tell him."

"I know," I agree. "I'm just..." I trail off, not wanting to voice my concerns.

"He's not going to turn his back on you. He won't even be angry. Shocked, dazed and confused, maybe. But he'll be standing beside you right through all of this, you know that, don't you?"

I nod, because, what else can I do?

"Good."

Alex takes a step forward, but before he gets anywhere, my hand darts out and grabs his upper arm. His eyes find mine, and I wince at the darkness within them.

"Thank you," I say honestly. "I couldn't have done the past week if it weren't for you. I need you to know how much I appreciate everything. I—"

"Always," he says with a sad smile before tugging his arm free and slipping into Daemon's bedroom.

A noise comes from the guest room, and with a heavy sigh, I head in that direction.

The last thing I want to do is hurt Alex. He was literally everything to me this past week. I know I will have always had my girls to keep me together. But he was just... he knew exactly what I needed every time and stood beside me like the loyal, incredible friend that he is. And I have no doubt that would have continued should Daemon not have miraculously reappeared.

I'm shaking my head as I walk into the guest room, still unable to process all of this properly. It's how I know it's not time to confess all to Daemon.

There's no way his head isn't as fucked up, if not more so, than mine is right now.

We just need things to settle, and then I'll find a way

to tell him. And I just have to convince myself that Alex is right. That he will stand right by my side when that confession finally passes my lips.

"Everything okay, sweetie?" Gianna asks, looking up from checking Ant's blood pressure.

"Y-yeah. I just..." I fall down onto the small sofa beneath the window and stare out at the city beyond. "All of this. It's..."

"Unbelievable?" Gianna finishes for me.

"Yeah. I just... I hoped, you know. Everyone kept telling me that they didn't believe it, that he would surprise us all and turn up like a ghost in the night. I refused to go along with it. Refused to believe that a miracle could happen, and yet—"

"It has. Do you know how he got back here?"

"Aside from the car you mentioned earlier? No." I shake my head.

"There will be plenty of time for talking. The most important thing is that he's back where he belongs and that he's not too badly hurt."

I bite down on my bottom lip as my concern for the guy in the other room grows.

"What is it, sweetie?"

"I'm worried about him. I know he's lucky, that his injuries will heal from this with time. But what about those that we can't see? He already struggles so much that I—"

"He'll get through this, Calli. He's got you with him this time. I have faith in both of you."

Her words are meant to reassure me, but since he

confessed to causing some of those scars earlier, my stomach has been knotted up tight.

What if he can't cope with this? What if he does it again?

"One day at a time, yeah? No one is going to rush his healing from this." I stare at her, one of my brows lifting. "I won't let them," she adds as if she can read my mind.

"What about his exams? Uncle Damien and Stefanos told him that—"

"He can retake them later in the year. Hell, they might even give him a free pass after this, who knows. Try not to worry about tomorrow. Focus on right now and being there for each other."

"Why isn't my mum like you?" I sigh, partly regretting saying it out loud and partly relieved that I have. Twisting around, I look out the door and toward the living area in the hope of seeing Jocelyn.

"Jocelyn had to go," Gianna says sadly. "She'll be back, though." She pauses, remembers that I asked her a question before she sighs. "Your mother has her positives."

"If by that you mean being a grade A stuck-up bitch, then yeah, I guess I could learn a thing or two."

"Well... now that you put it like that," Gianna laughs. I'm relieved that she's not trying to argue with me. "But I was more thinking of her interior design skills. Your house and her spas are very pretty to look at."

"Yeah, I guess we can give her that. There's got to be

more, my father isn't—wasn't," I correct painfully, "a stupid man, yet he fell for her."

Gianna shrugs, coming over and sitting on the arm of the sofa. "I guess love can be blind. Or she's really good in bed."

"Gianna," I gasp, shocked that she went there.

"What? Tell me you weren't thinking it."

"I was really trying not to," I mutter.

"You should talk to her once all of this has settled down. See if you can find some common ground to rebuild your relationship."

"Yeah, I guess. Although I'm not sure there's really anything to rebuild. There's never been much there. Since I started biting back and stopped doing everything she says, we have nothing."

Gianna smiles sadly at me. "Well, whatever happens, I'm always at the end of the phone, sweetie. Even if you do want to moan about my boys."

"I appreciate that. They're lucky to have you, you know?"

"I'm the lucky one. They're good boys. And seeing Daemon's face light up when he looks at you... It makes my heart so happy. Oh," she says, hopping up and pulling her phone from her pocket. "Looks like our food is here."

"What did you order?"

"I have no idea, Alex did it."

"Oh God, it could be anything."

"Or everything, knowing him."

She throws her head back and laughs. "I guess I'm

about to find out. I won't be long." She pauses at the door. "Antonio is going to be okay, Calli."

"Thank you for all of this." I have no doubt that she's probably meant to be doing her actual job right now, yet she is here caring for these two instead.

"My boys, and you, always come first."

She disappears before I get a chance to respond, and soon after, the sound of the front door opening and closing hits my ears.

My eyes land on Ant lying in the bed. Like Daemon, he's got a cannula in the back of his hand. His face is still as swollen, bruised, and completely horrifying as it was last night. As much as I might want him to wake up so that I can see with my own two eyes that he is okay, I think it's probably better if he's asleep right now, because I can't even imagine how much pain he must be in.

Pushing from the sofa, I walk over and sit on the edge of the bed beside him, slipping my hand into his in the hope that he can feel me here and know that he's not alone.

"I want to shout at you for this, for putting yourself in so much danger, but I can't because you brought him back to me. You'll never know how much that means to me," I whisper.

A soft groan rumbles in the back of his throat and my heart leaps.

"Ant, can you hear me?"

Another quiet groan.

"Oh my God, Ant. It's over, okay? You're safe."

His lips part and his eyes flutter, but as much as I might want him to open them and look at me, he never does.

"It's Calli," I say like an idiot in case he's so out of it that he doesn't know who's talking to him. "You're in Daemon's flat. His mum is a nurse. She's taking care of you. We're going to fix this, okay? Everything is going to work out."

His hand squeezes mine, but it's the only sign I get that he's still with me.

I sit with him, hoping he can take some strength from my support until the front door opens and closes and Gianna calls, "A little help, Calli."

"We're just out there if you need us, okay?" Leaning forward, I press a kiss to Ant's brow, careful not to cause him any more pain before I pull the door to and head down toward the kitchen.

"Oh my God," I gasp when I take in the bags that cover almost all of Daemon's counters. "He really did order everything."

"Good job I got a good deal out of our divorce, huh?" Gianna quips, making me smile. "Want to help me sort all this out? Hopefully, the scent of food will drag them all out."

"What if they're in the middle of—"

"Then they'll have to pause," she says with a vindictive yet cheeky smile.

"I like you, Gianna. I think we're going to get along well."

She chuckles at my praise. "Well, that's good to

hear, seeing as you're going to be my daughter-in-law one day."

"Uh... do you know something I don't?" I ask.

"Not at all, sweetie. I just know my boy, and now he's got what he wants, I have no doubt he'll do something crazy like put a ring on your finger."

"Um..." I hesitate, not knowing what to say to that.

"Let's just hope he waits a few years to put a baby in you though, hey? You'd like to get your degree first, right?"

My stomach turns over and I stand frozen in the middle of the kitchen.

"I... um... Mum sure wants me to," I mutter, focusing on the least heart attack-inducing part of her statement.

"You don't want uni, sweetie?" she asks, genuine concern on her face.

"Honestly, I don't know. I got sucked into my mother's web and stupidly agreed with her plan for me."

"But that's not your plan?"

"I don't have a plan. I'm lost. Floating out in the middle of the sea in a dinghy without a paddle kind of lost."

"University isn't for everyone. There is no harm in not going, or planning to do it later. I think we've all learned a lot in the past few days, and the most important is that we need to make the most of now. We never know what's around the corner."

"You're right."

"Forget about what your mother wants for you,

Calli. Focus on you. On what you want and the future you want to carve out for you and my boy."

"Wow," I breathe, stepping up to the counter and opening a familiar bag. Inside, I find all my favourite Chinese dishes that Alex ordered for me. My heart clenches at his thoughtfulness. "So you wouldn't think less of me if I didn't come with a degree?"

"You are a smart, funny, caring, and beautiful young woman, Calli. Do what makes your heart happy and forget about everyone else's opinions."

With emotion clogging my throat, I work silently, getting everything out as I think about my life.

Uni was probably going to be out of the question now anyway. I can hardly turn up in September with a bump and then take maternity leave.

If everything goes okay with this pregnancy, then the future my parents thought they had planned so nicely for me will be completely derailed. And actually, I'm okay with that. And more so, I think Dad would have been too.

15

DAEMON

"Ricardo is a dead man walking," Damien growls. "Every single one of those Italian cunts is for even thinking about doing this.

I stare at the boss with my heart in my throat. I have never seen him anything less than composed and in control of himself at all times, but having lost his brother, vital members of this Family, and then having to listen to my somewhat brief explanation as to what happened to me, he looks wrecked. Utterly fucking wrecked. His face is purple with anger and frustration, his eyes dark, the shadows beneath them heavy and bruised.

"Not all of them," I say in a rush, earning me confused and equally horrified stares from both Damien and my father.

"Bro," Alex warns, knowing where I'm going with this.

"No, they need to know, and they need to be protected."

"What's going on?" Damien asks.

"Antonio Santoro is in my guest room."

"What?" Dad barks, pushing from the wall and reaching for the door as if he's going to go and handle this situation alone.

"I'd be dead if it weren't for him. Or worse, still in that cell. He's a good guy, Dad. I fucking swear it to you."

He doesn't like it, that much is obvious, but he pauses.

"What's going on, son?" Damien asks, more willing than my father to hear my side of this.

"Ant is the reason I knew that Calli was in danger. He was also the one who pulled me out of that building before it crashed around my head, and he also orchestrated getting us out yesterday. Him and a friend."

"Why?" Dad barks suspiciously.

"He and Calli, they—"

"They're friends. They met before all of this started," Alex adds. "He's been good to her, kept her safe. Helped Daemon. He's also in a really rough way out there."

"He could have left me there to die and never had to suffer the consequences himself, but he promised her he'd do everything to make sure we were all safe. If he had the chance, I have no doubt he'd have gone back for Evan too. But he—we—were caught."

"Who's the friend?" Dad growls.

"Enzo Mariano."

"Jesus fucking Christ," he groans, scrubbing his hand down his face. "And where is he? Taking a fucking bath?"

"No, he's still there. As far as I know, they have no idea he helped us escape. Ant and I haven't really talked but—" The slamming of the front door makes me pause as fear rocks through me at the thought of Calli going out there, the thought of one of them waiting to take revenge for us breaking out.

"It's okay, man. It's just Mum getting the food I ordered. She's not going anywhere," Alex says, reading my mind.

"Can he talk?" Damien asks, sounding a little more sympathetic and understanding than my father. I want to think that's because of the state of me, of how the Italians treated me, but honestly, I'm not entirely sure it is.

"No," Alex answers for me. "He's in a worse state than Daemon. Mum's given him some really strong painkillers. He'll probably be out for a while yet."

"When he wakes and can talk, I want you to call me," Damien demands.

"Sure thing, Boss."

"In the meantime, we need to figure out how they're getting our intel before we even know it our-fucking-selves. Both of you," he says, gesturing to Theo and Dad, "I want new background checks on every member of this Family. If there is anything questionable, even the smallest fucking thing that smells a bit rotten, I want them dragged in and dealt with. Someone is feeding them our secrets, and they need to go.

"I will not have a repeat of last weekend, and I will not be losing anymore soldiers. This city is ours, and it's time we showed Ricardo fucking Mariano that we will not be beaten."

"We can't go to war, Dad. Now isn't the—"

"Did I say anything about war, Theo? We're going to squash any intel getting back and then focus on getting our own. Hopefully, Ant and Enzo will be the puzzle pieces we need and we can take them down quietly. Has their underboss got what it takes, or is he a corrupt piece of shit too?"

"Seems pretty loyal to me, Boss," Dad grunts.

"Well, we'll see what our new friends have to say and they can help us make a plan. We need the Italians, they're good for business. We just don't need that cunt at the helm."

"Amen to that," I mutter.

Silence falls over us as the scent of food hits my nose. My stomach growls so loudly that everyone—even Dad—cracks a smile.

"We should leave you to recover. I'm so fucking glad you're still with us, son," Damien says, reaching out to grip my shoulder.

"Thanks, Boss. I'm sorry about Evan." He nods, accepting my condolences. "Stefanos, I want Nico working closely with you on this. Theo, you too."

"But Nico is—" Theo starts to argue.

"Nico needs to focus, something to aim his anger at. Ricardo seems like the perfect target."

"He won't be up for taking him down quietly," Theo warns.

"He will if he wants a shot at being my underboss anytime in the future."

"You want Nico to be—" Damien cuts Dad off with a single look.

"It's time for our boys to step up, don't you think? This past week has proved to all of us that we don't know how much time we have. We need to look to the future. These boys are our legacy, and we need to make sure they're ready to handle everything this life will throw at them."

"But Nico is nineteen, you can't seriously be thinking about making him your second? I know he's hurting right now, we all are, but—"

"Keep questioning me, Stefanos, I dare you." The warning is cold, dragging the temperature of the room down a few degrees.

A soft knock on the door thankfully shatters the tension that just fell over us before it opens and Calli's head pops around the corner.

"I-I'm sorry, but food is here and Daemon needs—"

"It's okay, Angel. There's nothing that's being said in here that you can't hear."

Dad's face twists with anger, but Damien doesn't react, other than to get to his feet once again. He gives me a nod and a smile that says everything he's not saying with words before walking over to Calli and pulling her in for a hug.

"You look after our boy, yeah?"

"Of course. We'll have him as good as new in no time," Calli promises.

"And don't worry about anything, about Nico. We've got everything under control."

She nods at him as he slips from the room.

"We'll see you soon, Son," Dad says, his words clipped before he trails after Damien like a lost puppy.

"Well, that was fun," Theo announces, clapping his hands on his thighs and pushing to stand.

"You want to stay?" I offer. "Something tells me that if Mum left ordering up to Alex, there will be plenty."

"Thanks, but I need to get back. I've got a flat full of girls who are going to want to know that you're both okay," he says, looking between Calli and me.

"Tell them I'm sorry I've not called, it's just—"

"It's okay, baby C. No one expects anything of you right now," Theo assures her. "Just look after this one, yeah? He's gonna need plenty of TLC."

"I hope you know what you're suggesting there, man," Alex quips.

Wrapping his arm around Calli's shoulders, Theo turns to look back at me.

"You're weirdly okay with this. Should I be worried?" I ask somewhat nervously.

"I can't say it was something I saw coming, and if I found this out a few months ago, my opinion would probably be very, very different. But right now, I'm just glad we've got you back, man. And if you treat her right and make her happy, then what else can I ask for?" He turns back to Calli and drops a kiss on her head. "Call me if you need anything, okay? We'll be right upstairs."

"Thank you," she breathes, pulling him in for a hug.

"I'm going to go and check in with Nico," he says when she finally releases him.

"Are you going to tell him about this?" I ask curiously.

"I... uh... I don't know. I agree with Dad, he needs something to focus on. But I'm also terrified he'll grab his gun and head out on a suicide mission if we give him any more reason to want Ricardo dead."

Calli jolts at his words. "No, Theo. You can't—"

"I'm not going to put him at risk, Calli. Don't worry. We're going to get him through this, all of us."

"What if he keeps pushing everyone away?" she asks, a deep V forming between her brows.

"Then we'll push harder. We're not letting him drown, no fucking way."

She smiles up at him sadly, and it makes my heart clench.

"Things are going to be better from here on out, I promise you."

He's gone before any of us get to respond.

"I'm just gonna—" Alex says, heading for the door and slipping around Calli. Although I don't miss the way his fingers squeeze hers in support as he passes.

I've always loved my brother fiercely, but seeing the way he is with her, knowing that he'll have given anything to take care of her if I never returned settles something inside me. I just need to work on the jealousy that also floods me every time I watch him touch her, and we should be all good.

"Ready for some food?" Calli asks, stepping closer.

"Hell yeah." The biscuits Mum let me have earlier barely touched the sides.

"Shall we bring it down here or—"

"No, I'm coming out."

I force my eyes off the bed and slide to the edge.

She rushes to my side, proving that all the effort I put in did little to convince her that I'm okay, that moving anything more than an inch hurts like fuck.

"Daemon, you don't need to—"

"I do, Calli. I need... I need to be normal. I need to convince myself that this is real. That I'm not going to wake up and find myself locked back up in that cell with you as nothing but a memory."

She stares at me, sadness filling her eyes as she reaches for my hand.

"It's real, Nikolas. You're safe. I'm right there, and I'm not going anywhere."

'Thank you' I mouth, warmth spreading up my arm from her simple touch. "I love you," I breathe, making her eyes shutter with emotion.

Tears pool in her eyes and her bottom lip trembles.

"Shit, I didn't mean to—"

"They're happy tears, it's okay. I just can't believe I got you back. I thought that was it for us. That we were destined to be this dirty secret the world never got to find out about."

My stomach growls loudly.

"No more secrets and lies, Calli. This, us," I say, lifting our joined hands, "it's it now. I want everyone to know that you're mine."

"And I'm yours."

Leaning forward, she brushes her lips against mine in a simple kiss. It's nowhere near what I crave for her after going without for so long. But while she's here by my side, it'll have to do until I've healed and am able to show her just how much I really do love her.

"What do you need?" she asks when she pulls back regretfully.

I look down at myself. I'm still disgusting, and there's no denying that the stench in the room is coming from me, but until I get the okay from Mum to shower, I guess I'm stuck with it.

"Just grab me a zip-up hoodie," I say, desperately needing to hide the mess that is my chest and stomach.

"I love your body, Daemon. Never feel like you need to hide it from me."

"I'm not, Angel. I'm hiding it from myself."

Her lips part to respond, but she doesn't seem to have any words. So with a sad smile, she turns toward my chest of drawers and hesitates.

It occurs to me that the only time we spent here together was the weekend I stole her from Ant. But with them being here when I stumbled inside, and her wearing my clothes, it makes me wonder if she's spent the whole time I've been gone here.

The thought of her needing to be surrounded by my things makes a lump crawl up my throat, but as much as the meaning behind that thought hurts, it also fills me with everything I need.

She missed me. Really fucking missed me, and that knowledge wrecks me as much as it helps fix something inside of me that has been broken for so fucking long.

"In the wardrobe, Angel."

She nods before walking over. I expect her to pull one out, but she surprises me by grabbing two.

She unzips one and throws it on the bed before hanging the other on the wardrobe door and dropping her hands to the bottom of the hoodie of mine she's wearing.

My breath catches in my throat as she peels it up her body, exposing her perfectly flawless skin to me.

"What the fuck are you trying to do to me?" I breathe, my eyes taking in the tiny pair of lace knickers she's wearing before she pulls it over her head, revealing her bare tits. "Oh shit, Angel. Fuck," I grunt, reaching out and squeezing my cock. "Pretty sure I've lost too much blood to be sending everything I have down here."

"Whoops," she says innocently before pulling the clean hoodie from the hanger and dragging it over her head, covering up her tempting body. "Good to know everything is still working though." She winks cheekily.

"You're trouble, beautiful."

She comes closer, filling the air around me with her

mouth-watering scent before she lifts the hoodie and helps me into it. Or at least she does until she remembers the cannula in the back of my hand.

"Oh, I need to call your Mum," she whispers.

"Fuck that, I've got it," I grunt before she gets a chance to move away or call for her.

"Daemon," she gasps in horror as I rip off the plaster and pull the small tube from the back of my hand. "You can't just—"

"Barely felt a thing, Angel. It's all good."

"You need to stop doing that," she warns, her voice deep with pain. "You need to stop hurting yourself."

The memory of what I told her in the bathroom earlier comes back to me. "I haven't done that for years, beautiful. I found other outlets for my pain."

"G-good, but that doesn't mean you get to go around doing stuff like that." She gestures to the back of my hand as a small trickle of blood runs over my skin. "I want you fixed. I *need* you fixed."

"I will be," I say as she reaches for a cotton ball to wipe away the blood so I can push my arm into my sleeve. "In a few days, I'll be back to full working order, and I have some very good ideas as to what I want to do first."

"Oh yeah?" she asks coyly.

"Yeah, I'm going to lay you out naked on my bed and—"

"Sorry to interrupt that little visual, but the food's getting cold," Alex says, suddenly appearing in the doorway, amusement lacing his tone. His eyes drop to my sweats, and a knowing smirk plays on his lips.

"What? My girl's hot, and she showed me her tits."

"Really?" Calli hisses.

"Damn, I'm real sorry I missed that little show."

"You missed your chance, Bro. She's all mine again now."

"She's always been yours, man. You're right though, she has got good tits." Alex winks before wisely ducking out of the room before I can find something to throw at him.

"You two are going to make me grey early," Calli mutters as she closes the space between us once more and helps me to my feet.

I'm pretty sure I could easily do it without her help now, but that's not going to stop me from accepting her support. Having her arm around me and her warmth against me is more than I could ask for.

Mum's brows knit when we appear together. "Daemon, we could have brought it—"

"It's okay, Mum. I need this. I need to be normal and surrounded by family."

She looks at me with concern before her eyes drop to my un-cannulated hand and they roll. She doesn't chastise me for it. She knows me better than to waste her breath.

"How's Ant?" I ask once I'm sitting down.

"Still asleep. It'll just take time." An empty plate and a glass of water appear in front of me. "Take it steady, yeah? If you've not really eaten in a week, this is going to shock your stomach. Stick to plain things or—"

"I've got it, Mum," I say, reaching for her hand.

She stills, staring down at me with tears in her eyes.

Up until now, she's been in nurse mode, but now I'm up and about, I'm seeing more of my mum shining through.

"I'm so proud of you, Nikolas. And I'm so glad you found your way back to us." Her eyes fill with tears as she holds my hand tighter.

"Thank you," I say, hoping like hell she knows just how sincerely I mean that. "Now eat, you must be starving as well."

"If you're not fast, Gianna, Alex will have eaten it all."

"Hey," Alex mutters around a mouthful of something. "You make out like I'm a pig."

"Case in point," Calli says with a laugh.

I sit there and watch the three of them, Alex as he stuffs his face, and Mum and Calli as they load their plates with their favourite food. Contentment and happiness wash through me. I spent over a week wishing and praying that I could get to be surrounded by my family again. And by some miracle, I got it.

"What do you fancy, Daemon?" Calli asks, noticing that I haven't moved an inch.

My lips part, but I don't get a chance to say anything because Alex beats me to it. "Don't say it, Bro. Mum's sitting right there."

"I was going to say just some rice and noodles." I roll

my eyes. While the spicy dishes sitting on the table might call to me, I know Mum's right. My stomach is going to revolt if I throw too much at it too fast.

Calli is up and filling my plate before I get a chance to do it myself. Part of me wants to stop her, to make her eat her own, but the other part is just too fucking busy enjoying having her here.

The groan I let out when the egg fried rice hits my tongue is obscene, something that Alex helpfully points out, which makes Calli's cheeks burn bright red and Mum to throw a spring roll at his head.

Watching them is everything. Every-fucking-thing.

16

CALLI

Having Daemon sitting at the table and eating with us, even if he did only pick at his food despite the fact that he was clearly ravenous, was the thing dreams are made of.

I ate with one hand, preferring to keep one of them touching him at all times. I needed it. That reminder that this was real. That he really was sitting right next to me.

But as amazing as it was, and as insistent as Daemon was that he was okay, it was obvious only a few minutes in that the talk with Uncle Damien and his dad, along with the short trip here was taking it out of him, and before long, Alex and I were helping him back to bed. He almost immediately crashed the second his head hit the pillow.

"It's weird seeing him sleep. When I was a kid, I legit used to think he was the spawn of Satan or something. He just used to be awake all the time like some ethereal creature."

"Was he always like that?" I ask, not taking my eyes off Daemon's bruised face.

"No. As a young kid, he was just like me. But then our grandfather used to..." Alex trails off, clearly not wanting to go there.

"Lock you in his shed?" I ask, wanting him to know that I'm already aware of the heinous things that monster used to do to them.

"Yeah. It changed him. I mean, it had a pretty bad effect on me too, but nothing like it did to Daemon."

"If he weren't already dead, I'd go and kill him myself for hurting both of you," I promise.

"Daemon should have got the chance. He needed it after the years of abuse and torture."

"Did he... did he have it worse than you, do you think?"

"I don't think, Calli. I know. I did everything I could to prevent it. If Daemon just joined the football team, hung out with us more, then he wouldn't have needed to be there."

"Does your mum know?" I ask, already guessing the answer.

"No. Dad did, though. Never did a thing to stop the cunt. Don't tell her, Calli. It'll break her heart."

"Don't tell her what?" Gianna asks behind us.

"Fuck," Alex hisses.

"Do we need to have a chat, Son?"

"You okay with him?" Alex asks me.

"Of course."

"When he wakes, if he's feeling up to it, let him have that shower he's so desperate for," Gianna told me. "Wrap his dressings with this." She passes over some waterproof pads. "Then give me a shout and I'll come and change everything."

They both disappear down the hall, Alex leaving me with a pained expression etched onto his face. My gut knots, knowing that he's going to have to give her some of the truth, but I doubt he'll give her all the horror stories of their past. Hell, I'm pretty sure I don't have them. Daemon has only touched the surface of what he experienced as a young boy, and something tells me that I might never get to hear the worst. But as much as that pains me, I won't push him for it. He needs to deal with it all in his own time, and I will be right by his side as he does.

After using the bathroom, I crawl up beside him, gently wrap my arm around him and hold him as tight as I dare. The last thing I want is to hurt him, but also, I need him. I need him so much it hurts.

When I come to, I know instantly that he's missing.

A cold emptiness washes through me a beat before panic sets in.

Holy shit, it was all a dream.

I sit up in a rush, my heart pounding to an erratic beat in my heart.

I'm on the edge of the bed before I even know I've moved, my eyes scanning the room but not really seeing anything in my hysteria.

I'm at the door before I spot the zip-up hoodie I helped him put on yesterday, and then I look back over my shoulder, finding the empty saline bag that Gianna hooked him up to.

I breathe a sigh of relief before bolting through the door. The living room is empty, the only thing out of place is a handwritten note on the dining room table letting us know that Alex and Gianna have gone to Alex's flat to get some sleep.

When I glance at the clock, I find that it's seven AM.

"Jesus, how long did we sleep for?" I mutter to myself before heading down the hall on my quest for my boy.

I come to a stop in the guest room doorway, drinking in the sight before me.

Ant is still out cold on the bed, although I can't deny that behind the bruises marring his face, his skin seems to have a little more colour. Shifting my eyes from him, I find Daemon laid out on the sofa, his eyes closed, his cheek resting on his hands, a blanket haphazardly thrown over his body.

Seeing the two of them together is the biggest head fuck, but there's something so right about it. After everything Ant has done to protect me, he deserves for us to do the same in return.

Stepping farther into the room, I walk toward where Daemon is resting.

Crouching down in front of him, I reach out and attempt to push a bit of hair back from his brow. It instantly flops back into place and I sigh, giving it up as a bad job.

"I'm awake, you know," he says softly. "Been waiting for you to come find me."

"Is that right?" I whisper, dropping onto my arse as his eyes flicker open.

"I'm sorry, I was going to come back but—"

"Shh, it's okay," I soothe, reaching out to cup his cheek. "You have nothing to apologise for."

He leans into my hand, craving my touch as much as I do his.

"He woke up," Daemon whispers. "Was calling out for help."

"You should have woken me."

"It's okay, Angel. He wanted a piss. Probably for the best I helped with that, huh?"

"We owe him both our lives, Nikolas. I don't think either of us could refuse him anything after that."

"I'll take a million pounds and a villa on a secluded beach, if you're offering," Ant groans, and I hop to my feet so fast it makes the room spin.

"Ant," I cry, rushing toward him and crawling up the bed. "Oh my God."

"Hey, sunshine."

A sob rips up my throat as I stare into his dark eyes.

"I'm so sorry, Ant."

"Shush," he soothes, reaching out for my hand and squeezing it in support. "None of this is your fault. I made you a promise, and I had every intention of keeping it."

"But look what that cost you," I breathe as the bed dips behind me and a strong arm wraps around my waist.

"Jealous, devil boy?" I ask, twisting around and pressing a kiss to his neck.

He grunts in response and I can't help but smile.

"He's got nothing to be jealous of. I'm not here to fight for you, Calli. You're exactly where you belong. I said it before, I'll take your friendship."

"But why? I'm not worth all this."

"Angel," Daemon warns, obviously disagreeing with my statement.

"Because it was the right thing to do. Because I don't think anything my uncle does is right. Because he's the wrong person to lead our Family. Many, many reasons, Calli."

His eyes shutter and I panic.

"Are you in pain? Do you need something? Gianna left some pills for you if you woke up."

"Y-yeah, pills sound like a good idea."

Leaning over him, I grab the packet she left on the side and the glass of water.

It's awkward as hell, trying to get him into a position to drink it. Each of his movements has even more agony written on his face, but he does it.

"Thank you," he groans, falling back onto the pillow.

"They'll probably put you back to sleep. They're pretty strong," Daemon warns.

"Fine by me." He falls silent for a few minutes, his

eyes closed once more. And just when I think he's drifted off again, he startles me. "Does anyone know I'm here?"

"As far as we know, the Marianos have no idea. Damien, Theo, and my dad know, but I've ensured that you're safe," Daemon says. I bite my tongue when Jocelyn's name dances on the end of it, but I figure she's loyal to the core and would never do anything but support us, support me. "They're going to want to talk to you when you're up for it."

"I can do that. I assume they want my uncle gone?"

"Yes, and anyone who is part of his agenda."

"I have names," he confesses.

"What about Enzo?" I ask.

"He wants Ricardo gone as much as I do."

"But he's his brother," I gasp, stating the obvious.

"Yes, but that doesn't mean he has to like or agree with him. Ricardo is a power-hungry sociopath. He was the wrong person for the job. It always should have gone to Matteo."

"Is he going to be willing to help us?" Daemon asks.

"Yes. We just have to be smart. We need him on the inside."

"We can do that," Daemon agrees before Ant's breathing deepens as he slips back into sleep "Something tells me that things are going to get messy."

"Yeah, I'm sensing that. Just promise me something." I twist around to look at Daemon.

"Anything," he promises.

"Let the others handle it. Don't go rushing in for

revenge. I can't risk it, Nikolas. I can't for a second think that I've lost you again."

"I promise. I'm not going to do anything stupid. I think the best thing both Ant and I can do right now is to stay hidden."

"Are we safe here?" I ask, unease washing through me. "Is it the first place the Italians will come looking when they realise you've gone?"

"Possibly, but Damien has upped security, and if anyone gets a sniff of us being at risk, we'll move. We can go back to the beach house," he suggests.

"I'd like that."

"If it comes to it, we'll go. But I need to be here right now. And so do you. From what Theo said, Nico needs you."

A heavy sigh falls from my lips. "He won't even open his door to me."

"He just needs time, Angel."

"I know," I agree sadly. "I just want to fix him, you know? And now I feel guilty because I got you back and he's still drowning."

"You've both lost your dad, beautiful. You don't need to feel guilty. You've been through hell the last week, don't downplay what you've felt to make yourself feel better."

Twisting around, I wrap my arms around Daemon's shoulders and drop my face into the crook of his neck. But instead of embracing me like I'm desperate for him to do, he stills.

"What's wrong?" I ask, looking up at him with fear knotting my stomach.

"I need a shower."

"Well, lucky for you, your mum gave me some waterproof stuff to put over your bandages so you can."

"Yeah?" he says, his eyes lighting up like I've just told him it's Christmas morning.

"Yep. Are you going to be okay standing, though? I don't want to—"

"If it'll get rid of this smell and the dirt clinging to my skin, I'll do anything. Especially with your help." His smile gets wider at that thought.

"Okay, deal. But if it gets too much, you've got to tell me."

"I promise, but I have every suspicion that I'll find a whole new lease on life once you're naked with your hands all over me."

"You're trouble."

"You're only just figuring this out?" he quips.

"Come on," I say, quickly scooting off the bed and holding my hand out for him.

Before we get to the door, I look back over my shoulder at Ant.

"He's going to be okay," Daemon breathes.

"Now he is, yeah. But what if they get hold of him before we make our move?"

"We?" he asks, his brow quirking, one side of his lip twitching into a smile.

"Well, you know what I mean."

"Damn, the thought of you with a gun in your hand

putting an end to those motherfuckers gives me the warm and fuzzies."

"There is something very, very wrong with you," I say with a laugh.

"You love me anyway."

"Yep, the crazier the better, if you ask me."

I don't stop until we're standing in the middle of his en suite bathroom.

"Careful what you wish for, Angel," he warns.

"It's okay, you're not the only crazy one here."

My stomach knots as I think about our insane reality.

Both of us should be focusing on our futures right now, our exams. Yet here we are with him basically come back from the dead and me with a baby—

"What's wrong?" he asks, his brows knitting as he proves to me once more that he can read me better than anyone else.

"Nothing. Things just get on top of me every now and then. This past week has been... something else."

Not willing to give into it all yet, I reach for the tie on Daemon's sweats and pull the bow free.

"Hmm... I could get used to this kind of treatment," he whispers as I push my hands inside the fabric, finding him bare beneath.

Skimming my hands over his hips, I shove the fabric to the floor. My breath catches when I expose more bruises and cuts. But none of them are more savage than the blue and purple marks that wrap around his ankles.

Dropping to my knees before him, I brush the dark

skin gently with my fingers, images of what these could be from flickering through my head and making my stomach knot so tight I'm sure I'm about to throw up.

"It's okay, Angel. It's over now."

"They shackled you?"

"They obviously thought we were a flight risk."

"I wonder where they got that idea from?" I quip, desperately trying to keep the mood light as I help free his feet from his trousers. "You sure you're okay doing this?" I ask, sitting back on my haunches and looking up at him.

"More than okay, Angel." He grins down at me with a devilish twinkle before his cock bobbing catches my eye.

"Don't be getting any ideas, devil boy. We're getting you clean and that's it."

"You ruin all my fun," he mutters as I get to my feet and reach for the waterproof dressing Gianna gave me.

Once I'm happy that I've covered his bandages, I turn the shower on and drag my hoodie over my head.

"Fuck, I missed you, Angel." My breath catches.

His eyes hold mine as I push my knickers over my hips. The honesty in his tone, the love shining in his dark grey depths puts a few more of my broken pieces back together again.

He steps close, his hands cup my cheeks and he continues staring deep into my soul.

My skin pricks and my stomach turns over as words bubble up my throat.

But before I get a chance to say anything, he leans

forward, his lips brushing mine in the sweetest kiss that brings tears to my eyes and makes my hands tremble as emotions swell inside me.

He pulls back and looks at me with a smile. "I need to stop making you cry," he breathes.

"I hope you never stop making me feel like this."

He shakes his head as he can't believe what I'm saying.

"Come on, stinky. Let's get you all cleaned up."

"Are you trying to say I smell?" he jokes as I lead him into the huge shower cubicle that's billowing with steam.

Switching our position, I back him up until he's under the spray.

"Oh fuck, that feels good," he groans, the heat in his voice making my blood turn to lava.

I stand there staring as the water runs over his body, watching as the dirt washes away, the dark water swirling down the drain at his feet. If only the memories of what he went through could be banished so easily.

Reaching out, I grab his shower gel and a bath puff. Squeezing loads more than necessary onto it, I lather it up before running it over every inch of Daemon's body in gentle circles.

He watches my every move, his searing gaze burning my skin as I work.

His cock bobs hard and insistent between us, but neither of us makes a move to do anything about it. Although, it's not for lack of desire. My entire body burns with the need to feel that life-changing connection I became addicted to before I thought I lost him.

"Stop," he demands when I begin another pass over his chest, my eyes following the bubbles as I paint his body.

The puff is ripped from my hand and I gasp as my back hits the cold tiles when he flips our position.

"My turn," he growls, staring me dead in the eyes and allowing me to see the fire that's burning him up inside.

"N-no, you don't—"

"Don't argue with me, Angel. You won't win," he warns, his voice dark and deadly. "You like that, don't you, beautiful? You like me giving you little choice but to do what you're told. You might want to break free, but really, underneath it all, you're just a good girl who wants to please me, aren't you?"

"Jesus, Nikolas," I moan, my voice dripping with lust.

"I've got so many plans for you, Angel. So many ways I want to make you scream."

With nothing more than his words and the sight of his sinful body, I'm an aching ball of need. He knows it too, if the slight smirk that kicks up the corner of his lips and the twinkle in his eyes tell me anything.

"There," he says, throwing the puff to the floor. "All ready for me to dirty up again."

He steps closer, his large hand curving around my waist and his head dipping.

The heat of his body burns into mine as the hot water from above continues to rain down on us.

"I still can't believe you're here," I say, gently running my hands up his chest and linking them behind his neck when he presses closer still.

"Believe it, Angel. I'm here, I'm yours, and I'm not going anywhere without you right by my side."

His words steal my breath right before his lips claim mine, ruining me for him all over again.

I don't have any intentions of taking it further, despite my raging need to do so. But that doesn't mean I'm ready when a shrill female voice rips through the air, giving us little choice but to part.

"Daemon. Where the fuck are you?"

"Oh Christ," he mutters lightly. "Who let her in?"

"Hang on. I-I'm in the shower with Calli," he shouts back.

"You're meant to be at death's door, D. Not banging your girl in the shower."

"We're not... Th-that's—" I stutter before being interrupted.

"We'll be right there," he calls before gripping my chin in his hand and giving me little choice but to look into his heated eyes. "Mine," he growls, the low timbre of his voice making my body light up with desire.

"Yours," I agree, happily accepting his next kiss.

Hammering on the door makes us both startle.

"Yo, kids. I don't have all fucking day," Isla sulks. "I need to see this miracle with my own two eyes."

"I'm seriously reevaluating our friendship right now,

I," Daemon calls after kissing me on the tip of my nose and shuffling out of the shower.

My heart constricts when he has to reach out to the wall for support.

I kept him in here too long, made him do too much.

"You love me and you know it. Now get the hell out here," she demands.

"Wait," I say in a rush, running over to him to help when he reaches for the towel.

"I'm okay, beautiful," he argues when I try to help.

"No, Nikolas, you're not. Stop being such a stubborn prick." His brows rise in shock, but he doesn't argue as I wrap the towel around his waist. "Did you want me to go and get you some clothes before you—"

"No, it's okay," he says, but the way his Adam's apple bobs with a thick swallow after makes me wonder if it really is.

"It's just Isla," I whisper, running my hand up his chest and wrapping it around his neck.

"I know. I need to stop hiding," he says firmly.

Rolling his shoulders back, he takes a step forward. I move aside and watch as he reaches for the door.

His movements are slow, and I want to demand he gets back in bed to rest, but I know my concern will fall on deaf ears.

"Holy shit," Isla gasps when he emerges.

"Hey, I. Nice to see you too," he mutters.

By the time I get to the door, they're locked in an embrace. Isla's shoulders shake as her quiet sniffles fill the room.

I stand there awkwardly, wrapped in one of Daemon's towels, watching them.

"It's okay, I," he soothes.

Finally, she pulls back and looks up at him with dark make-up streaked down her cheeks.

"Fuck. It's so fucking good to see you."

"You too, I."

"Shit, you look—"

"Beautiful, huh?" he quips.

"Exhausted."

"Something like that."

"You should get into bed. Too much exertion in the shower." She winks, her eyes finally shooting to me as I watch them shamelessly.

"What's that?" Daemon leans in closer. "Is that a little jealousy I see in those green eyes?"

His words hit me like a baseball bat. Surely, he's not suggesting...

"Hell, yeah. I haven't seen any action in... too long. Especially nothing in the shower. Arsehole," she spits, amusement glittering in her eyes.

"You've got a one-track mind," Daemon scoffs, moving around her and toward his chest of drawers.

My breath catches when he stumbles in front of the unit and has to reach out to steady himself.

I bolt forward in concern but Isla stops me by stepping in front of me. She watched the exact same thing but doesn't seem to be in a rush to help.

"He's okay, Calli," she whispers. "He's also a hard-headed, stubborn arsehole. Sometimes, he needs to learn for himself that he's not Superm—"

"Batman," Daemon offers, making Isla's brow wrinkle in confusion.

"Yeah," I agree. "He's more Batman."

"Right, well..." Isla mutters, looking thoroughly perplexed before she shocks the hell out of me and throws her arms around my shoulders and pulls me in for a hug.

Her embrace is short, and although no words pass her lips, the gesture says a thousand words.

We've never been close despite our families spending a lot of time together while we were growing up, but something tells me that Daemon might be in the process of changing that, and he has no idea.

"You holding up okay?" she asks, sympathy oozing from her eyes. She understands, I know she does. She lost her brother a few years ago. She's been through something similar to what I am right now.

"Yeah, I'm a hell of a lot better now," I say, glancing over her shoulder to where Daemon is resting back against the chest of drawers, watching us intently.

His lips curl into a smile before he beckons me over with nothing more than a tilt of his chin. "Go start the coffee machine, I. We'll be out in a bit, yeah?"

"You got it, boss." She salutes him, much to his amusement.

"She's..."

"Batshit?" Daemon offers when I don't manage to come up with a word.

"Something like that, yeah."

"She's harmless." Her vicious shout cuts through the silence in the flat and Daemon barks out a laugh. "Or at least, she is until Alex is somewhere close."

"They don't get on?" I ask, unable to believe that anyone on the planet wouldn't like Alex.

"Nope. Not at all."

"But how? Alex is a human version of a golden retriever."

Daemon's laughter continues and it lights something up inside, banishing my concern for just a few seconds. "Don't let him hear you call him that. He thinks he's got a rep as a hard man."

"He might have outside these four walls. But deep down, he's the biggest softie in the world."

"You know that. I know that. But Isla... well, let's just say she's more of a cat person."

He pulls the top drawer open and drags out a pair of boxers.

"Maybe there's something more there?"

"Murder waiting to happen? No, there's nothing there, so don't go getting any crazy ideas."

"You did see what happened to Seb and Theo, right? Not so long ago, they were claiming that Stella and Emmie were nothing short of Satan."

"They probably still think they are to be fair."

"Well, yeah, maybe. But they also love them more than life itself so..."

"Just like I do you, Angel."

"Smooth talker," I quip, taking his boxers when he holds them out for me.

"I can't believe I'm going to ask this, but could you... help me get dressed?"

"For you, Batman. Anything."

I drop to my knees before him once more then hold the fabric out for him to step into.

"If you're lucky, I might even help you take them off again later."

"I'll hold you to that, Angel. Any more perks you're willing to offer?" he asks cheekily.

"Let's reassess if you're still awake."

"Deal."

17

DAEMON

Isla didn't stay long. She could see that I was struggling to keep my eyes open. So not long after she'd finished her coffee, she gave me another hug, whispering her relief for me being okay in my ear while making me promise to look after Calli, as if that really needed saying, and reluctantly let Alex see her out.

Mum redressed my cuts, and after she forced some more painkillers down my throat, I finally gave into my exhaustion from that shower with Calli and drifted off to sleep out on the sofa with Mum's, Alex's, and Calli's voices filling my ears.

For the first time in a long time, I slept peacefully with nothing but sweet dreams and hopes for the future filling my head.

When I finally came to, it was to the sound of Alex and Calli bickering in the kitchen over whatever they were cooking. I didn't really care what it was—it smelled insane and had my stomach growling so loudly, I have no doubt it was what woke me up.

The three of us ate the spaghetti bolognese with Ant in his room. After another day which pretty much only consisted of sleep, he was about as ravenous as me and ate the entire bowl with gusto before unsurprisingly announcing that he felt sick.

Thankfully, the bucket that Calli found fuck knows where in my flat was never actually needed, and the four of us spent a really nice and totally bizarre night together.

It seems that Calli might have been onto something, because he is just a decent guy. And despite Alex's initial concerns, he quickly fell under Ant's spell like the two of us have and we ended up laughing together until our stomachs hurt and Calli and Alex had tears in their eyes.

It was almost the most perfect night. The only thing that could have made it better was if I didn't pass out the second my head hit the pillow.

"Hey," I say, sliding my hands down Calli's arms, making her jump and yelp in fright.

"Daemon," she chastises, pulling her AirPods from her ears and dropping them to the table before twisting around to face me. "How are you feeling?" she asks, her eyes tracking over my cuts and bruises like she does multiple times a day. It's like she's hoping they might miraculously heal in front of her eyes.

"Good. Better," I say honestly.

"Really?" she asks, narrowing her eyes in suspicion.

"Yeah, really. Everything hurts a little less."

A smile curls up at her lips as she pushes to her feet. Her body brushes against mine, the softness of her curves making my blood heat for her.

"I can't wait to fuck you again," I confess a beat before a throat clearing on the other side of the room hits us.

"Ant," Calli cries.

"Looks like I'm not the only one who's feeling better," I mutter, shoving my hand into my sweats to rearrange my boner.

"Hey. Sorry, I didn't mean to interrupt, I just needed to get out of that room."

"Something wrong with my guest room?" I ask with a raised brow.

"Yeah, it smells," he confesses.

"Hate to break it to you, man, but that's you."

Ant flips me off as the front door opens and Mum and Alex appear, both of them smiling at the sight of Ant and I standing in the middle of the living room.

"Ah perfect timing. Alex, Ant needs a hand with something that I think is right up your street."

"Shoot," Alex says without missing a beat.

"Uh..." Ant hesitates, his eyes flicking to Calli instead.

"I don't fucking think so," I grunt, reaching for my

girl and pulling her into my side.

"Daemon," she complains. "Can we not get all jealous and possessive? If Ant needs help then—"

"Then Alex or Mum can help him. I'm not having you washing him like you did me."

She tilts her head to the side, looking entirely too cute.

"Whoa, I never said anything about washing him," Alex argues. "Sorry, man. I barely know you, I ain't fondling your sweaty balls."

"Oh my God," Mum breathes. "The guy nearly died getting Daemon back to us. You should be offering up way more than a fondling," she deadpans, earning herself laughs from all of us.

Alex huffs in irritation, but unable to argue with Mum's comment, he concedes. "I'll put the shower on, make sure you get there, and I'll even wait outside the door, but I'm not touching a loofah, even if it's only for your back."

"Dude, you're such a spoilsport. Enzo would have done it."

"Well then, call him," Alex quips, even though we know he can't. For the foreseeable future, the two of us are locked up in this building. At least it's a more comfortable prison than our previous one.

"Come on, bestie," Ant teases. "It'll be good for us to bond."

Mum, Calli, and I watch the two of them disappear down the hall, one of them much more excited than the other.

"What have I done?" Calli mutters.

"Aw, I don't know. I think it's time Alex got a new owner. Maybe he'll buy him a new lead and name tag."

Calli snorts while Mum glares at me.

"You're mean," Calli complains.

"Oh, because you've never said a bad word about your brother." I regret the words as soon as I've said them. "Shit, sorry, Angel."

"It's okay. If you're up for it, everyone wants to come and see you later," she says, plastering a smile on her face.

"Tell them that if they bring food, they can come."

"Something wrong with our cooking last night?" Calli asks, looking offended, while Mum ignores us and heads to the kitchen.

"Nope, it was perfect. I'd just rather not have to lose you to Alex as he tries to teach you how to cook."

"Daemon," she moans when I nuzzle her neck. "Your jealous streak knows no bounds."

"I want to teach you to cook," I confess as I kiss up her throat and down the line of her jaw.

"One spaghetti bolognese does not make me an expert, Nikolas."

"Good because I've got this fantasy," I whisper in her ear, low enough so Mum has no chance of hearing, "of you covered in icing sugar in my kitchen and me peeling your clothes from your body and licking every inch of your sweet skin until you're moaning my name and coming all over my worktop."

"Jesus," she moans, leaning into me a little more.

"You're picturing it, aren't you?" I spin her around so her back is pressed to my front and grip her chin, forcing her to look at my island. "Right there. Can you see me with my head between your thighs and your back bowing off the granite?

"Yes," she breathes, the movement of her chest increasing rapidly.

"Have you eaten yet?" Mum asks obliviously. Thankfully, her back is to us as she empties the dishwasher.

"N-no, not yet. I was waiting for Daemon to wake up," Calli says, her voice dripping with lust.

"I grabbed sausages, bacon, and eggs earlier. You okay to wait a little for it?"

"Sounds perfect, Mum. Thanks. While you do that, I need to steal Calli away for a bit."

"Okay, go do your thing." Calli tenses in my arms at Mum's comment. "Do your dressings need changing or anything?"

"Uh... not sure. I'll have a shower in a bit, then you can check them."

"Sounds good, Son."

Before she has a chance to say anything else, I steer Calli toward my bedroom with my hands on her hips.

She tries to fight it for a few seconds by attempting to plant her feet on the ground, but she soon realises that she has no chance of winning.

The second we're inside, I slam the door closed and drag my chair over, tucking it under the handle in case Alex thinks he's funny and tries to barge inside.

"Daemon, what are you—"

Her words are cut off when I step into her body and slam my lips down on hers.

She doesn't react to begin with, and I start to panic that she's going to refuse, to try and tell me that I'm not healed enough or some bullshit.

But thankfully, with the third swipe of my tongue against hers, she forgets about all the reasons she shouldn't be allowing this and her body relaxes against mine, her lips moving and her tongue joining in.

I kiss her with the need of our first and the desperation of it being our last, all the while walking her backward toward my bed. As soon as her legs hit the edge, I lean forward, giving her little choice but to lay back.

Her hands slide up my arms and gently push against my shoulder as if she wants to stop. But there is no way that's fucking happening.

"Angel," I growl into our kiss, and I force my way between her thighs and plant my hands on either side of her head.

My body hurts, but it's not the blinding pain I felt when I first woke up here. And anyway, I like a bit of pain, so it's nothing I can't handle—especially if it means I get to have my girl.

Our kiss is wet and dirty and everything I've craved since watching her walk out of the bathroom of that country club almost two weeks ago.

Her touch is so gentle it makes goosebumps erupt across my skin as she trails her fingers over my back.

"You won't break me, beautiful."

"No, but I might hurt you. Your cuts might—"

"Fuck that. I need you more than I care about a little pain."

She gasps when I hook her leg around my hip and grind my length against her pussy.

"And I know that you need me too. You're dripping for me, aren't you?"

"Daemon," she moans. "W-we can't. They'll... they'll hear us."

"I don't care, Angel. The whole fucking world could be watching for all I care. I need you. I'm fucking dying without you."

"I'm right here."

We stare at each other, our heaving breaths mixing as our fierce battle of wills continues.

She shudders as I trail my fingers down the inside of her thigh, and a smile pulls at my lips when I find the evidence of how much she needs this too.

Rubbing my fingers over the soaked fabric covering her pussy, she sucks in a sharp breath.

"Gonna continue telling me that you don't need this?"

"I... I never said—"

Hooking the fabric aside, I push two fingers deep inside her and curl them to find her sweet spot.

"Oh shit."

Finally, she forgets about reality and her grip on my upper arms tightens.

I grit my teeth against the pain of the cut on my left

arm, but thankfully, she doesn't notice. Not that I'd stop now even if she did.

My girl needs me, and I have every fucking intention of fulfilling her every desire.

"Daemon," she growls, her nails digging into my skin as she focuses on the sensations I'm unleashing on her body.

Sitting up, I reach for the zip on the front of my hoodie that she's wearing and drag it down.

"Fuck, I love knowing you're walking around like this," I mutter as I expose her bare skin.

Her chest is flushed red and her nipples are hard and desperate for attention.

My bruised ribs protest as I drop lower to suck one of them into my mouth as I finger-fuck her harder, feeling her climbing toward the release she needs.

"Oh fuck," she cries before slapping her hand over her mouth to stop herself when I flick her nipple with my tongue once again.

"So sensitive," I whisper, doing it again and again until she shatters, dragging a pillow over her face and screaming out my name.

It makes me feel like a fucking king as she clamps down on my fingers, her body quaking as pleasure surges through me.

The second she's done, I drag the pillow away, needing to see her beautiful face before I slide my fingers from her body and push them into my mouth instead.

Her eyes dilate as she watches me suck her juices off.

"Fucking missed you, Angel."

"Nikol—argh," she squeals as I flip us. "Shit. Stop doing that, you'll—" A moan cuts through her warning as I cup both her tits in my hands and squeeze. "Oh God."

Her hips roll, making her pussy grind down on my aching dick.

"If you don't want me overdoing it, beautiful, then I guess it's only right that you take charge."

I let my arms fall to the side as I thrust up, giving her an extra hint as to what I'm thinking.

"You... you want me to be in charge?" she asks as if it's the most absurd thing she's ever heard.

"Yeah, I'm sure you've got it in you."

"Well, actually... I haven't," she quips.

Shaking my head, I twist my fingers in the sides of her knickers and rip them away from her body.

"No, you haven't. Might want to fix that."

I can't help but laugh when she reaches for the tie on my sweats with the eagerness of a kid on Christmas morning tearing into their gifts.

Lifting my hips, I help her out, and she shoves the fabric just low enough to reveal my aching length.

She stares down at me with wide eyes, the tip of her thumb teasing my piercing.

"Angel," I growl, my need to sink deep inside her all-consuming.

Her eyes roll up my ruined chest before they lock on mine.

Lifting on her knees, she positions us before sinking down so fucking slowly on my dick that my fingers twist in the sheets and I swear my eyes cross.

"Better than I remember," I groan.

"Never leave me again. I won't survive it," she demands.

"I won't. Ever. We can just stay like this." I mean, it's not like I can so much as leave this building right now, so it would be a fucking incredible way to spend our time.

She rolls her hips, and I nearly fucking shoot my load from that small movement and the sight of her sitting impaled on me.

My heart pounds, swollen with so much fucking love for my girl I can hardly stand it.

"I want everything with you," I confess. "Every-fucking-thing."

Threading my fingers through hers, I drag her down to me so I can claim her mouth as she continues to fuck me slowly.

Each roll of her hips sends fireworks shooting around my body. After not thinking I'd ever get this again while I was locked in the dark and cold, brutalised by those fucking Italians, feeling her skin against mine, making her mine again... it's everything and so much more.

"I'm not going to last," I confess when she pulls back from our kiss to catch her breath.

"So don't. I want to feel your cum inside me, Nikolas. I want that reminder of who I belong to."

"Holy shit," I gasp. "Who are you and what have you done with my innocent angel?"

"You corrupted her, devil boy," she whispers in my ear. "Now, give me everything," she demands.

With a grunt of pain from my ribs, I push my hand between us and find her clit.

"Not without you. I want you coming all over my cock as I fill you up."

I pinch her clit and she sits down on me more forcefully, fully seating me inside her.

"That's it, Angel. Fuck me like a good girl."

She sits up straight and does exactly as she's told, all the while her eyes are locked on mine. They're filled with awe and love, and I find it hard to believe it's all aimed at me.

But it is. Because she's mine. I have no doubt.

"All fucking mine."

I pinch her clit once more and she cries out as she falls. The first tight clench of her pussy around my dick ensures that I fall right over that cliff with her.

"Fuck yeah," I grunt as I watch her ride out her orgasm.

The second she's done, she falls spent onto my body.

Her weight hurts, but it's so fucking worth it.

Wrapping my arms around her, I let her warmth seep into me as we both fight to catch our breaths.

"Do you think they know what we're doing?" she asks quietly.

Thankfully, she can't see me, because a wide, smug smile spreads across my face.

"Nah, they probably think we're just showering or something."

Sitting up in a rush, she glares at me, and my smile only gets wider.

"I don't give a fuck, Angel. I want all of them to know how much I love you and how you ruin me with everything you do."

She falls silent and her eyes leave mine as she loses herself in her thoughts.

"Nikolas, I—"

"Get your horny arses out here, breakfast is nearly ready," Alex shouts on the other side of the door.

"I don't think they had a clue what we were doing," I deadpan.

Calli's brow lifts as her soft look turns into a glare.

"They're going to have to wait. I'm not going out there smelling of sex, even if they know."

"I could go for a shower," I say, letting my eyes drop to her tits again.

Reaching out, I pinch one of her nipples. It makes her entire body jolt and my dick swell once more.

"Do not get any more ideas," she warns, as she sadly climbs off my body.

"How soon can we tell them all to fuck off? I need you and this entire flat to ourselves."

"Pretty sure your guest is gonna be here for a while."

"Nah, fuck that. He can move in with Alex so we can fuck on every surface of this place."

18

CALLI

The second I pull the door open, Seb and Toby come barreling their way into the flat with Theo only a beat behind them.

"Hey, baby C," Seb calls as they rush inside.

"Nice to see you all too," I call back, my heart so full at the sight of the guys so desperate to see Daemon.

Toby has the decency to give me a little wave behind him, not that I really care.

"Hey," Stella breathes, stepping into my space and gathering me up in her arms. "How are you doing?"

A second, and then a third set of arms wraps around me until I'm in the middle of a huddle.

"I'm good. I'm really good. He came back."

"Fuck, when Seb told me, I couldn't believe it."

"I knew he wouldn't go down that easily," Emmie says. "It takes someone really special to bring the devil to his knees, and the Italians aren't it. You, however..."

"I freaking knew you were banging him," Jodie says. "I sensed it weeks ago."

"And you didn't want to share the love?" Stella quips.

"I didn't want to point out everything that was right in front of your faces. I was new to the group."

"Oh, but you're happy to rub our noses in it now?" Emmie asks lightly.

"Fuck it, why not," Jodie jokes.

When they all finally release me, it's Jodie's wide smile that steals my attention.

"You look happy," I say, studying her.

"Sara woke up," she confesses.

"Oh my God, that's amazing," I sigh. "How is she?"

Her excitement falters a little and her eyes water. "Groggy. She's still mostly sleeping, but they've taken the majority of the tubes and stuff out and she's less medicated. It's still going to take time, but she's back with us. She opened her eyes, and squeezed my hand. It's progress, you know?"

"See," Stella says. "Miracles do happen."

My hand twitches at my side with my need to rest it on my belly.

It's weird, it's not a move I ever would have considered before. But knowing that I'm growing a little person in there has flipped some kind of switch in me. I guess it does with everyone. But knowing it and experiencing it are two very different things.

"Where's Bri?" I ask, looking around as if she's about to pop up.

"She's got a meeting at uni. Some issue with her new school placement." Jodie shrugs.

"Come on, it's not really me you want to be looking at, is it?" I joke as the guys' laughter fills the air around us.

"I just need to see it with my own eyes," Stella mutters as we turn to walk deeper into the flat.

"Well, well, well, aren't you a sight for sore eyes," Emmie says happily as the four of us spill into the living room.

"Hey," Daemon says, a playful smile pulling at his lips that makes my stomach knot.

Despite his desire to stop hiding, he's pulled on another zip-up hoodie for everyone's visit, and although I hate the thought of him not feeling like he's good enough, selfishly, I want to keep him to myself. Our biggest—okay, maybe not our biggest—secret has now been exposed, and I desperately want to keep a little bit of us just between us.

His eyes find mine and it only makes the love and desire flooding me even stronger.

Lifting his hand from the arm of the chair he's sitting in, he beckons me over with one simple flick of his fingers.

I hesitate, my skin prickling with all eyes in the room on me. But when someone, I suspect Emmie, gives me a little shove from behind, the magnetic pull between us becomes too strong and in a heartbeat, I've closed the space between us and am allowing him to drag me down onto his lap.

"You guys have met my girl, right?" he asks, looking nowhere but directly into my eyes as his fingers twist in my hair and he tugs me forward, crashing our lips together.

Whoops and hollers go up around us as Daemon's tongue pushes past my lips, deepening the kiss way more than necessary when we have an audience. An audience that includes my cousin.

Realisation hits me and I pull back.

"Where's Nico?" I ask, turning around to look at Theo, who is thankfully not watching us make out—unlike everyone else, it seems.

Daemon's grip tightens on my hip as I wait for an answer.

Theo looks up, his dark, unreadable eyes locking with mine. "He won't answer his door," he confesses sadly.

My lips part, suggestions for him to break the damn thing down right on the tip of my tongue. But as much as I might want them to override the security on his place and force their way inside, I know it's not the answer.

Twisting out of Daemon's hold, I march across the room before he can stop me.

"Calli, wait." His deep, demanding voice rolls through me, but it's not enough to stop me.

I'm out of the flat in the blink of an eye and racing toward the stairs.

Blood rushes past my ears and I run, my concern for my brother the only thing I can focus on.

"NICO," I shout, slamming my palms down on his door until they hurt. "NICO. It's me. Just open the fucking door," I scream, beginning to sound a little unhinged.

Desperation claws at me, emotion crawling up my throat.

I can't deny that having Daemon back has given me almost everything I need. And I'm pretty sure I can get on with my life without my mother's judgemental opinions, but I need my brother. As much as he might drive me crazy at every turn, I need him.

"Nico, please, I need—"

The click of a lock startles me and my hope soars.

"Nico," I sob when he pulls the door open a crack. It's enough to see that his flat is in darkness and only allows me to see one of his bloodshot eyes.

My breath catches as I take in his wrecked expression. I've seen him looking all kinds of fucked up in the past. Hell, I've helped him down to his basement while he's been off his face more times than I want to count—despite the fact he has no idea I was ever there for him when our parents weren't. But there's something about the darkness lingering in his eyes that tells me that this isn't just a bad hanger, bender even, but he's drowning. Truly fucking drowning.

Pain crackles between us as if it's a living, breathing thing, and it brings back everything I was feeling before Daemon crashed back into my life.

Guilt floods through my veins like poison as I think

about being downstairs, being so happy about his return, all the while my brother was up here—

"Is it true?" he growls, his voice rough, slurred and barely sounding like the one I'm so familiar with.

My brows pinch as I try to figure out what he's asking.

"Y-yeah, he's downstairs in his flat. It's—"

"Are you fucking him?"

My jaw drops at the vicious undercurrent to his voice.

"Uh... u-um..." I stutter. "It's more than—" Before I even get a chance to try and explain what I've found with Daemon, Nico's door swings closed, slamming right in my face. "NICO," I scream, my anger at his attitude and the ease he's able to block me out of his life with bubbling over, and I return to raining fury down on his door.

"Angel." Daemon's soft voice rips through me, halting my movements instantly.

Spinning around, my breath catches when I find him with Theo at his side, who looks ready to catch him at any moment should his body give up.

"H-he just—" I stutter, unable to voice what he just did.

"I know, beautiful. We were here." Faster than I've seen him move since I got him back, Daemon surges forward, Theo hot on his heels until he's close enough to pull me into his arms, holding me tighter than I'm sure he should. "It's going to be okay."

I suck in a shaky breath, tears balancing on my

lashes, desperate to fall but equally too stubborn to do so over my brother's bullshit opinion.

"He just needs time," Theo assures me, sounding much more sympathetic than I ever thought he was capable of. "He's not angry at you specifically, Calli. He's just mad at the entire world for taking your dad."

"Doesn't he think that I am too?" I argue.

"He can't see anything outside of his grief right now. He just needs to work through it, and all we can do is be here and show him that we're not going anywhere."

I swallow down my unease over the whole situation, but I can't get rid of the next thought that spills into my head. "And what if he can't?"

"He will. He has a job to do and a Family to help run. He will see through the dark cloud that has descended and realise that soon."

Daemon pulls me into his side while Theo steps up on my other side, and with one final look back at Nico's door, they guide me toward the lift and back down to the others, who are waiting anxiously in Daemon's flat.

"Did he ans— fuck," Stella surmises when she takes one look at my face when I'm guided back into the room.

"He answered. Demanded to know if I'm fucking Daemon and then slammed the door in my face."

The expressions of all my friends tighten in anger, and while I might be grateful for their support, really, I just want Nico to let me in and allow me to help him through this. Hell, I'd take him letting anyone in right now if it meant they could help him heal.

"Everything is still too fresh. I know you don't need

me to tell you how rough losing a parent is. But Evan was so much more than a dad to Nico. He was his ultimate hero, Calli," Seb says. "It hits real deep."

"I know. I get it, I do, I just wish..." I trail off, because none of it needs saying. I can see the same wish on all their faces.

"He just needs to let Bri in. I have no doubt she holds the medicine he needs right now," Jodie quips.

"You mean she'll suck it right out of him?" Emmie deadpans.

"Really?" I hiss, happily settling on Daemon's lap once more and curling myself into his warmth.

My heart aches over my brother, and grief still runs rampant through my body over the loss of our dad, but with Daemon's arms wrapped around me once more, everything just feels so much more possible.

Discreetly, I rest my hand on my belly. A secret thrill of excitement goes through me as I think about our reality.

That is, until the guilt takes over. I need to tell him, that much is obvious. I just... I need the right time. And that isn't when his flat is full of other people.

A bang sounds out from down the hall, cutting off everyone's conversations, and every set of eyes turns toward the hallway that leads to the bedrooms.

Ant's footsteps get louder before he emerges, his eyes widening when he takes in the number of people filling Daemon's living room.

"Uh..." he grunts, lifting his arm so he can rub at the

back of his neck, but his movements falter when his arm is halfway as his pain gets the better of him.

Unlike Daemon, he's still shirtless, showing off the artwork of bruises and cuts across his torso.

"Hey," he says, a lopsided smile appearing on his lips. "How's it going?"

Silence.

"I was just going to get a drink."

"Dude, come join us," Daemon encourages, and Ant looks around the room nervously.

"He's right. It seems like you're one of us now," Theo agrees, lifting Emmie from his lap and shoving her forward when he stands so Ant has a place to sit. "That's Seb, Stella, Toby, Jodie, and my girl Emmie," he says, introducing everyone, even though Ant is probably more than aware.

"Th-thanks," he stutters, moving over to the free seat slowly as if he's expecting someone to tell him it was a joke.

The front door slamming drags all our eyes away from Ant, and only a beat later, Isla comes bounding into the room, her eyes flicking around all of us before landing on our newest addition suspiciously.

"And you didn't think to tell me you were having a party?" she scoffs.

"And this is Isla," Daemon drawls. "Probably best to stay away from her though, she's been known to eat men alive."

"What the fuck, D?" she scoffs, marching toward the kitchen to help herself to a drink.

"What do you want to drink?" Emmie offers Ant.

"Whatever is in the fridge, if that's okay. No alcohol. These painkillers are already kicking my arse."

"So," I pipe up, more than ready to shatter the awkward tension in the room, "did you hear about Alex and Ant's little shower experience?"

"Shut the fuck up, baby C," Alex grunts. "We did not shower together," he points out when Stella and Emmie immediately show interest in this little story.

"Speak to Mum and you'll get a very different story. I heard you cleaned his balls up good," Daemon deadpans, making me bark out a laugh.

"You know, I really fucking hate you lot sometimes," Alex hisses, tipping his bottle of beer to his lips. "I ordered you all fucking Mexican, too."

"Just shows how little action you've been seeing if you're willing to shower with a dude, man. No offence, Ant. I'm sure you've got great balls and all that," Toby teases.

"It's Calli's fault," Alex grunts, dragging me back in.

"Don't even think about pulling that one," I warn. "I never said you couldn't go out and fuck any willing girl you could find just because you were looking after me."

"Bit inconsiderate, don't you think?"

"We all have needs, A," Daemon mutters. "I'm just glad you didn't try to make use of my girl while she was in your care."

"Nah, I knew you were coming back," Alex states proudly.

"Did you fuck," I mutter. "You were as shocked as me when he stumbled through the front door."

"Whatever." Alex looks around the room, a frown forming on his face. "I don't even have any wingmen if I wanted to go out and pull. You fuckers are all pussy-whipped. And you," he pins Ant with a look, "you're not even allowed out to play."

"You look like a kid who's had his sweets taken away, Deimos," Isla growls as she sits on the floor.

"Fuck the sweets. I need some pussy."

"Such a charmer," I quip while Isla scoffs in disgust. "I can hardly understand why they're not queuing around the street to offer themselves up."

"I need Nico. At least he still understands."

Silence ripples through the air as we all think of the member of our group who is currently upstairs alone drowning in his own misery and probably vodka.

"When I'm free, I'll take you out, man," Ant offers.

"Aw, even your boyfriend feels sorry for you," Seb barks.

"Fuck you."

"I'm good thanks, my girl keeps me nice and satisfied."

"Really?" Toby mutters.

"You still not over the fact I fuck your sister on the regular, Tobias? I'd have thought Hades would have forced you to get over that little issue."

"Yeah," I pipe up. "What actually did happen that night? And, when can we join you?"

"No," Theo barks. Absolutely fucking not.

"Oh, come off it. If Toby managed it with his sister somewhere in the vicinity, surely you can get over the cousin shit. I want to experience it."

Daemon's hot breath rushes over my ear. "Fuck them, Angel. I'll speak to Hera when I'm free and we'll go have a party for two, if you're interested."

"Um…" I hesitate. Who knows when he might be able to walk out the front door again, and just how pregnant I might be? The last thing he'll probably want to do is tie me up and have his wicked way with me. I'll be all swollen, fat and gross.

The banter between us all continues for hours. Everyone but Daemon, Ant, and I get happily drunk. Thankfully, everyone accepts my excuse of wanting to be sober so that I can look after both Daemon and Ant, who are quite clearly able to look after themselves now, but it was all I had.

We talk about everything from the week at school that Alex, Daemon and I have missed, to the guys' final football game of the season tomorrow night which could land Theo the championship trophy he's coveted all year.

By the time everyone leaves, Daemon can hardly keep his eyes open. Abandoning the mess and leftovers for tomorrow, I lock the door behind our guests, turn the lights off, and head toward Daemon's room.

When I round the corner, I find that he's stripped down to his boxers and is passed out flat on his back on the bed. The sound of his soft snores fills the room, and all I can do is stand there and smile.

Without having to worry about being caught, I lift both hands to my flat stomach as butterflies once again erupt within.

"I'm growing your baby, Nikolas," I whisper so quietly I doubt he'd even hear me if he was awake. "And I can't wait to see you holding him in your arms."

19

DAEMON

When I wake, it's once again to an empty bed and the sun shining in through the crack in the curtains.

I roll over, not interested in staying here alone any longer than necessary, and I'm shocked by how easily my body complies. Who knew sleep had such healing qualities?

I take a piss, brush my teeth and turn the shower on.

Glancing over my shoulder, I imagine Calli walking through the door to join me and my cock stirs.

Yesterday, watching her ride me was everything, but it only scratched the surface of my need to make up for lost time with her.

Moving back into the bedroom, I grab the new phone that Theo supplied me with, seeing as mine is fuck knows where. The fucking nerd even managed to ensure it was a direct copy of the one I lost—all my photos, my contacts, everything is in here. Thoughtful prick.

With a smile, I find the conversation I last had with Calli, my heart twisting when I find messages I sent her after we came back from my grandparents' place.

Locking down those less-than-memorable moments, I start tapping away.

Daemon: Any chance you could help me with something?

I rush back to the bathroom, push my boxers down my hips, and step under the spray.

I don't bother covering my bandages, I'm pretty sure everything is healed enough not to be an issue now, although if I'm wrong, something tells me Mum won't have an issue ripping me a new one. Or even Calli, for that matter, when she rushes through the door in a few seconds.

Over the sound of the water, I just about make out the click of the bedroom door opening.

"What's wro— oh," she says, the doorway darkening as her shadow fills the space before she appears.

Her dark hair is piled on top of her head in a messy bun, and she's got a pink pencil pushed through it. All she needs is a pair of glasses and she'd look like a hot little geek.

Once again, she's wearing one of my hoodies with her bare legs poking out the bottom, but today she must be cold, because she's got a pair of my Knight's Ridge PE socks pulled up to her knees.

"Fucking hell, Angel. You look like sin," I mutter, wrapping my hand around my painfully hard cock, working myself slowly as I continue drinking in the sight of her. "Tell me you're naked beneath my hoodie."

"What's wrong? Your message said you needed help. What—"

Her eyes drop to my dick and her lips form a perfect circle as I make a show of wanking myself off.

"Yeah, I really need your help with something, beautiful. You think you could get on your knees and help me out with it?"

"Feeling better again, I take it?"

"Good as new and desperate for my girl. So what do you say?"

"I was studying with Ant."

"And? He's a big boy, I'm sure he'll be okay for a few minutes on his own."

"A few minutes. You sure know how to please a girl."

"Angel, you wrap those luscious lips around my cock and you'll be lucky if it takes me a minute to blow."

"And what's in it for me?" she asks, stepping forward, her eyes lifting to find mine again.

"Well, once you've taken the edge off, I'm pretty sure I could fuck you as slow as you want for as long as you can bear, until you're gasping my name and begging for a release loud enough that this entire building can hear your screams."

She makes a show of thinking about my words before she whispers, "That sure is tempting. I had no idea Batman had so much stamina."

"Oh, Angel. He has more than you would ever believe."

"Sure would be a shame not to test that out."

I swallow thickly as she drags my hoodie up her body, once again revealing just a tiny pair of black lace knickers. The fabric gets caught on the pencil she's obviously forgotten is in her hair, and I get to stand there and watch her tits bounce while she fights with it.

"Oh for fuck's sake," she mutters, before finally freeing herself and throwing the fabric to the floor in a huff.

I can't help but smile at her as she lifts her foot to take a sock off.

"Wait," I cry. "Just the knickers."

She stills and looks up at me with the cutest baffled look on her face.

"You want me to leave the socks on?"

"Hell yeah. That's fucking hot."

"Okay," she whispers, pushing her thumbs into the sides of her knickers and shoving them down her legs, giving her hips a sexy little wiggle at the same time.

"Now come here, I need your lips on me."

Desire darkens her eyes as she stalks toward me and directly into the shower.

Misinterpreting my words, her knees bend, ready to sink to the floor, but I catch her with a fistful of hair before she drops.

"Not yet," I grunt, dragging her into my body and stealing a much needed kiss.

She moans as my tongue strokes hers and my hands roam around her body.

Everything outside of the room falls away and I lose myself in my girl, in everything she gives me. Her light, her innocence, her love.

I kiss her until we're both breathless, and once our chests are heaving and our bodies are begging for more, I pull her back and drop my eyes down her curves.

"Now you can get on your knees, Angel."

Her teeth sink into her bottom lip as she stares up at me through her lashes seductively.

"You say such sweet things to me," she teases.

"I can do sweet, but right now I want my cock so deep in your throat that you don't know where I end and you begin, and I want to watch as you swallow my cum before I bend you over and fill your cunt with more."

"Shit," she gasps, the blush that's already spread well down onto her chest only glowing brighter.

"They don't call me the devil for nothing, beautiful." She rolls her eyes at me as I wink playfully, but thankfully, she complies and sinks to her knees not a second later, wasting no time in doing exactly as she was told.

"Fuck yes," I bark when I hit the back of her throat.

She stares up at me the whole time, reminding me what a lucky motherfucker I am to get a second chance at life with my girl.

Just as I warned, I come embarrassingly fast. But

equally, just like I promised, after one more wet and dirty kiss, I demand she presses her palms to the tiles and sticks her arse out. I eat her until I'm hard once again, then I fuck her long and slow until she's trembling in my arms and her legs are threatening to give out as she pleads, whimpers and screams at me to let her fall.

By the time I spin her around again, crush her against the cold tiled wall and let her taste herself on my tongue, she's limp and sated.

My need for her means that before long, I'm grinding my cock against her thigh. My addiction to this girl knows no bounds.

"Again?" she breathes as I drop my lips to her neck.

"You have no idea," I confess. "I had over a week of nothing but thinking about getting back to you again and all the things I wanted to do to you. I got my wish, you're in my arms again, now I want to work my way through my imagination."

"Well, who would I be to stop you?" she moans when I nip at her soft skin.

Hooking her leg around my hip, I leave her standing on the other foot, aware that taking her weight might be pushing my limits right now, and guide myself to her entrance.

The moan that rips from her lips as I push inside her again is nothing but pure filth, and I eat it up as if I've been starved my entire life.

"You fucking ruin me, Angel."

"Nikolas," she cries, rolling her hips forward to take me deeper.

"Play with your clit, beautiful. I want to feel you coming all over my cock again."

I watch her hand as it descends down her stomach before her gasp rips past my ears as she finds her swollen clit. She squeezes me so tight, I have to grit my teeth to stop me from blowing. So much for her taking the edge off.

"That's it, beautiful. Take my cock like a good girl."

"Yes, yes," she cries. Her concerns about us being heard are long forgotten.

The fingers of her free hand twist in my hair and she drags my mouth down to hers so she can kiss me as we both find our climaxes.

"Fuck. Angel?"

"Yeah," she pants.

"Just so you know, I'm never letting you leave this flat," I say honestly into her neck.

"What? Ever?"

"If only," I mutter.

Pulling back, I look into her hooded eyes so she can see the seriousness of my next words.

"M-m-move in w-w-with m-m-me."

"What?" she gasps.

"I n-n-never want to be a-a-away f-from you again. And y-you can't tell me that y-you want to go home, y-you've been basically living in this building for over a week, from what I hear."

"Yeah, I have. I just never thought..." Her eyes shift from mine as she chews on her bottom lip.

"W-what is it?" I ask, my heart rate picking up again

but for an entirely different reason. "D-don't you w-w-want to?"

Her eyes jump back to mine, and whatever she reads on my face makes her entire body sag with regret.

"Oh, Nikolas," she breathes, taking my cheeks in her hands as fear drips through my veins that she's not as serious about this as I am. "Yes."

"Y-yes?"

"Yes, Nikolas. One hundred times yes. I was just wondering when we might get this whole place to ourselves."

"I'll get it sorted," I say confidently, but it doesn't have the effect I was hoping for, because she still looks a little bit like her puppy just died.

"Talk to me, Angel. What's going on?"

"Everything," she says with a pained laugh. "So much has changed in the past two weeks. It's just hard to keep up."

"I can't imagine what you're going through right now, and I'm not going to even try. But I'm here. Whatever it is, whatever you need," I wrap my hand around the side of her neck and press my brow to hers, "I'm right here."

"I need... I need it just to be us," she tells me quietly.

"Then I'll make it happen," I promise. "Anything else?"

"I'm really hungry," she confesses, making me laugh.

"You want me to cook for you, Angel?"

"Are you feeling up to it?" she asks, resting her arms over my shoulders and looking up at me hopefully.

"After that, I feel like I could do anything."

Stretching up on her tiptoes, she drops a kiss on my nose and reaches for the shower gel.

I watch her with my brows pulled tight. There's something else, I know there is. I push it aside when she moves toward me with a puff that's erupting in bubbles, trusting that whatever it is, she'll tell me when she's ready.

"Are you sure about this?" Calli asks, twisting her fingers with mine, staring up at me with a mixture of dread and excitement warring in her eyes.

"Yes," Emmie sighs behind me. "He's said like sixty billion times that it's okay. Now let's go. I don't want to miss kick-off."

"For someone who hates soccer, you sure seem clued up all of a sudden," Stella points out.

"At least I call the right name, Yank," Emmie scoffs. "It's football. You know... foot-ball." She mimics kicking a ball. "How you guys decided that a game where you throw a ball around should have the same name, God only knows." She throws her hands up in frustration.

"You sound just like the guys," I point out with amusement.

"No, I do not I— Fuck it. Can we just go now? We got you a special top and everything."

My eyes drop to the black hoodie she's wearing, and

for about the tenth time since she put it on, I spin her around.

I didn't see the dresses that Calli made for everyone when they first played All Hallows' but I heard plenty from the guys. I didn't really understand their excitement back then. But right now, staring at my girl with my name on her back and the girls' attempt at humour, giving me a position number of 666, a surge of possessiveness slams into me so strong that all I want to do is drag her down to my bedroom and take her all over again.

I hold her shoulders, staring down at the copper text announcing to anyone who gives a shit that she's mine. Even if to the outside world I've vanished off the face of the earth, this statement of who she belongs to is fucking everything.

Dragging her back into my body, I whisper in her ear, "Don't take this off later. I'm going to need to fuck you from behind while you're wearing my name."

"Now that's the idea," Stella announces. "The sooner we go, the sooner he'll be missing you and making plans to ensure you have a killer night."

"You guys really need to remember that you have a house guest," Ant pipes up.

"Aw, Ant. Are they making your stay hard? Pun totally intended," Emmie quips.

"It was much more peaceful when he wasn't fully functioning," Ant mutters.

"Only because you were in a fucking coma, man," I tease.

"I'm starting to see the positives of that situation."

"Well, the sooner we put your uncle in the ground, the sooner you can get out there and find some willing chick who's gonna dig the new scars."

"A-fucking-men to that," he announces as Calli is ripped from my grasp by Stella and Emmie and dragged toward the door.

"Bring her back to me in one piece," I order.

"You got it, boss." Stella salutes me before the three of them disappear, leaving me alone with Ant for the first time since we escaped hell.

"Get up," I demand, making his eyes widen in shock. "I've got a surprise for you."

"Uh..."

"Oh don't look so scared. It's a good surprise, promise."

20

CALLI

"**GO KNIGHTS**," Emmie screams at the top of her voice as our team runs onto the field.

The heady rush of the game that I'm used to from years of watching Nico, Theo and the guys tingles through me as the crowd around us goes wild.

It's a home game, so almost every single Knight's Ridge student is here along with parents and teachers, all hoping to watch our boys lift the trophy at the end of the night.

Theo and Nico might have had one foot in the Family during their time here, but football has always been their outlet. Their way to let go of the seriousness of their futures, their reality, and just be the easy-going, carefree boys they never got to be.

Obviously, it also helps that they're pretty talented. I mean, I'm not sure they're premier league-level talented, but they might have had a chance at going pro, or at least semi-pro, if their futures weren't already written in stone before they were even born.

I glance at my overly excited best friends, wondering what kind of alien has taken over Emmie's body as she continues to scream bloody murder for Theo when he finally emerges. It's a total one-eighty from the bored, why-the-hell-am-I-wasting-my-time-with-this expression she wore when we all travelled to Oxford earlier in the year.

"Oh my God," Stella gasps, grabbing my arm, shaking me violently so I have no choice but to look back to the field.

My breath catches in my throat when I spot the player who's just followed Theo out from the tunnel.

"Nico," I breathe. "He came."

I watch enthralled as the rest of the guys surround him and pull him in for a group hug.

"See, everything is going to be okay," Stella says, reaching for my hand.

"I knew he wouldn't let the guys down."

"HEY," a female voice shouts from the end of the row, and when I look over, I find Jodie and Brianna trying to squeeze their way down to us.

"Hey," Bri says, catching my eye once she's close and giving me a soft, knowing smile.

"Nico came," I tell her happily.

"We know. We brought him."

My chin drops in shock.

"Refused to move from his door unless he got his act together and came with us."

I shove Emmie none too gently, out of the way and throw my arms around Brianna.

"Thank you," I breathe in her ear.

"Anytime. How are you?"

"Good."

"And Daemon?" she asks quietly.

I pull back, shaking my head as a wide smile spreads across my face. "Incredible. It's just... I was too scared to wish for it, and I still can't believe it, but it's just..." I trail off, unable to explain exactly how it feels, having him back.

"Have you..."

"No, not yet. I haven't found the right time."

"There might not be one. You might just need to—" A whistle blows and the crowd goes wild once again, cutting off our conversation as the game starts.

I move back into my space between Emmie and Stella, but not before Jodie catches sight of my hoodie.

"Love your number," she shouts, flashing me a shot of her back which proudly displays Toby's name and number.

As gutted as I am that I didn't get the chance to make these myself for the girls, I love that I've got a little bit of Daemon with me.

Reaching into my pocket, I pull my phone out and find our chat.

Calli: Miss you. *heart emoji* Is everything okay?

Devil boy: Everything is fine. Stop worrying and enjoy yourself. Are we winning yet?

I look up, watching as Theo heads toward the goal. Seb and Alex race up the other side of the pitch toward the box.

Calli: Not yet, but Nico is playing. Jodie and Bri dragged him here.

Devil boy: That's awesome. Now enjoy yourself!

Calli: So demanding.

Devil boy: You know it.

The crowd erupts and the stand beneath me vibrates as Knight's Ridge celebrates the first goal of the night.

"Who scored?" I ask not catching which of our players is at the bottom of the pile of bodies.

"You weren't even watching," Emmie chastises.

"It was Theo," Stella adds helpfully.

"He's gonna get my best skills tonight if he brings this home."

I once again stare at Emmie like she's grown a second head, but as the guys resume the game, I figure fuck it. She's happy, I've got my boy back, Nico has left his flat, and Uncle Damien and the guys are going to deal with the Italians. I have to believe that it's all going to be enough for our lives to return to some kind of normality soon.

The game passes in a blur of goals from both sides as they duel, both teams equally matched, but in the end, just like the last time they met, we stole the victory in the final few minutes of the game, earning Theo the win and the title he's craved for years.

I can only hope that it's only the beginning of success for them all. With our exams starting in only a few weeks and the threat of the Italians as dangerous and real as ever, I think we're going to need all the luck we can get.

I'm enthralled, watching the guys celebrate down on the pitch. Everything inside me begs to be down there, to be able to jump into Nico's arms and assure him that everything is going to be okay.

But I can't.

Excitement buzzes in my veins as I watch Theo lift the trophy while the rest of the team bounces around him, chanting for their captain.

Emmie, Stella, Jodie, and Brianna shout and scream for their boys, shocking the crowd around us with filthy promises of the best night of their life once they get home later. If it weren't for the looks on the faces of those around us, I might be slightly horrified, but as it is, I can't stop laughing.

Eventually, the excited crowd begins to thin out and the guys disappear down to the locker room.

"Oh my God, that was insane," Stella cries, a wide smile on her lips.

"I need a drink," Emmie announces. "You're coming to the party, right?" she asks, turning her eyes on me.

"Uh..."

"Calli, no. You need to come and celebrate."

"Oh don't worry, I'm planning on celebrating." I wink. "Just... from a distance."

All four of them stare at me, sadness but understanding in their eyes.

"I need to get back to him."

"Okay fine, we can't really argue with that. But you are coming down to see the guys first, and then we're going to have a repeat of the party at our place another day. After all, a little birdie told me there are some birthdays coming up."

"Really?" I groan. Honestly, other than ensuring that Daemon celebrated his big day in spectacular fashion, I was hoping that mine might just float under the radar. I've got too much going on right now to think about the day my mother put in a little effort and pushed me out.

Anger burns low in my belly as I think about her lack of care and effort in the past two weeks. I always knew she was a selfish bitch, but this whole thing really has opened my eyes.

"Oh hell yeah, we're not letting that pass us by, baby C," Stella says happily as we head for the stairs.

"Does it mean we can drop the baby C shit? Emmie is the baby anyway," I mutter, much to her horror.

"Age is just a number. I'm more mature than any of you motherfuckers," the girl in question barks.

"Oh sure, whatever you say," Stella mutters as the crowd loitering in front of the locker room exit appears before us. "Are they having a fucking laugh?" she barks. "These stupid bitches should know by now that those boys belong to us. Ex-cuse me," she hisses, shoving some unsuspecting year twelve out of the way.

As a group, we force our way through the crowd until we're front and centre.

Girls complain, but one vicious look from Emmie or Stella and most of them wisely shut their mouths. Both of them have earned some seriously fierce reputations since starting at Knight's Ridge, and I couldn't be prouder.

My phone buzzes in my pocket as we wait for the guys. I'd messaged him the second the final whistle blew to tell him the score, but although he'd read it, he didn't immediately respond. I told myself it was because he was mid-Xbox battle with Ant, but it didn't stop a little concern creeping in.

I know that Uncle Damien has the building surrounded and being watched 24/7, but that doesn't stop my unease that somehow the Italians will manage to get inside and take back what belongs to me.

Devil boy: Does that mean you can come back and celebrate with me? *tongue out emoji*

Calli: Soon. Just going to congratulate the guys and I'll be home. *winky emoji*

Devil boy: Fuck, that sounds good.

A smile curls up at my lip at the thought of always coming home to Daemon. It just... it feels right.

Devil boy: You've always been my home, Angel.

My heart swells as I read his words, emotion crawls up my throat, and tears burn the backs of my eyes.

"I hope he's not making you cry again," Bri whispers in my ear and I lower my phone, looking up at her through glassy eyes.

"He is, but only in the best way."

"I'm glad it all worked out for you," she says. "Although I must admit, I was sceptical when I found you running that day."

"You weren't the only one," I mutter. "Everything happens for a reason though, right?" I say, although I can't deny the painful tug at my heart as I wonder, and not for the first time, what the possible reason could be that we're being forced to live without Dad now. Nothing about that seems to have any kind of justification.

"We can only hope, right?"

The doors open before us and any chance of

continuing our conversation is obliterated as the screaming starts.

"Wow, these hussies really want some Knight's Ridge cock, huh?" Brianna shouts in my ear.

Glancing over her, I smirk. "Because you don't?"

"Callista Cirillo, I have no idea what you're talking about," she gasps, as if my suggestion shocks her. I see the truth, though. It shines brightly in her eyes, as I'm sure my love for Daemon does in mine.

"He's not going to be an easy one to crack if you're serious," I shout.

"Serious? Nah, Calli. I'm not serious about anything when it comes to your brother other than the screaming orgasms he's able to dish out like sweeties."

"You know, sometimes you really don't need to be so honest."

She bursts out laughing as I'm jostled to the side.

Looking around, I watch as both Emmie and Stella surge forward and jump into Theo and Seb's arms.

Toby appears next and Jodie takes off while the crowd shouts and screams.

"Bet this lot of hungry girls never thought they'd see the day their beloved knights handed their balls and hearts over," Brianna mutters in my ear.

"Probably not, no. Lucky for them though, there are more members of the team."

She laughs, but it's soon cut off when Nico emerges behind the three couples who have zero consideration for the sheer number of people who are watching their PDA.

"Shit, he looks rough," I whisper under my breath. "Go to him." I elbow Brianna in the ribs, but she doesn't move.

"It's not me he needs right now."

With her hand pressed between my shoulder blades, she pushes me forward until my legs have little choice but to follow orders.

I come to a stop right in front of my brother and stare up into his dark eyes.

The rest of the team emerges from the locker room and disappears into the desperate girls behind us.

"Good game, Bro."

He glares down at me, his expression completely blank and unreadable for a few seconds before he finally cracks and gives me just a glimpse of the pain he's trying to battle through.

"Thanks, Sis," he whispers before pulling me into his arms.

His grip on me is so tight I have to fight to suck in the air I need as his embrace continues longer than would usually be acceptable.

The world continues around us, but the noise of the excitement blurs as our pain melds together and we cling to each other.

"I'm sorry," he breathes in my ear.

I nod, too choked up to be able to reply.

When he finally pulls back, I make quick work of wiping away the tears that slipped from my eyes without permission, hoping like hell that they haven't ruined my make-up.

"Are you going to the party?" I ask my brother.

As is tradition after the final game of the year, almost the entire sixth form at Knight's Ridge parties in the woods behind the school grounds.

There's a huge bonfire, barbecue, music, and most importantly for everyone who attends, more alcohol than they can handle.

It's something of a rite of passage to go and get fucked up for the year thirteens who have exams right around the corner. And I'm sure it's something that Nico's been dreaming of for years, and obviously, after tonight's performance and with three of the guys being taken, he'll have a whole line of girls wanting his attention. Alex will, too.

The thought of both of them having a good night after all the shit they've been through brings a smile to my face.

Shooting a look over Nico's shoulder, I catch Alex's eyes as he watches us, and my smile widens.

"Nah, I'm just gonna head home. I'm not really in the mood for people. You?"

I shake my head, sadness washing through me that he's intending on bailing on tonight. "You should go. You deserve it."

"Baby C," Alex sings after ducking out on the conversation he was having with Toby and Jodie. He sweeps me up in his arms and spins me around. "We're motherfucking champions." His smile is wide, his happiness infectious. "Surely that deserves a kiss," he teases.

"Yeah, you're right," I agree, shocking him.

Clapping my hands to his cheeks, I force his lips to pucker for me, his eyes twinkling with wicked intent as I lean in, but at the last minute, I plant a wet kiss on his brow.

"Baby C," he sighs. "You're a tease," he pouts, putting my feet back on the floor.

"And you're too pretty to be killed by your own brother."

A throat clearing behind me forces me to look back, and when I do, I find Nico's eyes locked on my back.

"Nice hoodie," he mutters.

"Uh... Thanks." Awkwardness descends around the three of us. "Are you really not going to the party?" I ask again.

"What the fuck, man? You have to come. You're my wingman," Alex argues.

Nico studies him for a beat before his shoulder drops and he lowers his head.

"Sorry, I'm just gonna—"

"You want a lift home?" I offer, making him glance back up from beneath his lashes at me.

"Uh..."

"I'll see you tomorrow, yeah?" I say, turning to Alex. "Be good, and have fun. And be safe," I quickly add.

"Oh, sound advice there, Calli," he mutters with a smirk, low enough that Nico won't hear. Although, when I look back, I find him walking in the direction of the car park.

"Careful, the position on godfather is yet to be decided," I quip, turning back to Alex.

"Oh fuck off, that's mine and you know it."

I shrug. "Too early to tell."

"I guess it is, seeing as daddy is still clueless." He pins me with a look.

"Don't start," I mutter.

"Calli, if you don't do it soon, then I will," he warns.

"Don't even think about it." I narrow my eyes in the hope he can see the danger lingering in them.

But when he just glares back, I realise that I'm probably nowhere near as scary as I need to be to affect him.

"Fine, whatever. Have a good night, yeah? Try not to get herpes or whatever." I take off in the direction Nico disappeared with a smile on my face.

"Love you too, Calli."

"Yeah, yeah," I call before spinning around and blowing him a kiss.

I catch up with Nico where he's looking out over the cars that are left.

"Where's yours?" he asks, looking confused.

"Still at Mum and Da— I've got Daemon's," I explain, changing tack.

"You've got... Jesus, Calli. I feel like I don't even know who you are right now."

His words rip my heart in two.

But he takes off again before I respond, having spotted Daemon's Audi a few spaces down.

I unlock it as he gets closer and watch as he drops into the passenger seat and tips his head back.

"I'm still the same person, Nic," I assure him. "I just—"

"How long have you been fu... seeing him?"

I blow out a long breath, nowhere near prepared to explain everything that's happened between Daemon and me to my big brother.

"It started at Halloween. But I didn't know who he was, he was wearing a costume and—"

"See. The Calli I know would never do something like that."

"Nico, the Calli you've lived with all this time has been smothered until she was barely a person. Did you ever consider that it's only now I'm actually being myself? I never wanted to be locked away, kept as far away from everything as possible, and wrapped in so much cotton wool that I could barely breathe.

"Daemon he... he saw through that somehow, and he offered me a way to break free, to be me, to embrace what I really want."

"And that's him? Out of everyone we know. It's Daemon?"

"Yeah, Nico. It is. He's—"

"Dark. Twisted. Dangerous?"

"Well, yeah," I agree with a laugh. "But that barely scratches the surface. That's the soldier he shows the world, but behind closed doors he's... sweet, caring, vulnerable."

"I'll take your word for that," he scoffs.

"Dude, you are no fucking different. Don't think I don't remember you crying the first time you watched *The Notebook* with me. You're not exactly tough to the core."

"I did not cry," he argues fiercely, like he does every time I bring this up. "I had something in my eye."

"You're so full of shit," I mutter as I bring Daemon's car to life and put it into reverse.

I might be focusing on where I'm going as I back out of the space, but that doesn't mean I miss the way my skin tingles.

"You look weirdly good driving his car."

Daemon would probably say I look better riding his cock.

I can't help but laugh at my own thoughts, and when I glance at Nico before putting the car in drive, I find him frowning at me like a baffled puppy.

"What?" I ask.

"We totally underestimated you, didn't we?"

Palming the wheel, I press my foot to the accelerator a little harder than necessary as a smirk pulls at my lips.

"Are you really only just figuring that out?"

"Fucking hell," he sighs, finally looking away from me and focusing out the window.

The silence that falls between us is filled with a million and one unspoken words, but I guess that's nothing unusual when it comes to me and Nico. We're close, I guess. But with him always keeping me on the periphery of his life, it's meant that there has always been a wall between us.

I pull to a stop at a set of traffic lights and look over once more.

Nico's fists are curled tight on his lap, and when I get up to his face, there's a deep frown marring his brow and his jaw is ticking.

"I really love him, you know," I blurt. "He's it for me."

My words do little to help him relax. But when he turns to me, he doesn't say any of the things I expect him to.

"How do you know that? I've heard Seb, Theo, and then Toby say the same thing over the past few months. But how? How do you know that?" he asks, finally dropping his walls a little.

"I... um... I don't think there's an answer for that, Nic. It's not a decision you get to make, it's just... it's the feeling that's buried so deep inside that there's no other option but to accept it."

"Why is it Daemon and not Alex?"

I can't help but laugh as the lights turn green and I move forward once more. "At the beginning of all this, I asked myself that question more than I thought possible. It's just... it's Daemon. I don't know. He makes my heart race and my—"

"I swear to God, if you say pussy wet then I'm going to throw myself out of this car no matter how fast you're driving."

"I was not going to say that, but I might be tempted now I know what your reaction is going to be."

"I wanted better for you than this life, Calli," he confesses.

"But don't you see? This *is* my life. Even if I ended up with someone like Jerome, then my life would still be surrounded by danger, violence, and the risk of someone I love dying at any moment. We can't stop living or doing what makes us happy because we're scared."

"Can't we?" Nico whispers as I pull toward the underground garage beneath our building.

"I know this is hard, Nico. Truly I do, but you can't let it beat you."

"Easier said than done," he mutters as the roller door lifts, allowing us to disappear beneath the building.

"Have you spoken to Mum?" I ask hesitantly.

"No. You?"

"No. And I can't say I want to either."

"Something is going on with her. She never used to be this much of a selfish bitch," he mutters.

"Not to you maybe. This is pretty standard for me."

"She loved him though, right?"

Nico's question forces all the air out of my lungs.

"Uh... I mean, yeah. I always assumed she did. But since—"

"He worshipped the ground she walked on. If she was the one to die that night, he'd be a mess. But the way she was on Monday, I dunno. Something just doesn't feel right."

"It's probably just shock or something. Grief, it's..."

"An even bigger bitch than she is?" he asks, his

attempt at a joke falling flat. "You're going to have to go back at some point. You can hardly stay here for—"

"I'm moving in with Daemon," I blurt.

Nico scrubs his hand down his face. "Of course you are. Have you told her yet?"

"No. But I don't care what her opinion is. I'm eighteen next week, school is nearly over. I'm done following orders."

"What about uni?"

"What about it?"

"You're still going to go, right?"

I shrug. "Don't know. What about you?"

"What's the point? What's the point in any of it? All we're going to do is end up dead."

My lips part in shock, and as much as I want to find some words to respond with, I can't form any.

"You should go to the party tonight, Nic."

He pushes the car door open. "I'm not very good company right now. They'll be better off without me."

He's gone before I get a chance to stop him.

"Nico, wait," I call, but it's too late. The door leading toward the lift is already closing. "Fuck," I hiss, falling back against the seat and tipping my head back.

Pain and grief war within me as the hopelessness I feel over how to help Nico knots at my stomach.

Forcing it all aside, I think about the boy upstairs waiting for me and my sorrow is thankfully replaced by excitement and nerves.

As if he knows I'm thinking about him, my phone buzzes.

Devil boy: I've got a surprise for you.

My hand finds my stomach. "Not as big as the one I've got for you."

Climbing out of the car, I lock it up and head for the lift.

The hallways are as quiet as ever, but knowing that everyone else is out at the party makes the place feel even emptier than it usually does.

My excitement to get inside and hopefully let Daemon come good on his promise of what he wanted to do to me while I'm wearing his name gets the better of me, and the second the little red light on the biometric scanner turns green, I shove through the door, more than ready to find him.

Only, I quickly come to a stop when the scent hits my nose. My stomach turns over as I get swallowed up by the sweetness.

Sucking in a deep breath through my lips, I try to shove the unwelcome feeling down.

Feeling a little more in control, I step toward the door that will lead me to the living area, but my movement falters when the flickering light beyond the door catches my eye.

A smile pulls at my lips, and I rush forward to see what he's done.

"Oh my God," I breathe when I emerge in a room full of flickering candles and my boy sitting nervously on the edge of the sofa in just a pair of sweats. "Nikolas, this is—"

"Romantic, huh?"

"Y-yeah, it's... amazing."

"I thought it was only right that we spend our first official night living together the right way," he says, pushing to his feet and stalking toward me, his cocky bad boy swagger back in full force. It hits me right in the libido.

"Jesus, you're hot," I blurt like an idiot.

"I'm a mess, Angel. But luckily, you're beautiful enough to make up for it."

"Bullshit. You couldn't be any more perfect to me."

His large hands cup my face as he stares down into my eyes. So much love pours from them it makes my heart ache in the best way.

"I love you, Angel."

Reaching up, I brush my lips against his and he pulls me closer into his body.

"I could kiss you forever," he says, teasing me by holding back and just the simple brush of his lips.

"Where's Ant?" I ask, desperate to take this further but not willing to do so if we're ultimately going to be walked in on.

"He's got a new home," Daemon confesses.

I pull my head back, my brows pinching. "He left?" I ask, concern instantly cooling my previously heated body.

"The flat, yeah. Not the building though. Damien got one of the flats downstairs finished off for him?"

"What?" I ask in disbelief. "He's got his own place?"

"Yeah, but more importantly, we've got our own

place. So I can fuck you anywhere I want, as often as I want, and you can scream as loud as physically possible, and no one will hear you."

Desire tightens everything south of my waist and my mouth waters at the picture he paints.

"Now the only question is, where do we start?"

Tightening my arms around his shoulders, I thread my fingers through his hair and reach up on my toes.

"Right here," I breathe, my lips brushing his.

"Fuck, yeah," he grunts, dropping his hands and sweeping me off my feet.

"Daemon, no," I cry, terrified that he'll hurt himself or rip the few stitches Gianna put in.

"I'm good, Angel. You don't need to worry about me."

My arse hits the edge of the kitchen counter before his hands slip around to my back and he steps between my thighs.

"I didn't think you were ever going to get back. Fuck, I missed you."

Before I even think up a response, he's claimed my lips in an all-consuming, filthy kiss that has me writhing on the counter.

Dragging me right to the edge, he presses closer, ensuring I can feel just how desperate he is for this too.

"Nikolas," I moan, my head dropping back as he grinds his hard cock perfectly against my clit. His lips kiss down my throat before he makes his way back up, nipping and sucking at my sensitive skin. "Please. More."

"I love it when you beg. Tell me what you need, Angel."

"You. I need you," I gasp as his hips continue to roll at a dizzying speed.

"More specific. My fingers? My mouth? My cock?"

"Yes, yes. All of them. I want all of it, Nikolas. All of you."

"Are you wet for me?"

He drags his fingers over my thighs, pinching the soft fabric of my leggings.

"You know I am," I moan when he begins walking them up to where I need them most.

"I think I need evidence. Then I'm going to push my fingers deep inside you and have you coming right up here on the counter, so the next time I make you food, I'll remember watching you fall."

"God."

"Then I'm going to lay you out and eat like you're my favourite meal until you're screaming my name."

"Yes."

"And then, when your legs are trembling and your cunt can barely take any more, I'm going to fuck you nice and slow, just like I did in the shower until you're begging me for another release, desperate for me to push you over the edge."

"Why are you still talking, devil boy? Actions speak louder."

"Fucking love it when you're desperate for me."

"Which is always. Now do something, please."

"Whatever happened to my sweet, innocent angel?"

"You corrupted her and dragged her to the dark side," I moan as he tucks his fingers around the waistband of my legging and hooks them over my arse.

"Fuck yeah, I did. And I'm going to do it all over again."

My Converse hit the floor a second before my leggings and knickers are dragged from my ankles and discarded.

"Open your legs for me, beautiful. Let me see you."

Heat blooms up my neck, spilling onto my cheeks.

Shamelessly, I spread my thighs and drag the bottom of my hoodie up, letting him see just how badly I need him.

"You own me, Angel. Fucking own every inch of me."

His previous plan seems to go flying out of the window as he pushes my thighs even wider and drops to his knees before me.

Dragging his nose through my folds, he breathes me in. Embarrassment washes through me and I fight to close my legs, but he doesn't let me.

"Mine. All fucking mine."

"Nikolas," I scream when he sucks my clit into his mouth, grazing it gently with his teeth, and I fall back onto the counter.

"Louder," he demands before licking up the length of me. "I want every motherfucker in the world knowing that you're mine."

"Yes, yes," I cry as he sinks two thick fingers inside

me, curling them exactly how I like while his tongue lavishes my clit.

In only minutes, he's bringing me to ruin, and I scream out his name as I shatter all over his countertop. My back arches and my fingers twist in his hair until I'm sure I'm about to pull it clean out, but he never even tries to stop me.

"Fucking need you, Angel," he growls, pulling back and wiping his glistening mouth with the back of his hand.

He stands, his movements faster than they have been all week, but it's not quite smooth enough to make me forget.

"Are you ok—"

"Perfect, beautiful. Now do as you're told and take my cock like a good girl."

His grip on my hips is bruising as he drags me off the counter, but I wouldn't want it any other way. The second he has me on my feet, he pulls my arse back and immediately slides inside me.

Aftershocks from my release shoot around my body as he seats himself as deep as he can.

"Fucking addicted to you, Calli. You're everything to me. Everything."

"Same," I gasp. "I love you, Nikolas. I love you so much."

"I'll never get tired of hearing that."

Every drag of his cock lights something up inside me until my legs no longer feel like they're going to hold me up. But Daemon's grip on my hips never falters, keeping me exactly where he wants me, playing my body to perfection and giving us both what we so desperately need.

"Fucking love this hoodie. All your clothes should have my name on them so everyone knows who you belong to."

"Most guys make do with a ring," I blurt, immediately feeling like an idiot. I blame my hormones and the endorphins shooting around my body for my loose lips.

"Now there's an idea. Callista Deimos. My very own angel."

His grip on my hips tightens, sending a biting pain through my body that mixes with the pain and sends me crashing over the edge.

"Fuck, fuck, Calli. Fuuuuck," Daemon groans as his cock jerks deep inside me, filling me with his cum.

"I'm pregnant."

21

DAEMON

My entire body tingles with the strength of my release as I thrust my hips forward once more, marking Calli as mine on the inside just like I crave to out on the outside.

Images of her standing in her shower all those weeks ago painted in my blood float through my head, stopping my cock from softening as quickly as it usually would.

But as the high from my release starts to fade, those two words that just spilled from her lips begin to register in my brain.

A smile twitches at my lips before laughter breaks free.

"I know that was good, Angel. But I think that might be pushing it."

Stepping back, I reluctantly pull out of her and spin her around, desperate to look into her eyes.

But the second I do, a weight I wasn't expecting presses down on my shoulders.

"W-what's w-w-wrong?" I stutter, panic quickly spilling through my entire body, turning my blood to ice.

She sucks her bottom lip into her mouth as she reaches for me, her hands skimming down my forearms until her fingers twist with mine.

"That wasn't a joke," she confesses.

My eyes narrow as my head continues to spin. The haze of my intense release still stops my brain from functioning quite right. But as my blood begins to travel north once more, my thoughts clear and reality sets in.

"Y-you're p-p-p-p-p—"

"Nikolas," she whispers. "Take a breath."

I do as she suggests while everything around me begins to spin out of control.

"You're pregnant?" Despite being able to say it clearly this time, the words sound alien as they fall from my tongue.

"I'm sorry, I didn't mean for it to come out quite like that. I've just been waiting until we're alone and... I dunno... it couldn't stay in any longer."

"You're p-p-pregnant. Like... with an actual human baby?"

A small smile creeps onto her lips.

"Yes, or at least I hope so, because it'll be fucking weird when I give birth otherwise."

Her grip on my hands tightens as I take another huge step back.

"It's okay. Trust me, I know this is a shock, but—"

"You're pregnant?"

"Nikolas," she breathes, but her soft tone does little to calm me down.

"I-I'm sorry, I-I-I j-j-just need—"

I'm across the room and heading for the safety of my bedroom before I've even registered that my legs have carried me there.

Fuck.

Fuck.

Reaching for the door, I swing it closed behind me, the slam of it echoing through the entire flat.

"Fuck. Fuck. Fuck," I chant, marching toward the bathroom.

Stopping in front of the basin, my fingers curl around the edge and I hang my head.

I can't be a fucking father.

I can't.

I can barely look after myself. Let alone another person.

I can't... but Calli...

Fuck.

She'd make the most fantastic mother. She's so gentle, kind, caring. Compassionate, understanding. All the fucking things a mother should be.

Yet the father of that child is me and—

The sound of the bedroom door opening rocks through me.

"Daemon?" she calls softly before light footsteps pad my way.

"I'm sorry," I force out, unable to move from my position.

"No, it's okay. I'm the one who should be apologising. Of all the ways I've thought about telling you, none of them looked like that."

"You mean you didn't plan on me fucking it out of you?" I deadpan, risking a glance over at her.

"No, I guess I didn't."

Pushing from the basin, I turn around to face her.

All the air rushes from my lungs as I take her in. She's standing there in just her hoodie, probably with my cum running down her thighs. Her eye make-up is smudged and her lipstick is everywhere, half of it probably over my face as well.

"You're perfect," I whisper. "Everything."

She takes a hesitant step closer, her eyes dropping to my feet before they crawl up my body.

"I had no idea," she confesses. "It didn't even register that I was late. And then I opened my diary and there it was. I was a week late. I'm never a week late. Barely even a day late."

"When was this?"

"The night of Mum's birthday."

"Shit, you knew before—"

"No. I took a test before we got to the country club, but I never got a chance to look at the result. I didn't until later that night when the guys came back and you, Dad, and Nico weren't with them."

"Fuck, Angel."

I move closer, unable to contemplate how she must have felt in that moment.

"I was terrified, Daemon. I thought I'd lost the three

most important men in my life in one night, and then I opened my purse and my fate was right there staring back at me. But..." Her voice cracks with emotion and it shatters something inside me. A lump crawls up my throat and the backs of my eyes burn with what I can only assume are tears. "I had a little bit of you growing inside me. Even if you were gone. Something of us remained, and I... shit," she whispers, lifting her hand to wipe away her own tears. "I've never been more grateful for anything in my life until you came stumbling through that door again."

My arms wrap around her a beat before her sobs fill the room.

"I wanted to tell you straight away, but there was always someone else around, something more serious to talk about and—"

"Shh, Angel. It's okay. It's okay," I repeat, pressing my lips into her hair. "I've got you, beautiful."

"I was so scared, Daemon. Scared of being alone, of having to do this by myself. And then you came back and I was still terrified, but for an entirely different reason."

"I'm here," I say, cupping her cheek and giving her little choice but to look up at me. "I'm here, and nothing in the whole world could drag me away from you now."

"I was scared you'd be mad that I let it happen. I was scared you wouldn't want it, or me. We're so young and—"

"Whoa, calm the fuck down, Calli," I say softly when she starts to lose her grip on reality. "Get all that shit out of your head, Angel. There is nothing that could make me not want you. Nothing. And you didn't let this happen. It took two of us to do this, that's not on you."

"But it had to have happened that first time. I didn't take my pill, and I should have thought about it and—"

"You did take your pill," I state.

She rears back, staring at me through confused eyes.

"I was handcuffed to your bed. There's no way I could have—"

"I made you take it, Angel." My thumb shifts from her cheek and brushes over the pillow of her bottom lip as I think back.

"After I tied you to my bed, I went back out. I only really tied you there so I knew you'd be there when I got back, but fuck, one look at you and I was so fucking gone for you." I shake my head, remembering all too well the strong surge of emotions that rocked me to my core as I stood in the doorway of the room behind her now and stared at the girl I'd craved my entire life but never thought I'd be able to have.

"I went back to the warehouse, made sure Ant was okay, and grabbed your bag."

"Wait," she says. "You were the one who took my car back home?"

"Yeah, Angel. There was no fucking way I was leaving it in Italian territory for anyone else to find."

"The messages to Emmie and Stella."

I smile at her coyly.

"Nikolas," she warns, although she can't fight the beginning of a smile that wants to break through.

"You, Calli, are always my first priority. Keeping you safe will always be the single most important thing to me."

She stares at me, her chest heaving as she accepts my words.

"Although now," I say, dropping to my knees before her and shoving her hoodie up around her ribs, exposing her stomach. "It seems you're not the only one I'm going to have to worry about."

Wrapping my hands around her slim waist, I lean forward, pressing my lips to the soft skin beneath her belly button.

"Oh God," she sobs as I kiss her stomach, my eyes on hers the whole time.

"I'm not mad at you for this, Calli. I could never be. It was just... a shock. I'm sorry I freaked out and made you think—"

"It's okay," she whimpers. "I get it. It's... a lot."

"It's everything," I promise her, getting back to my feet, sliding my fingers into her hair, and claiming her lips. "And it's ours."

"Nikolas," she moans into our kiss.

I break it long before I'm ready to and take a step back.

Tears still cling to her lashes, but I'm pretty sure they're happy ones, so I let them go. Her lips are swollen from my kiss and her chest heaves with her need for more.

"Clean up, Angel," I say regretfully, still slightly

obsessing about the mess that's between her thighs, but there will be plenty of time for a repeat.

Walking back to the basin, I wash my hands before heading into my bedroom and climbing onto the bed to give her some privacy.

My heart beats to a steady rhythm as I lie there with all these new crazy thoughts running around my head.

My hands tremble as more fear than I'm sure I should be feeling grips me in its clutches. I try to shove it away and focus on how fucking hot Calli is going to look with her belly swollen with my baby. But fuck, my confidence levels with all this are fucking shot.

I'm still trying to get my head around how Calli thinks I can be what she needs when movement in the doorway catches my eye. When I look over, I find her watching me as she chews on her bottom lip.

"Hey," I say, rolling onto my side so I can study her.

A shy smile pulls at her lips and does all kinds of crazy shit to me.

"Hey. Are we... are we okay?" She takes a step forward as if she's going to come to me but quickly changes her mind.

Pushing up onto my elbow, I stare at her.

"Yeah, Angel, we are. I meant everything I said in there." I shoot a look over her shoulder to the bathroom.

She nods. I'm not entirely sure she really believes me, but she quickly turns toward a bag full of her things that's sitting in the corner of her room.

"You need to put all that away." She pauses for a

beat, half bent over, giving me just a tiny glimpse of what's hiding beneath that hoodie.

She grabs a pair of knickers and pulls them up her legs before crawling up the bed and resting on her side in front of me.

"Are you sure you really want me to move in?" she asks, a frown wrinkling her brow.

"More than I've ever wanted anything in my life."

"But it's not just going to be me."

"No, it's going to be you and our baby." Tucking my hand under her hoodie, I press it against her stomach.

"Fuck, Daemon. This is crazy."

"You're telling me."

"My mum is going to flip her lid."

I can't help but laugh. "Do you care?"

"No, but—"

"Then it doesn't matter, does it?"

"I guess not," she whispers before falling silent, getting lost in her thoughts.

"What is it?"

"I... I don't want to go to uni," she confesses quietly.

"Okay, so don't."

Her eyes widen. "Just like that?"

"Yeah, why? Did you think I'd have a problem with it?"

"I don't know. I just... all my life, everything has been planned for me. It's weird to think not everyone marches to the beat of my mother's drum."

"Trust me, I don't give a shit about your mother's hopes and dreams. I care about yours. And if uni isn't what you want, then don't do it. I want you to be happy, Calli. That's all that matters to me."

"I love you," she whispers, more tears balancing precariously on her lashes.

"I love you too. So... what happens here exactly?" I ask, rubbing her belly.

"Well, I think it's gonna get bigger, and then at some point, I'm going to have to expel it somehow."

I can't help but laugh at the horrified look on her face as she says that last bit.

"Okay, but that's like ages away, right? You're only like... three weeks or something out of... nine months?"

"I'm almost seven weeks."

"Seven?" I ask, rearing back in shock.

"Yeah, according to my app."

"An app? Why isn't it according to a doctor?"

"Because I haven't seen one yet."

"What? Why not? You need looking after. There might be something we need to do or—"

"Nikolas," she breathes, placing her hand on my cheek. "It's okay. Everything is okay. Alex and I have done all the research and—"

"Alex?" I ask, reality hitting me upside the head that I could be the last person to find out about this. "Alex knows?"

Guilt passes across her face.

"Yeah. He was trying to hold me together when I looked at the result. He's been amazing. Everything I needed while you couldn't be here. Please don't be pissed at him for stepping into your place for a little while."

Jealousy burns red hot through me.

"I made him promise that if anything happened to me, he'd make sure you were okay."

"He stood by that promise, Nikolas. Without him, I'd have crumbled."

I nod, happy that he was there for her but hating that I couldn't be.

"Who else knows?" I ask, terrified that she's going to say everyone and that they've all been talking behind my back since I returned.

"Brianna. She figured out something was wrong when we were at the spa and I broke down and told her. She went out and got me the test. And Jocelyn. I'm not sure how she knows, but she does. And now you, Daddy."

My chin drops and my heart pounds.

"Fuck, I..." Slipping my hand around her back, I drag her closer, keeping my eyes locked on hers. "Say that again."

"Kiss me, Daddy."

"Fuck, that really shouldn't get me as hot as it does," I mutter before doing as she demands and losing myself in my girl.

With our bodies tangled together, we make out, whispering promises for what's going to come next for us until we pass out, still locked together with hope filling our hearts.

22

CALLI

"And we'll be able to park in the underground car park, right?" Daemon asks, his deep voice flowing through me, making goosebumps erupt on my skin.

I woke this morning feeling so much lighter. Finally, he knew the truth, and despite an initial freak-out, I think it went pretty well.

Obviously, I never planned to just blurt those words out as I rode out a mind-blowing release. But I can't regret it, because the truth is out now, and I have every confidence that it's going to be okay.

He might have been shocked, but he said the sweetest things to me, the kind of supportive things that I've only been able to dream of since I discovered the truth.

My stomach rumbles as I get closer to the kitchen, my mouth watering to discover what he's in the middle of making.

"Okay, that's great. Thank you. Yes. We'll see you then."

I frown, trying to work out who he's talking to and not entirely liking the sound of him planning to leave this building, but knowing that if he's set his mind to something then there is no point in me even attempting to change it.

"Morning, Angel," he says the second I emerge as if he knew I was loitering and listening to his half of that phone call. "I hope you're hungry. Take a seat."

"What's all this?" I ask, looking at everything he's been making.

"Everything you need."

I raise a brow at him as I take in the array of food.

"You're not expecting me to eat all of this, right?" I ask, slightly horrified.

"Well, no. I just haven't put it away yet. But I did some research and found out all the nutrients you and the baby need in the first trimester, and voila." He gestures to the small supermarket of food that covers every counter of his kitchen.

"Okay... um... this is insane, you know that, right?"

"Nothing is too much for you and our baby, Angel."

"I've created a monster," I mutter lightly. "How did you even get all this here so fast?"

"I ordered it while you were sleeping and sent Alex down to collect it all. Figured he owed me one, or a million for keeping me in the dark about this all week. I don't know how you did it, but that boy is incapable of keeping secrets so—"

"Oh, I don't know. He kept ours pretty well," I add.

"Pretty sure you have some magical voodoo or something. You've got us both wrapped around your little finger."

"And I'm not even fucking him," I joke, although I'm not sure Daemon appreciates it if the serious expression on his face is anything to go by.

"You better bloody not be."

"Chill out, caveman. There's only one man on the planet who's had an all-access pass to my body, and he's standing right in front of me."

"Only one?" he asks, his brow lifting. "Because, correct me if I'm wrong, but I've witnessed someone else getting pretty up close and personal to what belongs to me."

"And in case you forgot, you shot him before he had a chance to do anything."

"Fair point."

"Have you spoken to him? Is he okay down there?"

"Not since I moved him in. But he's probably more than happy not to have been forced to listen to you screaming last night."

"Or you freaking out," I quip, making him take a step closer.

His previous amusement vanishes from his face, and the cold, closed-off mask that I haven't seen in a while slides into place instead.

I'm pretty sure more sane people would be terrified. But I've seen too much of Daemon's vulnerable side to even bat an eyelid at his attempt to scare me.

Squaring my shoulders, I step right into his body.

"What are you going to do, soldier? Punish me?"

He gasps when I reach out and wrap my fingers around his cock. It instantly hardens and I can't help but smile up at him.

"Seems like someone's up for some fun," I tease.

Reaching up on my tiptoes, I drag my tongue along the line of his jaw until I hit his throat.

"Your big bad soldier act doesn't scare me, Daemon."

"No, it just makes you wet, doesn't it, Angel?"

"Maybe."

I kiss down his neck and nip his collarbone before moving lower.

"Who were you talking to, Nikolas?"

He swallows, his Adam's apple bobbing.

I kiss and lick lower as his cock continues to harden as I rub him gently through his sweats.

"Jesus, Calli," he groans, twisting his fingers in my hair as I trace his abs with my tongue.

"Answer my question."

"I-I b-booked you an appointment with a doctor."

"Nikolas, I said it was okay," I warn as my knees hit the floor and I untie the bow in his sweats with my teeth.

"Fuck. Yeah, I know. I just... fuck, Angel," he groans when I drag his trousers over his hips and free his cock.

"You know, I am kinda hungry," I whisper before dragging my tongue up the length of his shaft.

"You look it," he mutters, reaching for the counter

with one hand as if he needs it to hold him up while the other twists in my hair.

"Think I'll have you for starters, then your cooking for after."

"Sounds good to meee." The final word turns into nothing but a feral growl as I suck him into my mouth. "Fuck. Never leave me."

I can't help but laugh around him as I up my speed, challenging myself to get him off in record time, because, honestly, I am kinda hungry for some real food too.

"You do know I'm not actually eating for two, right?" I ask when I push my plate back and rest my hands on my bloated belly.

"Quantity wise no, but you need to load up on all the nutrients you both need," Daemon says, walking back into the kitchen head to toe in black.

"That makes it sound like so much less fun." I pout. "You look like you're heading out to rob a bank," I point out.

"No need. I've got enough for both of us."

"I don't want your money, Daemon," I say, knowing that this is something we're going to need to talk about. It's all well and good me saying I'm not going to uni, but also, I can't just move in here and provide nothing but daily blow jobs—not that I think he'd have an issue with that.

"I know."

"Don't you think you should just stay here? I can video call you so you can hear everything." I say, knowing that now isn't the time to discuss money.

"Argue all you like, Angel. It's not happening. I'm going through all of this with you whether you like it or not."

"I love it, but are you sure it's safe? If someone sees you, or if Uncle Damien finds out, he'll lose his shit."

"He'll understand when he learns about his great-nephew."

"Nephew? It could be his niece. I can just see you playing princesses and being forced to wear a tutu."

His chin drops as if he's about to argue, but then a smile curls at the corners of his lips, and the image in my head becomes even more vivid.

"You want a girl, Angel?"

"I don't mind as long as it's healthy." The second I say that, all the blood drains from Daemon's face. "What? What's wrong?"

"What if... what if it's born like I was?"

"Perfect?" I ask, trying to lighten the mood, but it has little effect.

"Calli," he warns.

"It's not hereditary, is it? I thought it was just one of those things. And anyway, if that happens, then you're living proof that it's not an issue."

His hand lifts to the scar that's hiding behind his hoodie. "I don't want—"

"What you went through, the scars you have, they

make you you, Nikolas. They show the world how strong you are, and how determined you are. I wouldn't change an inch of you and I hope that one day, you'll find a way to accept that.

"If there's an issue and our baby follows in your footsteps, then I'll spend every day of its life teaching him or her to embrace those scars, to be proud of them, because they'll be a Deimos and they'll be so fucking fierce."

"Okay, next issue," he says, skirting over that and the emotion swimming in his eyes. "What if it's twins?"

I can't help but laugh. "Did you get any sleep last night, Daemon, or did you spend all night researching, menu planning, and worrying about all the what-ifs?"

"I got a couple of hours," he confesses. "But Mum is a twin and—"

"Okay, well, Alex and I looked it up and there's no proof that identical twins are hereditary. It's usually random. So we've got as much chance as anyone else out there. And even if you were fraternal twins, then it usually comes down the female line, so we'd be okay."

He steps closer and cups my face in his hands. "And you're teasing me for thinking of all this," he quips.

"I had a week of knowing and needing a distraction from my life. I looked up all kinds of weird shit. But the point is, whatever happens, we'll deal. We've got each other, and that's all we need, right?"

"Yeah, we'll deal. We're not going to be the first or the last clueless eighteen-year-olds figuring out what to do with a baby."

"That's the spirit," I say with a laugh before the beep of the door unlocking sounds in the hallway.

"If you're fucking, this is your one and only warning," Alex shouts before bursting into the room two seconds later. "Damn," he mutters when he finds us just standing there.

"You know, a warning usually precedes a little time to cover up," Daemon mutters.

"I've already seen you both naked." Alex shrugs as if it's no big deal.

Daemon moves faster than I'm expecting, and in less than a heartbeat he's in front of Alex and has his t-shirt twisted in his fist, his nose damn near touching his brother's as he growls his frustration.

All the while, Alex looks as cool as fucking ever.

Weirdo.

I might claim not to be scared of Daemon, but Alex's calmness while the devil is glaring down at him takes it to a whole new level.

"Daemon, don't be a di—" My words falter when Daemon's hard mask suddenly falls away, and instead of throwing the punch that I was convinced was coming next, he pulls Alex into his body and wraps his arms around him.

"Thank you."

"I've got you, man. Both of you. Always."

By the time they part, I'm sobbing like a fool.

"Baby C," Alex sighs before the two of them drag me into the middle and crush me between their hard bodies.

"Right, are we doing this then, or did you decide to go boosting cars and mugging old women instead?" Alex asks, echoing my comments about Daemon's outfit when he pulls a cap from his pocket and drags it over his hair, and then tugs his hood up for good measure.

"Fuck off, Bro. I'm just being safe. I've got too much to live for now. Those Italian cunts aren't getting anywhere near me again."

"Good to hear it. Still think it's overkill."

"And as ever, I don't give a shit what you think. I'm doing this for my girl and my kid, so you can just shut the fuck up or I'll call someone else to help."

"And tell them that you're going to some fancy-arse doctor on a Saturday, why exactly?" Alex asks smugly as he heads back toward the front door.

"How did you get someone to agree to this last minute?" I ask, shoving my feet into my Converse and following Alex.

"I have my ways," Daemon admits cryptically.

"You threatened to kill them, didn't you?" Alex deadpans.

"I wasn't quite that blunt, but it's safe to say that my reputation precedes me."

"You hear that, baby? Your daddy has a rep around town as the bogeyman. You got some big shoes to fill, kid."

"What if it's a girl?" I argue.

"I thought you were all about equal rights, baby C. Your little princess could be a bad-arse motherfucker too."

"Fuck yeah," I agree.

"Unless anyone else is harbouring secrets in this building, she's gonna be our first heir. Lady Boss incoming."

I glance over at Daemon as he steps up beside me and throws his arm around my shoulders, and I find a wide smile splitting his face.

"Oh my God, you're considering it, aren't you? Our baby girl running the family?"

"It would be fucking epic, yeah. Maybe I should take your name when we get married, so she'll still be a Cirillo."

"Wait a fucking second," Alex barks, spinning around to glare at both of us after he's hit the call button for the lift. "You're putting a fucking ring on it too?"

Daemon and I both just stare at him for a good five seconds before we both fall about laughing.

"One day, yeah," Daemon says as if it's already a sure thing. Which I guess it is. Because I can't deny that if he were to drop to one knee right now, then I'd say yes in a heartbeat.

"Who are you and what have you done to my twin?" Alex mutters, stepping into the lift.

"Fell in love, man. It'll happen to you one day. With any luck, it'll make you less fucking weird."

"What?" he balks while I chuckle. "I have never been the weird one here. You've claimed that every day since we were born."

"Don't I fucking know it," Daemon mutters, but

when I squeeze his hand and look up, I find him smiling still.

"I can't wait for a girl to knock you on your arse," I say, joining in.

"Well, she'd better be strong is all I'm saying, because I ain't going down easy."

"That's what they all say. The second she opens her legs, you'll be on your knees like a good little puppy."

"Oh my God," I snort.

"What?" Alex asks, looking between the two of us as we laugh. "Why do I feel like I'm missing something here?"

His confusion only makes me laugh harder.

"You know, it's not nice being replaced." He points. "Not so long ago, it was me and you having these silent conversations."

"Bro, don't worry," Daemon forces out between his laughter. "You are utterly irreplaceable."

"Good, I should hope so."

"How was last night?" I ask, changing the subject. "You get lucky?"

When all he does is let out a sigh, Daemon reaches over and scruffs his hair like he's a little kid.

"There's no shame in overusing your hand, man. Just remember to use lube, no one wants blisters."

Daemon darts out of the lift a beat before Alex lunges toward him.

I watch the two of them chase each other around the underground garage with a smile on my face.

Alex is obviously taking it easy on Daemon—his

movements are still a little slow, but it won't be long before he's able to put his ordeal behind him. Well, physically, at least. I'm sure the mental side of what he went through will linger a while longer.

"Are you two kids coming or am I driving myself to this thing?" I shout, making them both pause instantly.

"We're coming, Mummy," Daemon calls, making Alex gag.

"You look happy," I say as he bounds over to me and pulls me into his body.

"That's because I am. I'm with my two favourite people in the world and about to go and find out more about a third who's going to fight you both for the top spot."

"If Alex is right and it's a girl, neither of us stands a chance."

"Nah," he says, nuzzling my neck, and making me giggle. "You'll always be my number one girl."

"Hmm... we'll see."

"Your carriage awaits, baby C," Alex announces, pulling the back door of a black town car open.

"Not your usual style, Deimos," I mutter.

"Nope, but this arsehole wanted the most blacked-out car I could find."

"Fair enough." I climb into the back and Daemon quickly follows me, or at least I thought he was. But when I glance over my shoulder, I find Alex holding him back.

"You do anything you shouldn't be back there, and I will not be held responsible for my actions."

"You still bitter about Seb screwing Stella while you were driving?" I ask with a laugh.

"Just don't. I'm warning both of you."

"Jeez, Alex. We're not animals, we can control ourselves."

Daemon rips his arm from Alex's grip and finally climbs inside.

"Or at least, we would have been able to if you didn't point out just how much space there is back here. I could lay my girl out on these seats and—" The door slamming cuts off what I'm sure was going to be a very vivid description of the image playing out in Daemon's head right now.

"You're mean."

"Yeah, and Alex is a liar," Daemon states, shocking the hell out of me.

"What?"

"Don't tell me that you didn't see the hickey on his neck. He totally got laid last night. What I can't figure out is why he's not bragging about it."

"Hmm... interesting," I murmur as the guy in question drops into the driver's seat, the red mark on his neck more than obvious now I'm sitting behind him.

We stay silent as Alex brings the car to life and pulls out of the underground garage.

"So, how was the party last night? Any drama we need to know about?" I ask innocently.

23

DAEMON

I sit next to Calli as the doctor who was unfortunate enough to be on the wrong end of my demands when I called the private clinic on the Cirillo payroll earlier this morning checks her over and asks her a bazillion questions about her health and the date of her last period.

"Okay, so that would make you almost seven weeks pregnant then. And as long as your blood work comes back okay, then everything looks good from where I'm sitting."

Every few seconds, his eyes shift from Calli's to mine, as if he's worried I'm going to pull a gun out on him at any moment.

Pussy.

A knock at the door makes him practically jump off his seat. With a quick apology, he walks toward our visitor.

Calli squeezes my hand in support. I don't think it's a secret to her that we're here purely for my benefit. My need to know that everything is okay, that she's healthy, that the baby is as good as he can be tucked up in the warmth of her body has been all-consuming. But hearing the doctor's assuring words, even if he looks like he's going to shit his pants every time he so much glances my way, does help to settle things inside me.

"You okay?" she asks.

"Yeah. Mostly just glad he's not going to be the one delivering the baby. He's got the nerves of a skittish kitten."

"Leave him alone, and stop trying to scare the piss out of him."

I shrug. "Habit. Plus, he keeps touching you."

"Seriously," she hisses, glaring at me.

An obnoxious squeak fills the air before the timid doctor wheels a machine into the room.

"It's very early, so there won't be much to see. But I can do an ultrasound if you would—"

"Yes," I bark, startling him once more.

"Okay, Calli, if you would like to hop up on the bed. You'll need to lift your top and lower your waistband."

"Daemon," Calli hisses when my growl of disapproval fills the room.

In only seconds, she's in position and the doctor has the machine set up.

"If your dates are wrong, then we might not be able to see anything with an external exam."

"They're not wrong," Calli confirms confidently.

"Okay, well. Even so. It's early, so we'll just see how it goes. If this doesn't work, we can use the internal wand."

"Internal?" I balk.

"Yes. An internal ultrasound at this early stage can give—"

"A woman would come and do that though, right?"

"Oh my God," Calli mutters. "Ignore him. Can you please just..." She gestures to her exposed stomach and the doctor swallows nervously. "Hopefully, it won't come to that."

"This will be cold."

"Nothing I can't handle."

"So it would seem," the doctor mutters bravely.

I shift on my seat, but Calli's tight grip on my hands stops me.

'Chill out, yeah?' she mouths as the doctor squirts some clear gel on her belly that looks suspiciously like lube.

"What is that?" I blurt.

"It's... uh... ultrasound gel. It's water-based. Entirely safe for both mum and baby."

"I knew this was a bad idea," Calli mutters to herself.

"Right, let's see what we've got here."

Ignoring me, the doctor presses a plastic wand to Calli's belly and stares at the screen as it flickers black and white.

Now, I'm not an idiot. I'm not expecting to see a

baby or anything really that is recognisable, but I was expecting something a little more than just haze.

"There we go," he says proudly as if he's just won the fucking Olympics.

"Where? What are we looking at?"

He moves the wand a little to the side, and suddenly a black circle appears, and right in the middle is—

"Is that it?" Calli asks, her voice full of awe.

"Yep." He goes on to explain exactly what we are seeing, but the words just pass me by as I stare at the little white blob on the screen that will one day be an actual living baby. Half of her, half of me, and a whole lot of fucking perfect.

"Would you like a printout?"

"Yes."

"Please," Calli adds. "Yes, please."

He taps a couple of buttons before moving the wand from Calli's belly and placing it back in its holder. Once the printer has finished, he gently places the photos on the end of the bed and pushes to his feet.

"Well, unless you have any more questions, I can leave you to clean up and you can then book your next appointment with Louise out at reception."

"With you?" I ask.

"I'm sorry?"

"The next appointment, it'll be with you?"

"That will all depend on our rota, Mr. Deimos." With a tight smile and a nod, he says goodbye to Calli and all but runs out of the room.

"Was that really necessary?" Calli asks, wiping at her stomach with some blue tissue.

"Here, let me."

With a huff, she lets her hand drop, allowing me to clean her up.

"What? He wanted to put something inside you. That's my job."

"Jesus. You're something else."

Cupping her over her leggings, I stare into her eyes.

"Mine. Remember?"

She glares right back at me. "You're going to need to get over all this, or you're never going to cope when I deliver this baby."

"The midwives and doctors will all be female."

"Of course they will. And will it also be 1922?"

"You're not funny."

"Neither are you. Now help me down, this thing is crazy high."

"Anytime, Angel."

"At last," Alex says, jumping from his seat in the waiting room the second we emerge. "How's our lil' one doing?"

A throat clearing on the other side of the room cuts through the air.

"Everything looks good," Calli says before Alex steals her from my side and wraps his arm around her shoulders.

"See, dunno what you were stressing about, Bro. Calli's got this baby growing shit in the bag."

He steers her toward the more-than-curious woman who's staring at the three of us with her chin practically on the floor.

"We need to book another appointment," I say, ignoring my brother's antics.

"Um... all t-three of you?"

"Hell yeah, I'm not missing any of—"

"Please ignore him," Calli says, fighting to shove Alex off her. "Dr. Wilcox said we need to book another appointment for—"

"Your twelve-week scan. Yep, it's right here."

"You're an idiot," I mutter to Alex while Calli and the receptionist discuss dates.

"Bro, it was too funny. She legit thinks we're tag-teaming her."

"Yeah, can you not?"

"Dude, it gets easier and easier to get to you every day."

I snarl at him, more than ready to lay him out right here in the middle of the deserted clinic.

"Okay, kids. Are we about done?" Calli asks, having sorted her next appointment.

"Yep, let's go," I say, reaching for her hand that's not clutching the photos of our little blob.

"Can you just give me a sec?" Alex asks, darting toward the reception desk and leaning forward on his elbows.

"Oh my God, is he chatting her up?"

"Christ, let's go."

The journey down to the basement car park is in silence. I have no idea about Calli, but everything we just learned and saw is spinning around my head on repeat.

Reaching across her body, I grab the photos.

"This is really happening, huh?" I ask, staring at the top image with wide eyes.

"It really seems that way. It's terrifying, isn't it?"

"You could say that," I mutter as the lift dings, announcing our arrival. "Come on, we've got something else we need to do today."

Tugging her forward, I lead her to the car and climb in behind her.

"What else are we doing?"

Before I get to confess to the next part of the plan. Alex pulls open the driver's door and hops inside.

"Any luck, man?"

"A player never tells, you know that, Bro."

"She said no," Calli surmises.

"Wha— You have no faith in my skills, baby C."

"I've seen you in action, Alex. And there's a reason you're single."

"You know, it's a really good job I love you both," he huffs.

"Where are we going?" Calli asks again.

Turning to her, I twist my fingers with hers.

"We're going to your parents' place," I confess.

"Why?"

"Thought you wanted to move out."

Her chin drops before the colour drains from her face.

"I do, but—"

"You don't want to tell your mum," I predict.

"We've got you, baby C," Alex assures her.

"Does she even know you're alive?" she asks me.

"No. No one but those who need to know are aware."

"So where the hell are we telling her I'm moving?"

"Into my flat. She just doesn't need to know that you're not there alone yet."

"She's going to lose her shit," Calli warns.

"We'll take that risk. We're just going to go and pack up your stuff, and then you can tell her and leave. She hasn't bothered to check in on you. I think the time for her to have an opinion on any of this is long gone. Plus, you're eighteen next week. She doesn't have a leg to stand on," Alex assures her.

"Tell her about uni while you're there as well, if you want. Really kick her while she's down."

"What about uni?" Alex asks.

"I'm not going."

"Oh... I mean, I guess that makes sense with everything. What are you going to do?"

"Aside from pushing a human out of my vag?" Calli asks while I wince at the thought. Babies, even newborn ones aren't really that small. I can't even begin to imagine how much that must hurt.

"Well, yeah. Aside from that teeny-weeny little task."

Leaning forward, Calli slaps him upside the head. "Teeny-weeny. Don't compare our baby to the size of your cock."

"Holy fuck. Yes, Angel."

Fuck. If I didn't already love her more than life itself, that one comment would have done it for me.

"Fucking hell, I love you," I bark, barely able to force the words out through my laughter.

"Why did I encourage this coupling? I should have known it would come back to bite me in the arse. I should have fucked you first when I had the chance," Alex sulks while we continue to laugh.

"When did you ever have a chance?"

"You were totally up for it that weekend we crashed Toby and Jodie's party," Alex states.

"Was I really? Pretty sure if I was gagging for it, it would have happened. As I remember it, we went to bed, chatted for a bit and fell asleep."

"I was being a gentleman and waiting for you to make the first move," he argues.

"How very noble of you."

"You should be thanking me. If she'd hopped on my cock before yours then there's no way she'd lower her standards and be happy with yours after."

"Pfft, I think you'll find—"

"Bro, you had to add accessories. Clearly, it ain't up to the job."

"Oh no, that is not the point. Tell him, Angel. Tell him how much better it is."

"Sorry, I don't have a comparison. I'm a one-dick-only kinda girl."

"And thank fuck for that," I say, dragging her closer. "Alex will just have to take our word for it that I'm a better lay than he is."

"Fuck you."

"Nah, I have no interest in testing you out. You could, however, tell us who gave you that nice little hickey on the back of your neck, and she and Calli could compare notes. For research purposes, of course."

"Yeah, not happening."

"You resorting to old women again?"

"Leave him alone. The wrinkles and grey hair might be his thing," Calli teases.

"I can assure you, they're not."

"Didn't stop you following around our old housekeeper."

"Okay, can we stop now?" Calli begs. "I don't need to hear about that again."

"Yes, thank you. Let's change the subject."

Silence falls around the car as we close in on Calli's parents' place.

"I'm not sure I really want to go in there," she confesses when Alex slows to a stop on the street before the Cirillo estate.

"I know, Angel. But you need to do it. Stand up to her like you've wanted to do your entire life. It's time to grab hold of your life and steer it in the direction you want."

"Huh," Alex mutters from the front.

"What?"

"You're weirdly good with the advice for someone who's never followed any in his life."

"And ignore him," I add.

Calli sucks in a deep breath as Alex turns into the driveway, bringing the colossal house into view before us.

"Is your mum just gonna live in this place alone?" he asks.

"Probably. She can be the queen of her own castle."

"Sounds lonely," he breathes.

"I'm sure she'll find enough opportunities to throw dinner parties," Calli says bitterly, staring out of the window. "Even from out here, the place just isn't the same."

Neither of us says anything. There are no words that would make her feel any better about this, so I just have to hope that our silent support is enough.

"Come on, baby C. Jocelyn is waiting for us."

"Is Mum in?" she asks hesitantly.

"As far as we know, yes."

"Great. Let's get this over with then."

She reaches for the door handle so she can escape, but I pull her back.

Gripping her chin between my fingers, I hold her steady.

"You've got this, Angel. Then it's just you and me, okay?"

Tears swim in her eyes before she blinks them away.

"Yeah. Me and you."

"I love you, Angel."

"I hate this, that you've got to hide," she whispers, sadness dripping from each word.

"I know. But hopefully, it won't be for much longer."

"I love you too. We won't be long."

24

CALLI

Dread sits so heavy with me as I walk beside Alex toward the front door, I'm amazed I manage to put one foot in front of the other.

"You've got this, Cal," Alex says, reaching for my hand and twisting our fingers together.

He might not be who I really want standing beside me right now, but he's a solid second.

"Thank you for doing this with me."

"It's time for us all to have a fresh start. And that means we need you with us. You always should have had a flat in our building, Cal. I just never thought you'd end up living with one of us."

"Daemon's flat feels more like home than this place ever has."

"I can see that."

Just before I climb the final step, I look back. I can't see him through the blacked-out glass, but I know he's watching us. My skin tingles with awareness, the magnetic pull I always feel when we're close as strong as ever.

"It won't be long and you can tell the world. Just a few more weeks, hopefully."

"Weeks? What about his exams? He worked so hard and—"

"Everything will work out, baby C. Have faith."

I blow out a long breath, trying to follow his advice.

I reach out to press my hand to the scanner to let us in, but it's not necessary, because the door opens for us.

My heart sinks, and I suck in a breath in preparation for coming face to face with my mother, but obviously, it's not her.

"Oh, sweetheart," Jocelyn soothes, stepping out of the house to wrap her arms around me. She's been back to visit us at the flat briefly, but she's mostly kept away, giving us the space she can so clearly see we need.

"I'm okay," I say, fighting to keep my voice steady.

"Come on, I've already made a start with the things I know you're going to want to take."

"Where's Mum?" I ask, following Jocelyn toward the basement stairs with Alex by my side.

"Up in her room, getting dressed."

"How is she? Has she said anything about—"

"She's as you probably expect."

"So she barely noticed I left?"

"I'm sorry, sweetheart. She's... shut down."

"Shut down, or doesn't care?"

"Honestly, I'm not sure. She's..." Jocelyn sighs. "I

have no idea. Everything is a mess. This house without your father, without you, it's... it's just wrong."

"I know. I feel it too." I wait until we get to the bottom of the stairs where I know we're safe from prying eyes, and I pull the scan pictures from the pouch in my hoodie. "Look."

"Oh, Calli," Jocelyn gasps, her eyes immediately filling with tears. "Oh, my sweet girl. How are you feeling?"

"Terrified. Overwhelmed."

"And how about Daemon? I'm assuming he's aware."

"I am," a deep voice rumbles from the other side of the room before he emerges from the shadows.

"Wait. How did you..."

"I have my ways, remember?" he says cryptically, walking over, wrapping his arms around my waist and resting his chin on my shoulder.

Jocelyn lifts her hand to cover her heart as she stares at the two of us.

"I'm so glad everything worked out for you both. I know you have your mum and dad, Daemon, but if either of you need anything, all you have to do is call me."

"Thank you, Jocelyn. We really appreciate it," Daemon says, his voice rumbling through me.

"Right," she says, clapping her hands together and banishing her sadness. "Are you ready to get packed and fly the nest?"

I look around my basement. It only feels like

yesterday I packed up all my stuff and moved down here. But while there might be some lingering sadness about leaving this place behind—mostly memories of my dad, of the fun times we had as a family, and of course Jocelyn—I know I'm doing the right thing.

My place is with Daemon now. It's in the building with the rest of my family. The place I'm going to be able to build my future.

Boxes litter the space where Jocelyn has already started, and my wardrobe doors are open, showing the empty space inside.

"Are you sure your flat can handle all of this?" I ask Daemon, only half-joking.

I got rid of loads of stuff when I moved down here, mostly all my old awful clothes that Mum insisted I wear. But since having my own space and finding my love of sketching and creativity, I've acquired a whole new host of things.

"We'll make it work."

"Maybe it should be Cassandra who's moving out. You guys could take over this place instead," Alex suggests.

"Uh... no, you're okay. Daemon's flat is perfect for now."

"Come on then, before we disturb the wicked witch of the west," Alex quips before Jocelyn takes over, giving each of us jobs to do.

In record time, we have the entire basement boxed up and ready to go.

"Did you have a plan for how to move all this?

Because it is not fitting in that car," I ask, staring at the sheer number of boxes, cringing as I think about where it's all going to go.

"Do you even know us at all?" Alex mutters lightly. "Backup should be arriving…" he pulls his phone from his pocket and stares down at the screen. "Any second now."

A door opens on the other side of the basement before a loud voice booms, "Did you order a man with a van?"

Turning around, I find Theo and Seb standing there with smiles on their faces. And not a second later, Uncle Damien joins them too, making my eyes widen.

He lightly messes up Daemon's hair, looking unsurprised to see him out in the wild, as he strides through the space as if he owns it, which I guess he kind of does.

"How are you holding up?" he asks, pulling me into his arms.

"I'll be better when I'm out of here."

"Don't blame you, kiddo. I hate to say it, but I always wondered what my brother saw in your mother."

"You aren't the only one."

"Does she know yet?"

"Nope," Jocelyn says when Uncle Damien looks over at her.

"We're going to clear the place out and then go and tell her," Daemon explains.

"I sincerely hope you're not going to be involved in that."

"I'm not an idiot, Boss. I know the rules."

"Right, so why is it that you're standing here right now when you shouldn't be stepping outside of your building?"

"Uh…"

"Anyway. Shall we?" He gestures to the boxes and Alex, Seb, and Theo grab one each and head toward the back doors while Daemon, Jocelyn and I watch them.

"The end of an era," Jocelyn muses.

When neither of us speaks for a few seconds, she continues.

"I know it all seemed a long way off when we've talked about it before, but if you need me for housekeeping, nannying, anything, Calli, all you need to do is call me. I'll drop this place and be at your door in minutes."

"Thank you, Jocelyn. You have no idea how much that means to me."

We stand there as the guys come in and out, and before long, the place is empty aside from the furniture, the contents of my almost eighteen years on this earth locked into the back of a van and driven across town.

"That was the easy bit. Are you ready for what comes next?" Daemon asks.

"No, but it's not going to stop me."

I step away from him and move toward the stairs.

I hold my head high and roll my shoulders back.

"Wait, I'll come with you," Alex says, but he stops when I look back and hold his eyes.

"No. I need to do this by myself. I'll meet you both out in the car in a few minutes, okay?"

"Angel, you don't need to do this."

"I do."

I hold Daemon's eyes for a beat, and he nods before I turn back around and head up the stairs.

With each step I take, I drag up a little more confidence, and by the time I'm on the first floor and standing outside my parents' bedroom, I feel like the bad-arse mafia princess I was born as, like the woman who is strong enough to stand by Daemon's side as we embrace whatever the future, this life, is going to throw at us.

I take one final deep breath before I lift my hand and knock.

"Come in," she calls and I march forward, needing this done sooner rather than later. I'm done hiding, pretending that I'm okay with the way she wants me to live my life.

In a few days, I'm going to be an adult, and I'm fully prepared to face the consequences of this decision... I think.

"Callista, what are you... this is a nice surprise," she says, quickly changing tack.

"Yeah, I'm sure it is," I mutter under my breath as I study her.

She's wearing a deep red silk robe, her hair and make-up is on point as ever, and there is absolutely no sign that she is suffering, missing my dad in the slightest. She just looks like she does every other day. As if losing her husband, the love of her life, the father of her children, hasn't changed her life in any way.

"You could have dressed up if you were going to travel across town," she chastises, eyeing my hoodie and leggings combo with disgust.

"I'm good, thanks. The last two weeks have been... hell. I'm not really in the mood to make myself look all pretty."

"Right, well. Did you have something important to say? I need to get to the spa. I'm hiring a new manager."

"Why? What happened to—"

"It's none of your concern, Callista." She waves me off, effectively shutting the conversation down.

"But she's been at your London spa since you opened it."

"Yes, well. Not everything works out quite how you plan it now, does it?"

I grip on my scan pictures in the pouch of my hoodie. "N-no. I guess not. Talking of plans, I've come to tell you that I've made some significant changes to mine in light of what's happened recently."

Now that gets her interest and she finally looks back over at me instead of searching through the endless racks of clothing in her walk-in dressing room. "Oh?"

"I'm moving out," I blurt before I chicken out.

Mum's eyebrows shoot up, but thanks to the amount of botox that's been pumped into her face, her brow doesn't so much as twitch. "Y-you're moving out?"

"Yes. Actually, I've *moved* out. The basement is

empty already and my things are on their way to their new home."

Her lips press into a thin line, but I refuse to cower. This is my decision, the right decision, and I'll stick by it no matter her reaction.

"And where exactly are you going?"

"To live in Daemon's flat."

A bitter laugh falls from her lips. It's full of disbelief and disgust.

"Your father told you that you couldn't move into that building."

"My father is no longer here, if you hadn't noticed. And I'm going to be eighteen in a few days. I get to make my own decisions from here on out. And while we're at it, that includes me not going to the university of your choice to do the course that you think would be suitable for me."

The dress that's in her hand drops to the floor at that confession and she storms toward me, her eyes full of fire.

"Now just you wait a minute, young lady."

"No, I'm not waiting for anything. You haven't cared about anything but yourself and your reputation for years. Your selfishness is the only reason Dad is no longer here. If you didn't need to have that stupid party when the threat from the Italians was so strong, then none of this would have happened. Not that you seem to *care* that it's happened.

"How is your son, Mum? Nico looked up to Dad like he hung the moon in the sky, yet you haven't even tried to call him to see how he's coping, have you? Have you even noticed that I haven't been here for almost two weeks?"

"Of course I noticed," she spits.

"And not just because you haven't had someone other than Jocelyn to boss around, to try to control? I'm done, Mum. If you need me, then you know where to find me. You have my phone number, if you ever care to look."

And with that said, I take off, not even bothering to look back when she barks my name as if I'm nothing more than her lap dog that she's only interested in when she's lonely.

My footsteps race down the stairs, my need to get out of this house and away from her all-consuming.

Jocelyn is right there at the bottom of the stairs, waiting for me. I half expected Alex and Daemon to be standing with her, but Jocelyn is a force to be reckoned with when she wants to be, so maybe I shouldn't be surprised that she got her way.

"Calli?" she questions when I don't say anything.

"It's done. I've told her what I'm doing, and made it clear that her opinion on the subject means jack shit."

"I'm so proud of you, Calli." She opens her arms to hug me, but as much as it pains me to do so, I put my hands up to stop her. If she holds me, then I'm going to break, and I don't want to do that here.

She nods in understanding and takes a step back.

"You're welcome anytime."

"Focus on getting your man better and your exams. And then I'll take you up on that offer."

"Deal," I say with a soft smile, wishing for the millionth time that she was my mother and not the cold-hearted bitch upstairs who hasn't even tried to chase me to argue with me. "Thank you for everything, Jocelyn."

"You're welcome, my sweet girl. Now go and start your new life with your sexy man."

"We need to find you a fella, J. You deserve to have some fun too."

"Whatever you say. Now go. And have fun. You're only eighteen once, you know."

"Thank you," I call, running out of the house and toward the town car that I know is hiding my boys from me. "I did it," I cry the second I jump inside. "I did it, and I've left, and it's over."

Daemon looks at me with awe etched into every inch of his face. "Yeah?"

"Yeah. Told her I'd already left and that uni wasn't happening. I'm free."

He studies me as if he can't believe what I'm telling him—that or he was expecting me to break. To be fair, I might. But right now, I'm riding the high of my success.

"Take me home. I'm ready to start our new life together," I demand.

"Hell yes to that," Daemon agrees before reaching for me and giving me little choice but to straddle his lap. "Drive carefully, yeah, Bro? We've got precious cargo on board."

"Daemon, don't you even think about—"

His lips claim mine, and anything other than the two of us ceases to exist. All I can do is hope that Alex took Daemon's demand seriously, because I'm too lost to care about anything but the man between my thighs right now.

25

DAEMON

"After everything I've done for you," Alex grunts, throwing the door open the second he pulls the car to a stop and bolting.

As soon as he's far enough away that he won't hear us, Calli and I both fall about in peals of laughter.

"That was mean," she gasps through her joy.

"He can take it, he's a big boy."

My hands flex on her arse, rocking her over my hard-on.

We might have happily teased Alex with our kisses and loud moans, but that was as far as it went. While I may have zero issues in staking my claim over Calli whenever I get the chance, I know that it's not necessary with Alex. I also didn't want to fucking die. I know what he's like behind the wheel when he's distracted, and I wanted all of us to see another day, thank you very fucking much.

"Mmm... I can take it too," she growls in my ear.

"You, Callista Cirillo, are a bad, bad girl."

"That's what happens when you get taken by the devil," she groans, making my cock ache for her.

"I should get you upstairs," I confess. She's too good for this. Fucking in a car in the middle of an underground garage.

"Don't treat me like that girl, Daemon. Not when you know she's so far from the truth," she warns.

"Oh, Angel. I'm more than aware that you've got a little devil inside you." I grasp her throat and she startles, her shocked gasp ripping through the air. "I've seen him."

Her hips roll hard, more insistent at my words.

"You were an arsehole to the doctor."

"He wanted something that was mine."

"Daemon, he really, really didn't. He was fucking terrified of you."

"I know, I liked it," I confess.

She shakes her head, chastising me, but in contrast, her hands reach out and she pulls the zip of my hoodie down, exposing my ruined skin to her.

Habit makes my muscles tense with my need to cover up, and the second she pulls back, her eyes holding mine, I know she felt it.

"Never hide from me, Nikolas. And in return, I'll never hide from you. Ever." She leans forward, running her nose up the side of my throat. "I want all of you. The good, the bad, and the ugly. The dark, the dangerous, and the deadly. And everything in between. Your scars don't scare me, and neither does your darkness. The only thing that truly terrifies me is the thought of you shutting me out, of losing you."

"Fuck, Angel. You wreck me."

"Good. The feeling is entirely mutual. Now, are you going to do anything about this," she rocks her hips again, "before we head up to our flat and embark on our new life? Together."

A deep growl of approval rumbles in my chest.

"Say that again," I demand.

"Together."

"Yeah, the other bit," I groan as she continues to grind on me.

Her brows pinch as she thinks back before a lightbulb goes off.

"Our flat?"

"Fuck, yeah. Ours."

With my restraint in tatters, I flip us, laying her out on the seat beside me and dragging her leggings and underwear down her legs.

"Daemon," she cries in shock as I shove my sweats down over my arse, freeing my cock.

The tip glistens with precum from all her grinding.

"Please."

"Fucking love it when you beg for my cock, Angel."

Throwing one of her legs over my shoulder, I lift her hips from the seat and slam home inside her.

"Yes," she cries, her pussy contracting around me and trying to suck me deeper.

Fuck. My eyes roll back as my grip on her hips tightens, forcing her body onto me until I'm fully seated.

"Yes, yes," she chants when I circle my hips, hitting that sweet spot inside her with every rotation. "Fuck me, Daemon. I need it, I need you."

Looming over her, I rest my hand beside her head while keeping her hip locked in the other one.

"Never can deny you of anything, Angel."

I thrust inside her hard, and if it weren't for me holding her, she'd have slammed her head into the door.

As I laid there last night, running through all this crazy shit in my head and Googling like a mad man trying to squash my panic, this was one of the things I looked up.

Since I'd been back, I hadn't taken her all that hard. My body hadn't been able to. But fuck if I didn't want to, and the thought of doing something, of hurting her or the baby fucking terrified me. But after reading more about having sex during pregnancy than I ever thought I would in my life, I learned that thankfully, I don't need to hold back on my girl. At least, not yet. She might have something else to say about it a little further down the line. But right now, she'll continue getting the worst—or the best, she might argue—of me. Because fuck... I needed her something fierce.

Her nails claw at me, scratching up my shoulders after shoving my hoodie down my arms as I take her with wild abandon.

"Mine. Mine. Mine," I chant with every thrust.

"Yes. Yes. Daemon. Nikolas. Fuck."

"Come for me, Angel. Then you're going to walk

back into our flat and start our future together with my cum dripping out of your pussy."

"Oh God," she whimpers, her cunt tightening down on me. "I love you."

Sitting up, I change our angle slightly and press my thumb against her clit. The second I roll it, she detonates, filling the silence of the underground garage with her cries for me.

Three more thrusts and I fall over the edge, my cock jerking deep inside her, coating every inch of her with me.

"Fuck, Angel," I pant, falling over her and claiming her lips.

"I need a shower," she complains, making me laugh.

"I'm sure that can be arranged. I fucking love showering with you."

"To get clean, Daemon," she argues. I'm still inside her, so there's no way she doesn't feel me hardening again.

"Sure. We can totally do that too."

She laughs, but it's quickly cut off when I push my tongue past her lips and steal one last kiss before I let her pull her clothes back on and we head upstairs.

"You know, Nico will catch you one day, and he'll kill you," Calli mutters lightly as we walk hand in hand out of the lift and toward our front door.

"I'd like to see him try. I'm a better soldier than him, hands down," I state confidently.

"Might not want to let him hear you say that."

"He'd need to leave his flat first, beautiful."

She stills at my words, but she can't exactly argue.

"He'll be okay, you know. We won't let him drown," I assure her as we walk through the hallway and into the living room.

"I know, I just—" Her words falter when we find someone sitting on the sofa who immediately commands both our attention.

"Uncle Damien."

It was immediately obvious when he turned up in her basement that he wasn't shocked to find me there. And I know that's not because Theo called him in for help.

He's got eyes fucking everywhere. He probably knew I was planning to leave the flat before I actually stepped foot in the hallway.

I bet he fucking knows where we went and why, too.

I didn't give a shit if Damien knew I defied orders and left. Alex and I had set the whole thing up to be as safe and discreet as possible. And fuck, to get the chance to see our little blob and to ensure Calli was okay, I'd do it again in a heartbeat.

"What do the words *do not leave this building* mean to you, soldier?" Damien growls, putting on a show.

Calli tenses beside me, clearly a little terrified by Damien's boss façade. I, however, am not so affected. I can see the lightness in his eyes. This isn't a serious warning. If it were, I'd already be staring down the barrel of his gun. Or worse.

"Extenuating circumstances," I say, pulling Calli

into my side and wrapping my arm around her protectively.

"So I understand."

Calli sucks in a breath as her uncle confirms what I already knew.

Slapping his hands down on his knees, he pushes to stand.

"I guess congratulations are in order," he says with a smile. "Gotta be honest, kid. I didn't think you'd be the first one to give us an heir, but stranger things have happened, I guess."

My lips part to respond, but Calli beats me to it.

"It wasn't planned," she blurts.

"As I suspected. But these things happen for a reason. Selene and I weren't all that much older than you both when we found out she was expecting Theo. Being young doesn't always need to be a bad thing. I became a better man the day I became a father, and I've no doubt you will be too, son," he says, his eyes holding mine.

I nod, grateful for his words.

"But," he pushes, needing to keep the façade of being the hardened mob boss that he is, "if you defy my direct orders again, you might not get to see the day that happens."

Calli gasps in horror.

"He's joking," I assure her.

"Am I?" Damien asks ominously.

I really fucking hope so.

"We've got things in place with the Italians. Let us

do our jobs while you stay here and do yours, looking after my niece."

"Sure thing, Boss," I agree.

"And please remember I have access to all the security footage in the communal areas of this building. Including the garage."

I bite down on the inside of my cheek to stop the smile that wants to break across my face.

He's teasing us, I know he is. We were in the back of a blacked-out car. But we were locked inside for quite some time, and I can only assume he has a decent imagination.

"We'll remember that, Boss."

He steps closer and wraps his hand around Calli's shoulder. "I know things are... strained with you and your mother right now. But if you need anything, our door is always open for you. If you need any advice, anything, Selene is right at the other end of the phone, okay?"

Callie sniffles as she nods.

"Th-thank you."

"Okay, now. You look after my future boss in there," he instructs. "I'm going to see your brother, see if I can talk some sense into him."

He takes off before we get a chance to reply.

"Good luck," Calli calls after him. "I've been trying to do that for years."

The slam of my front door reverberates through me before I reach out and pull Calli into my body.

"Right, where were we?" I murmur, brushing the tip of my nose against hers.

"I can't believe he knows everything," she whispers.

"Calli," I sigh. "Knowing Damien, he probably knew you were hanging out with Ant to begin with. Not a lot happens in this Family that doesn't land on his radar."

"But he never said anything."

"Probably figured out what I didn't straight away."

"Oh yeah, what's that?"

"That he's not a threat. He's an ally."

"Really?" she asks, her nose wrinkling in suspicion.

"I guess we'll never know. And really, it doesn't matter. As far as I'm concerned, we all ended up exactly where we should be." Okay, so maybe not Evan. But our world... it's brutal, cruel, and painful. Sometimes, the innocent fall, but we have to believe it's for the greater good. Calli will heal, Nico will find his way again, and who knows, he could be standing at Damien's side far sooner than any of us believed. He just needs to remember that he's Nico motherfucker Cirillo, step up, and do his father proud. Because, despite him being a bit of a moron most of the time, he's a fucking awesome soldier, and I suspect an even better underboss. But I guess, only time will tell on that one.

"So, Angel," I murmur, my lips brushing hers with every word. "I've been thinking about this shower," I confess.

"Oh yeah?" she breathes, looking up at me through her lashes.

"There's a tub in the master bathroom that's never been used. What do you say to soothing water, fluffy bubbles, flickering candles, and sharing it with one of the scariest arseholes in his city?"

"I say... bring it on. But I should warn you, I'm Callista Cirillo. It'll take more than one scary arsehole to take me on."

She shrieks as I lift her into my arms.

"Good," I mutter, kissing down her neck. "I should hope I've already trained you better than that."

Her moan of pleasure rips through the air when I suck on the sensitive skin beneath her ear.

"I love you, Nikolas."

"I love you too, Angel. Always have, always will."

EPILOGUE

Calli

I'd had one of the best weeks of my life since officially moving in with Daemon. He was everything I needed, the perfect distraction and the best housemate I could have asked for.

His return might have helped take my mind off my grief. Hell, it halved my grief in an instant. And throwing myself into taking care of him in those first few days really helped me push my pain aside in favour of focusing on him.

But as we fell into our reality, the massive hole that Dad has left in my life began to open up again.

Everything came crashing down around me the second Daemon pulled me into the bath he promised me after we got back on Saturday. The reality of what I'd just done, the feelings I'd smothered while inside the house Dad had loved and surrounded by all his things just erupted.

Daemon was a rock as he lowered us further into the water and held me while I cried, told me how much he loved me and how incredible I was.

It was everything. He was everything.

My everything.

As much as I might not have wanted to, I got up Monday morning, allowed Daemon to cook me breakfast, and headed into school.

Reentering my life was weird. It was like going back in time, as if the past few weeks hadn't happened.

As if I hadn't been abducted by my now baby daddy who was hidden away from the rest of the world while we pretended something between us might be a possibility. That my dad hadn't paid the ultimate price for the life we live. That my mother hadn't checked out on her parental responsibilities, and that I was going to take them on instead in just a few short months.

I always knew that life can change in the blink of an eye, but I'd never really experienced it so brutally before.

Hands wrapped around both of my arms as the warmth of my two best friends surged down my sides, and together the three of us walked back into Knight's Ridge College as if everything was right in the world.

Alex was there waiting for me along with Theo and Seb. Nico was unsurprisingly absent, Damien's chat with him on Saturday seemingly having little impact.

But alongside them was Jerome, with a small smile playing on his face.

Guilt tugged at my insides as I realised how much I'd abandoned him. He was suffering too, although in a different way, and I'd checked out on all our study sessions without so much as a message to cancel.

As far as I knew, he was as in the dark about the Daemon situation as Mum was, and I was more than willing to keep up that façade as long as it kept him and Ant safe while Uncle Damien and the others came up with a plan to put the Italian threat to bed for good.

Much to everyone's disappointment—especially Alex's—we insisted that we spent both our birthdays this week locked up in our flat with each other. And that's not just because Daemon couldn't go anywhere else, but because we didn't want to.

We'd nearly been ripped apart for good before we even started. Our time together as a couple was precious, especially as it wasn't going to be just the two of us for all that long.

We ordered takeout, we lazed on the sofa watching movies, and we fell into bed in a tangle of limbs and enjoyed each other until the early hours of the morning. I could barely open my eyes the following morning, but I fought through the tiredness of my first trimester and focused on school. I might have made the decision to forgo university, but that didn't mean I wasn't going to put my all into my exams. And Daemon supported me the whole way, helping me study, and keeping me well fed while I worked.

DARK LEGACY

We'd banned anyone from our flat this week, telling them all that we just wanted to settle in, much to everyone's irritation. So neither of us was overly surprised when the buzzer went off first thing this morning and we found Gianna and Jocelyn on the other side of the camera, lifting bags full of breakfast and presents for us to see.

They brought every kind of pastry they could find, and the four of us stuffed our faces while Daemon and I opened our presents and laughed along with their stories. Thankfully, Jocelyn kept any talk of Mum out of our conversation, allowing me to keep her pushed to the back of my mind.

"For the love of God," Daemon groans into my neck where we're twisted up together on the sofa after Jocelyn and Gianna left less than ten minutes ago. "Did they make a fucking schedule or something?"

"We did give them a free pass today," I say, reluctantly untangling my legs from his so he can go and see who it is this time.

It's clearly someone who lives in the building, seeing as they're knocking on the door. Really we should just be grateful they bothered and didn't just barge straight in like Alex seems to enjoy doing. One day, he's going to get an eyeful of something he doesn't want to see, and hopefully, it'll shock him out of the habit. I love that he and Daemon are close, but there are limits.

"Oh shit, Angel. Alex got a girl for his birthday," Daemon calls with a laugh when he gets to the door.

"No shit. Nico bought him a hooker?" I shoot back

with a wince, knowing it's something my brother would have done prior to Dad's death. Now, I'm not even convinced he'd have remembered all our birthdays this week if the others didn't ensure he knew.

He poked cards under the door for us on our big days, and I got a message, but that was the extent of his effort.

I can't blame him—he was drowning in grief and barely allowing any of us close enough to even try to support him. But it still hurt.

It was more than I got from our mother, though, so I guess it was something.

"Fuck off, no one bought me a hooker," Alex grunts, his voice louder as he gets closer.

"Still celibate then?" I ask when he rounds the corner.

"You know, baby C, I used to like you," he grunts before rushing over, sweeping me off my feet and spinning me around the room.

I squeal as my stomach bottoms out.

"Stop, stop," I cry before I puke all over him.

As far as pregnancy symptoms are concerned, I think I've been pretty lucky so far. But every now and then I get this strong surge of nausea that washes over me and I have to get ready to run. I haven't needed to yet, but I think the time is coming.

"Alex, put her down," Daemon commands, his voice leaving little room for argument, and Alex, the good little pup that he is, places me back on my feet almost instantly, while the world spins around me and my stomach lurches.

"You okay?" Daemon whispers in my ear, pulling me into his body.

"Y-yeah. I'm good."

"And he's right, Kas isn't a hooker," a very familiar female voice says from the doorway. "And she prefers her men a little... older, with more ink, and a little rougher around the edges."

"You saying that my cock isn't good enough for you, tiny?"

I gasp at Alex's words, but the second I catch sight of the smirk she shoots his way, I relax, realising that they know each other.

"What the hell is going on?" Daemon barks, clueing me in to the fact that he's as in the dark as I am here.

"Kas is here for your birthday present."

"We always said we wanted a repeat of that night, Bro. So I thought..." Alex wiggles his brows suggestively and my eyes widen.

I'm not an idiot, they've both alluded to sharing in the past, and I've heard enough over the years about the guys'... activities that it's hardly a surprise.

Brazenly right in front of me was not what I was expecting.

"Puh-lease. Neither of you could afford me. You are gonna need to get those tops off though. Show us those abs, boys," Kas, the stranger in the room says, immediately getting my back up.

"Oh no, I don't think so," I argue, standing in front

of Daemon as if I'll be able to protect him from showing anyone his scars.

But when all he does is chuckle behind me, embarrassment burns through me, making my cheeks heat.

"I fucking love you, Angel. But I think I know what my brother has done," he says a little loudly, while Alex laughs.

"We made a deal, Bro. We lose our V cards on our eighteenth."

"I'm afraid you're a little late for that," I mutter.

"Yeah, about four years," Alex agrees, and Daemon tenses.

"Four?" I balk.

"Yeah, but let's not go there now, it's not a pretty story," Alex says in an attempt to brush past it.

"But we all now want to hear," Emmie says, speaking my exact thoughts.

"Not now," Daemon grunts, but the way his hand grips my hips tells me that no one other than me will be privy to that information. And something tells me it might just be one of those things that he's stuffed away in that lock box inside him in the hope he never has to talk about it again.

"Can someone please tell me what is going on?" I ask, desperate to get to the bottom of this.

Kas steps forward and holds her hand out to me. Hey, Calli, I'm Kas. I'm an artist, and I work with Emmie's dad. Apparently, these two want birthday ink."

"Ink?" I ask, glancing back at Daemon.

He just shrugs, a small smile playing on his lips.

"Yep, we made a pact when we were kids that we'd get our first ink together on our eighteenth birthday. And seeing as we're stuck in this... situation, I found a way to bring the ink to us."

"Is this safe?" I ask.

"Of course, I'm a professional," Kas says with a smile. "I know I look young, but I can assure you—"

"N-no, that's not what I mean. Sorry, I wasn't suggesting that you can't..." I trail off, my cheeks blazing that she assumed I was questioning her skills.

"Kas is solid," Emmie assures us. "Right, Kas?"

"Yep, my lips are sealed. I was never even here." She winks. "So, which one of you big bad soldiers do I get to try to make cry first?"

I'm weirdly excited as Kas gets Daemon in a chair and thankfully doesn't require him to pull his top off when I discover that the twins' matching tattoos are going on their biceps.

"You know, I shouldn't be going over such a fresh scar," she chastises as she cleans Daemon's skin.

"So don't tell anyone." He shrugs. "I need this thing gone."

Unable to argue with my stubborn boys, Kas just lets out a sigh and continues until both of them are inked up.

"You nearly ready, Angel? Stella is threatening to come and drag us upstairs at gunpoint," Daemon mutters as he walks into our bedroom, finding me curling my hair.

"Yep, almost good to go." I smile at him in the mirror, my stomach fluttering when his eyes meet mine.

Switching my tongs off, I turn around and close the space between us.

"Hey," I breathe.

"Hi, Angel." Excitement and mischief twinkle in his eyes.

"What are you thinking?"

"About how much fun we'll have after I peel this dress from your body later."

"Mmm... maybe we should skip this party."

"As tempting as that is, I'd rather Stella didn't blow my balls off for keeping her best friend locked up in my castle."

"I'm the furthest from being locked up these days. I just prefer being here and having 24/7 access to your body."

He growls when I reach out and cup him through his jeans.

"I can't complain about that, Angel. But our friends don't seem to have the same opinion."

"Our friends?" I ask, unable to keep the smile from my lips.

Since he's been back and everyone learned the truth

about us, he's embraced everyone's friendship like I wished he'd done years ago.

He's no longer keeping everyone at arm's length and refusing help when it's offered. Instead, he's starting to learn just how good it is to be surrounded by ride-or-die friends.

Our family.

And for now, that still seems to include Ant.

He appears to be more than content living downstairs and hiding out from the rest of his Family while Uncle Damien and the others do whatever it is they're doing.

From what I've heard, all the guys have been down to hang out with him in the past week and keep him company. I've even heard a rumour that Isla has been caught fleeing.

I guess everyone's appreciation for what he did for Daemon overrules any suspicions about his heritage.

I'm happy living in ignorant bliss about the Italian plan while having my boy safe in my arms.

They haven't asked him to come back to work yet, and nothing has been said about school or his exams, so I'm just taking every day as it comes. As a blessing.

"Yeah, turns out, they're all right," he confesses.

"All right? Don't let them hear you say that," I joke, reaching up and brushing my lips against his.

The second I do, his phone vibrates between us.

Slipping my hand into his pocket, I find a FaceTime call from Stella.

Wrapping my arm around Daemon's neck, I swipe the screen to answer.

"Damn, I was hoping to catch you mid fuck, because there is no other reasons as to why you should be so late getting your asses upstairs."

"Jeez, Stel. Seb not putting out today or something?" I joke.

"Don't get me started on him," she spits.

"Whoa, what did he do?" Daemon asks.

"Nothing," a deep voice rumbles somewhere close to the phone. "I did nothing."

"Exactly my point."

"We're coming now. Please don't kill each other."

"They'd better bloody not in my flat. I'm not getting their blood off my solid wood floors," Theo warns.

Reaching out, Daemon cuts the call.

"Christ, they sound like a barrel of laughs," Daemon quips.

"Get some drinks down them and Theo won't be worrying about their blood on his floor."

"He'll lose his shit if they make up in his flat."

"I know. We need to go so we don't miss it."

With our fingers locked together, we make our way upstairs and toward Theo's penthouse.

The second we push the door open, loud music floods my ears, and when we make it to the living room, it becomes instantly obvious that the drinks have already been more than flowing.

"I know we're late, but we're not that late," Daemon jokes behind me as we watch Seb and Stella grope each other in time to the music behind Theo's back, where he sits with Emmie on his lap, Toby, Jodie, and Bri beside him, and Ant, Alex, and Isla opposite. The only person missing is Nico, and it breaks my heart.

"Oh shit," Isla cries the second she sees us.

"Fuck," Emmie barks before they all hop to their feet and pull party poppers from Christ knows where. They release them over the two of us while shouting 'happy birthday' and falling about laughing. I'm assuming at the look on Daemon's face. I soon get that confirmed when I turn around to him stunned motionless.

"You look like you've seen a ghost," I cry, my own amusement getting the better of me.

"I just wasn't expecting that," he says with a shrug, trying to play it off as if this is an everyday occurrence. He needs to get used to it, because it's going to be. Well, maybe not the party poppers, but the hanging with our friends part will be.

"Cocktails," Bri announces happily. "You both need a Brianna special."

She winks at me as she makes her way toward the kitchen, letting me know that she's got me.

"Where's Nic—"

I don't get a chance to finish my question, because movement from the other side of the room catches my eye.

"Nico," I cry, rushing toward him.

"And you couldn't wait another minute so I could

take a piss," he mutters as I wrap my arms around him, holding tight.

"It's good to see you, Bro."

"You too, Sis. He still treating you right?"

"You know it. Come on, let's party."

Pulling back, I find him glaring death at Daemon, not that Daemon is fazed in the slightest by the warning. But I also don't miss the way he glances over at Bri, who's busy shaking her booty as she mixes a cocktail.

"Just go over there. Enjoy yourself," I say, unable to believe I'm encouraging my brother to go and hook up.

"I... I can't, Cal," he says cryptically before stalking toward a bottle of vodka that's been abandoned on the coffee table and lifting it to his lips, swallowing down more than anyone should be able to in one go.

"What's going on?" Daemon asks, the elastic connection between us only stretching so far.

"I have no idea," I admit, watching Nico closely as he continues to glance at Bri every few seconds.

"He'll figure it out. Let's just have fun, yeah? You ready to fool everyone in the room into thinking you're getting drunk?" he teases. We talked about telling everyone now that we've had a scan and seen that everything is okay. But we quickly discovered that we're not ready to share our secret yet. We're not going to be able to keep it covered up much longer, but I want to try.

"Shouldn't be too hard. They're all half cut already. Plus, when they get wasted, all they do is fuck, so I guess I just need to jump you and let you take me against the wall."

DARK LEGACY

His eyes darken at my suggestion, and I'm half expecting him to take me up on it right here right now.

"Might hold you to that, Angel. But for now, dance with me?"

"Dance? With you?" I ask, quirking a brow.

"What? You think I can't dance?"

He steps away from me and then spins me back into his body.

Someone cranks up the music and Brianna delivers our drinks while the other couples and even Alex, Isla, and Ant get up to join us.

Happiness flows through me as I look around at all my favourite people in one room. But that's nothing compared to when I glance over my shoulder at the man behind me, his hips moving with mine in time to the music with his hand splayed possessively over my stomach.

This is it. This is exactly where I was always meant to be. Right in the centre of the world I was born into.

Spinning in Daemon's arms, I reach up on my tiptoes and brush my lips against his.

"It's me and you, devil boy," I promise him.

"Always, Angel. Always."

Nico

I sit on the sofa with my fists curled so tight my nails begin to pierce my skin as my eyes shift from where my sister is trying to suck Daemon's face off—gross—to the woman who's driven me to the point of insanity since the first moment I laid eyes on her in that dive bar with Toby all those months ago.

Her body moves perfectly in sync with the music, her hips rolling temptingly in her skintight jeans. But then my eyes lock on the pair of hands that's gripping her hips.

Rolling my eyes up his arm, I pause at the bandage over his bicep but give it little thought. It'll be the least of what he's got to deal with if gets too fucking handsy.

Alex is off his face, that much is more than obvious when I get to his eyes. They're blown wide, telling me that he hasn't just stuck to the potent cocktails Brianna has been delivering to everyone since way before I got here, if their levels of intoxication were anything to go by. Not that I could really comment. I had my first taste of alcohol long before lunchtime. And if it weren't for me trying to do right by my sister right now, then I'd already be blacked out and locked in my flat alone in the hope another bottle of vodka might just be the key to making everything stop hurting so fucking much.

As if he can feel my burning stare, Alex's eyes find mine over Brianna's shoulder. But if he senses the warning, then he completely misreads it because he smiles wide at me. Motherfucker knows exactly what he's doing.

Not in the mood to be tormented by one of my best friends, I push to my feet and storm toward the kitchen. I need more vodka after all. I've got some E in my pocket that I've been saving for tonight, knowing that I'll need the extra help if I'm going to convince any of these drunk idiots that I'm even slightly enjoying myself.

I'm not.

I don't want to be here.

I don't want to be anywhere.

No, that's not true. I want to go back a few weeks so that I can tell my dad he's a fucking idiot for allowing Mum to cloud his judgement. I want to shake him until he had no choice but to listen to me that Mum was his weakness and always letting her pull the shots was going to get us all killed when it came to the Italians.

Even fucking Daemon knew it.

But what was I meant to do? Go against the boss's orders?

I couldn't, no matter how fucking suicidal I thought their plans were. Fuck knows why Damien agreed.

He said he had intel. But fuck did that turn out to be wrong.

I just wish I could have done something. That I was closer to him when the building came down, that I could have got to him, dragged him out before it fucking buried him alive.

The angry, bitter beast inside me roars in anger as I think back to that night.

I failed.

I failed him.

And I'll never forgive myself for not being there when he needed me.

I should feel better that that night didn't claim Daemon too. Especially now the truth has come out about him and Calli. And while I might be glad to see him put a smile back on her face, it does little for me.

The grief and pain within me are too deep, too all-consuming for anyone else's happiness to have any effect on me.

I pull the baggie from my pocket, but movement across the room catches my eye before I even take them out.

A flash of dark hair and a mouth-watering arse have my legs moving before I know what I'm doing.

Anger surges through me, the bitter taste of betrayal right behind it.

Alex has barely noticed his dance partner has left. He's already turned around and started dancing with Ant and Isla.

Fuck knows why we're partying with a fucking Italian, but I figure I don't have a lot of say in anything right now. I just need to turn up, plaster a fake smile on my face, and pretend I'm not falling apart one painful crack at a time.

He moves slowly, the beating he took at the hands of his leaders still causing him issues, but he doesn't seem all that bothered by the pain as Isla wraps herself around him like a snake, Alex pressed in right behind her as the three of them laugh and enjoy themselves as if he belongs here.

With no one paying me any attention, I follow my deceitful siren down toward Theo's bathroom and slam my hand on the door a beat before it closes.

She shrieks in shock but quickly jumps back before the door hits her in the face.

But she doesn't cower.

She never does.

No matter how much I might want her to get on her knees for me, she never will. Not in the submissive way I want, anyway. She always holds too much power for that.

Just like today, when she swiped the world from beneath me with just her mere presence.

No one should have that kind of power over me.

Ever.

"What do you want, Nico?" she asks.

Ignoring the fact that I'm standing here, and that the door is now wide open, she hooks her top up and undoes the button on her jeans as if she's going to continue like I never stormed in.

"What the fuck is wrong with you?" I bark, reaching out and collaring her throat before she has a chance to shove her jeans down.

Stepping forward, I get right in her face.

It's a fucking mistake, because her sweet mango scent fills my nose, and fuck if my mouth doesn't water.

"Me? What is wrong with me?" she asks incredulously. "The only one of us with an issue here is you, you arrogant twat. Now, will you get out of my fucking way? You can watch if you want," she offers, clawing at my forearm in the hope I might release her.

"Oh yeah. Shall I take a photo too? I could take it to your new boss so he has a better understanding of who he's just employed," I threaten.

"Fuck you, Nico. I'm not scared of you and your empty threats," she growls.

Goddamn it, her fire gets my cock rock hard.

She's the only one who has since that night in The Spot. And I fucking hate her for ruining me like that.

It makes me need her.

And I don't need anyone.

Ever.

"Empty?" I taunt. "None of my threats are empty, Brianna. I thought you knew who I was. What I'm capable of."

She snarls at me, and my cock jerks in response, wishing those full lips were being put to better use.

"You need to get yourself out of my life, Brianna Andrews, or you can bet your fucking arse I'm going to shatter everything you've spent years working toward faster than you can get on your knees to suck my fucking cock."

"Cunt," she hisses.

"Takes one to know one. *Miss Andrews.*"

Now, there's going to be a little break in our beloved Knight's, but I promise they're coming.
Nico and Brianna's story is coming this winter!

PRE-ORDER NOW

But do you need a little more Batman? Or maybe even a little bat baby?

Yeah, I thought so.

DOWNLOAD Dark Knight Legacy NOW

But please... do not share the cover or any details of this story, it's a little treat for Batman lovers and I don't want to spoil it for readers who haven't got this far yet.

Enjoy! xo

ABOUT THE AUTHOR

Tracy Lorraine is a *USA Today* and *Wall Street Journal* bestselling new adult and contemporary romance author. Tracy has recently turned thirty and lives in a cute Cotswold village in England with her husband, baby girl and lovable but slightly crazy dog. Having always been a bookaholic with her head stuck in her Kindle, Tracy decided to try her hand at a story idea she dreamt up and hasn't looked back since.

Be the first to find out about new releases and offers. Sign up to my newsletter here.

If you want to know what I'm up to and see teasers and snippets of what I'm working on, then you need to be in my Facebook group. Join Tracy's Angels here.

Keep up to date with Tracy's books at
www.tracylorraine.com

ALSO BY TRACY LORRAINE

Falling Series

Falling for Ryan: Part One #1

Falling for Ryan: Part Two #2

Falling for Jax #3

Falling for Daniel (A Falling Series Novella)

Falling for Ruben #4

Falling for Ein #5

Falling for Lucas #6

Falling for Caleb #7

Falling for Declan #8

Falling For Liam #9

Forbidden Series

Falling for the Forbidden #1

Losing the Forbidden #2

Fighting for the Forbidden #3

Craving Redemption #4

Demanding Redemption #5

Avoiding Temptation #6

Chasing Temptation #7

Rebel Ink Series

Hate You #1

Trick You #2

Defy You #3

Play You #4

Inked (A Rebel Ink/Driven Crossover)

Rosewood High Series

Thorn #1

Paine #2

Savage #3

Fierce #4

Hunter #5

Faze (#6 Prequel)

Fury #6

Legend #7

Maddison Kings University Series

TMYM: Prequel

TRYS #1

TDYW #2

TBYS #3

TVYC #4

TDYD #5

TDYR #6

TRYD #7

Knight's Ridge Empire Series

Wicked Summer Knight: Prequel (Stella & Seb)

Wicked Knight #1 (Stella & Seb)

Wicked Princess #2 (Stella & Seb)

Wicked Empire #3 (Stella & Seb)

Deviant Knight #4 (Emmie & Theo)

Deviant Princess #5 (Emmie & Theo

Deviant Reign #6 (Emmie & Theo)

One Reckless Knight (Jodie & Toby)

Reckless Knight #7 (Jodie & Toby)

Reckless Princess #8 (Jodie & Toby)

Reckless Dynasty #9 (Jodie & Toby)

Dark Halloween Knight (Calli & Batman)

Dark Knight #10 (Calli & Batman)

Dark Princess #11 (Calli & Batman)

Dark Legacy #12 (Calli & Batman)

Corrupt Valentine Knight (Nico & Siren)

Ruined Series

Ruined Plans #1

Ruined by Lies #2

Ruined Promises #3

Never Forget Series

Never Forget Him #1

Never Forget Us #2

Everywhere & Nowhere #3

Chasing Series

Chasing Logan

The Cocktail Girls

His Manhattan

Her Kensington

THE MISTAKES YOU MAKE

Have you read the FREE prequel for Letty and Kane's story?
Scan the code to download your e-copy now.

THE REVENGE YOU SEEK SNEAK PEEK

Chapter One

Letty

I sit on my bed, staring down at the fabric in my hands.

This wasn't how it was supposed to happen.

This wasn't part of my plan.

I let out a sigh, squeezing my eyes tight, willing the tears away.

I've cried enough. I thought I'd have run out by now.

A commotion on the other side of the door has me looking up in a panic, but just like yesterday, no one comes knocking.

I think I proved that I don't want to hang with my

new roommates the first time someone knocked and asked if I wanted to go for breakfast with them.

I don't.

I don't even want to be here.

I just want to hide.

And that thought makes it all a million times worse.

I'm not a hider. I'm a fighter. I'm a fucking Hunter.

But this is what I've been reduced to.

This pathetic, weak mess.

And all because of *him*.

He shouldn't have this power over me. But even now, he does.

The dorm falls silent once again, and I pray that they've all headed off for their first class of the semester so I can slip out unnoticed.

I know it's ridiculous. I know I should just go out there with my head held high and dig up the confidence I know I do possess.

But I can't.

I figure that I'll just get through today—my first day—and everything will be alright.

I can somewhat pick up where I left off, almost as if the last eighteen months never happened.

Wishful thinking.

I glance down at the hoodie in my hands once more.

Mom bought them for Zayn, my younger brother, and me.

The navy fabric is soft between my fingers, but the text staring back at me doesn't feel right.

Maddison Kings University.

A knot twists my stomach and I swear my whole body sags with my new reality.

I was at my dream school. I beat the odds and I got into Columbia. And everything was good. No, everything was fucking fantastic.

Until it wasn't.

Now here I am. Sitting in a dorm at what was always my backup plan school having to start over.

Throwing the hoodie onto my bed, I angrily push to my feet.

I'm fed up with myself.

I should be better than this, stronger than this.

But I'm just... I'm broken.

And as much as I want to see the positives in this situation. I'm struggling.

Shoving my feet into my Vans, I swing my purse over my shoulder and scoop up the couple of books on my desk for the two classes I have today.

My heart drops when I step out into the communal kitchen and find a slim blonde-haired girl hunched over a mug and a textbook.

The scent of coffee fills my nose and my mouth waters.

My shoes squeak against the floor and she immediately looks up.

"Sorry, I didn't mean to disrupt you."

"Are you kidding?" she says excitedly, her southern accent making a smile twitch at my lips.

Her smile lights up her pretty face and for some

reason, something settles inside me.

I knew hiding was wrong. It's just been my coping method for... quite a while.

"We wondered when our new roommate was going to show her face. The guys have been having bets on you being an alien or something."

A laugh falls from my lips. "No, no alien. Just..." I sigh, not really knowing what to say.

"You transferred in, right? From Columbia?"

"Ugh... yeah. How'd you know—"

"Girl, I know everything." She winks at me, but it doesn't make me feel any better. "West and Brax are on the team, they spent the summer with your brother."

A rush of air passes my lips in relief. Although I'm not overly thrilled that my brother has been gossiping about me.

"So, what classes do you have today?" she asks when I stand there gaping at her.

"Umm... American lit and psychology."

"I've got psych later too. Professor Collins?"

"Uh..." I drag my schedule from my purse and stare down at it. "Y-yes."

"Awesome. We can sit together."

"S-sure," I stutter, sounding unsure, but the smile I give her is totally genuine. "I'm Letty, by the way." Although I'm pretty sure she already knows that.

"Ella."

"Okay, I'll... uh... see you later."

"Sure. Have a great morning."

She smiles at me and I wonder why I was so scared to come out and meet my new roommates.

I'd wanted Mom to organize an apartment for me so that I could be alone, but—probably wisely—she refused. She knew that I'd use it to hide in and the point of me restarting college is to try to put everything behind me and start fresh.

After swiping an apple from the bowl in the middle of the table, I hug my books tighter to my chest and head out, ready to embark on my new life.

The morning sun burns my eyes and the scent of freshly cut grass fills my nose as I step out of our building. The summer heat hits my skin, and it makes everything feel that little bit better.

So what if I'm starting over. I managed to transfer the credits I earned from Columbia, and MKU is a good school. I'll still get a good degree and be able to make something of my life.

Things could be worse.

It could be this time last year...

I shake the thought from my head and force my feet to keep moving.

I pass students meeting up with their friends for the start of the new semester as they excitedly tell them all about their summers and the incredible things they did, or they compare schedules.

My lungs grow tight as I drag in the air I need. I think of the friends I left behind in Columbia. We didn't have all that much time together, but we'd bonded before my life imploded on me.

Glancing around, I find myself searching for familiar faces. I know there are plenty of people here who know me. A couple of my closest friends came here after high school.

Mom tried to convince me to reach out over the summer, but my anxiety kept me from doing so. I don't want anyone to look at me like I'm a failure. That I got into one of the best schools in the country, fucked it up and ended up crawling back to Rosewood. I'm not sure what's worse, them assuming I couldn't cope or the truth.

Focusing on where I'm going, I put my head down and ignore the excited chatter around me as I head for the coffee shop, desperately in need of my daily fix before I even consider walking into a lecture.

I find the Westerfield Building where my first class of the day is and thank the girl who holds the heavy door open for me before following her toward the elevator.

"Holy fucking shit," a voice booms as I turn the corner, following the signs to the room on my schedule.

Before I know what's happening, my coffee is falling from my hand and my feet are leaving the floor.

"What the—" The second I get a look at the guy standing behind the one who has me in his arms, I know exactly who I've just walked into.

Forgetting about the coffee that's now a puddle on the floor, I release my books and wrap my arms around my old friend.

His familiar woodsy scent flows through me, and

suddenly, I feel like me again. Like the past two years haven't existed.

"What the hell are you doing here?" Luca asks, a huge smile on his face when he pulls back and studies me.

His brows draw together when he runs his eyes down my body, and I know why. I've been working on it over the summer, but I know I'm still way skinnier than I ever have been in my life.

"I transferred," I admit, forcing the words out past the lump in my throat.

His smile widens more before he pulls me into his body again.

"It's so good to see you."

I relax into his hold, squeezing him tight, absorbing his strength. And that's one thing that Luca Dunn has in spades. He's a rock, always has been and I didn't realize how much I needed that right now.

Mom was right. I should have reached out.

"You too," I whisper honestly, trying to keep the tears at bay that are threatening just from seeing him—them.

"Hey, it's good to see you," Leon says, slightly more subdued than his twin brother as he hands me my discarded books.

"Thank you."

I look between the two of them, noticing all the things that have changed since I last saw them in person. I keep up with them on Instagram and TikTok, sure, but nothing is quite like standing before the two of them.

Both of them are bigger than I ever remember, showing just how hard their coach is working them now they're both first string for the Panthers. And if it's possible, they're both hotter than they were in high school, which is really saying something because they'd turn even the most confident of girls into quivering wrecks with one look back then. I can only imagine the kind of rep they have around here.

The sound of a door opening behind us and the shuffling of feet cuts off our little reunion.

"You in Professor Whitman's American lit class?" Luca asks, his eyes dropping from mine to the book in my hands.

"Yeah. Are you?"

"We are. Walk you to class?" A smirk appears on his lips that I remember all too well. A flutter of the butterflies he used to give me threaten to take flight as he watches me intently.

Luca was one of my best friends in high school, and I spent almost all our time together with the biggest crush on him. It seems that maybe the teenage girl inside me still thinks that he could be it for me.

"I'd love you to."

"Come on then, Princess," Leon says and my entire body jolts at hearing that pet name for me. He's never called me that before and I really hope he's not about to start now.

Clearly not noticing my reaction, he once again takes my books from me and threads his arm through mine as the pair of them lead me into the lecture hall.

I glance at both of them, a smile pulling at my lips and hope building inside me.

Maybe this was where I was meant to be this whole time.

Maybe Columbia and I were never meant to be.

More than a few heads turn our way as we climb the stairs to find some free seats. Mostly it's the females in the huge space and I can't help but inwardly laugh at their reaction.

I get it.

The Dunn twins are two of the Kings around here and I'm currently sandwiched between them. It's a place that nearly every female in this college, hell, this state, would kill to be in.

"Dude, shift the fuck over," Luca barks at another guy when he pulls to a stop a few rows from the back.

The guy who's got dark hair and even darker eyes immediately picks up his bag, books, and pen and moves over a space.

"This is Colt," Luca explains, nodding to the guy who's studying me with interest.

"Hey," I squeak, feeling a little intimidated.

"Hey." His low, deep voice licks over me. "Ow, what the fuck, man?" he barks, rubbing at the back of his head where Luca just slapped him.

"Letty's off-limits. Get your fucking eyes off her."

"Dude, I was just saying hi."

"Yeah, and we all know what that usually leads to," Leon growls behind me.

The three of us take our seats and just about manage

to pull our books out before our professor begins explaining the syllabus for the semester.

"Sorry about the coffee," Luca whispers after a few minutes. "Here." He places a bottle of water on my desk. "I know it's not exactly a replacement, but it's the best I can do."

The reminder of the mess I left out in the hallway hits me.

"I should go and—"

"Chill," he says, placing his hand on my thigh. His touch instantly relaxes me as much as it sends a shock through my body. "I'll get you a replacement after class. Might even treat you to a cupcake."

I smile up at him, swooning at the fact he remembers my favorite treat.

Why did I ever think coming here was a bad idea?

Chapter Two
Letty

My hand aches by the time Professor Whitman finishes talking. It feels like a lifetime ago that I spent this long taking notes.

"You okay?" Luca asks me with a laugh as I stretch out my fingers.

"Yeah, it's been a while."

"I'm sure these boys can assist you with that, beautiful," bursts from Colt's lips, earning him another slap to the head.

"Ignore him. He's been hit in the head with a ball one too many times," Leon says from beside me but I'm too enthralled with the way Luca is looking at me right now to reply.

Our friendship wasn't a conventional one back in high school. He was the star quarterback, and I wasn't a cheerleader or ever really that sporty. But we were paired up as lab partners during my first week at Rosewood High and we kinda never separated.

I watched as he took the team to new heights, as he met with college scouts, I even went to a few places with him so he didn't have to go alone.

He was the one who allowed me to cry on his shoulder as I struggled to come to terms with the loss of another who left a huge hole in my heart and he never, not once, overstepped the mark while I clung to him and soaked up his support.

I was also there while he hooked up with every member of the cheer squad along with any other girl who looked at him just so. Each one stung a little more than the last as my poor teenage heart was getting battered left, right, and center.

With each day, week, month that passed, I craved him more but he never, not once, looked at me that way.

I was even his prom date, yet he ended up spending the night with someone else.

DARK LEGACY

It hurt, of course it did. But it wasn't his fault and I refuse to hold it against him.

Maybe I should have told him. Been honest with him about my feelings and what I wanted. But I was so terrified I'd lose my best friend that I never confessed, and I took that secret all the way to Columbia with me.

As I stare at him now, those familiar butterflies still set flight in my belly, but they're not as strong as I remember. I'm not sure if that's because my feelings for him have lessened over time, or if I'm just so numb and broken right now that I don't feel anything but pain.

It really could go either way.

I smile at him, so grateful to have run into him this morning.

He always knew when I needed him and even without knowing of my presence here, there he was like some guardian fucking angel.

If guardian angels had sexy dark bed hair, mesmerizing green eyes and a body built for sin then yeah, that's what he is.

I laugh to myself, yeah, maybe that irritating crush has gone nowhere.

"What have you got next?" Leon asks, dragging my attention away from his twin.

Leon has always been the quieter, broodier one of the duo. He's as devastatingly handsome and as popular with the female population but he doesn't wear his heart on his sleeve like Luca. Leon takes a little time to warm to people, to let them in. It was hard work getting there, but I soon realized that once he dropped his walls a little for me, it was hella worth it.

He's more serious, more contemplative, he's deeper. I always suspected that there was a reason they were so different. I know twins don't have to be the same and like the same things, but there was always something niggling at me that there was a very good reason that Leon closed himself down. From listening to their mom talk over the years, they were so identical in their mannerisms, likes, and dislikes when they were growing up, that it seems hard to believe they became so different.

"Psychology but not for an hour. I'm—"

"I'm taking her for coffee," Luca butts in. A flicker of anger passes through Leon's eyes but it's gone so fast that I begin to wonder if I imagined it.

"I could use another coffee before econ," Leon chips in.

"Great. Let's go," Luca forces out through clenched teeth.

He wanted me alone. Interesting.

The reason I never told him about my mega crush is the fact he friend-zoned me in our first few weeks of friendship by telling me how refreshing it was to have a girl wanting to be his friend and not using it as a ploy to get more.

We were only sophomores at the time but even then, Luca was up to all sorts and the girls around us were all more than willing to bend to his needs.

From that moment on, I couldn't tell him how I

really felt. It was bad enough I even felt it when he thought our friendship was just that.

I smile at both of them, hoping to shatter the sudden tension between the twins.

"Be careful with these two," Colt announces from behind us as we make our way out of the lecture hall with all the others. "The stories I've heard."

"Colt," Luca warns, turning to face him and walking backward for a few steps.

"Don't worry," I shoot over my shoulder. "I know how to handle the Dunn twins." I wink at him as he howls with laughter.

"You two are in so much trouble," he muses as he turns left out of the room and we go right.

Leon takes my books from me once more and Luca threads his fingers through mine. I still for a beat. While the move isn't unusual, Luca has always been very affectionate. It only takes a second for his warmth to race up my arm and to settle the last bit of unease that's still knotting my stomach.

"Two Americanos and a skinny vanilla latte with an extra shot. Three cupcakes with the sprinkles on top."

I swoon at the fact Luca remembers my order. "How'd you—"

He turns to me, his wide smile and the sparkle in his eyes making my words trail off. The familiarity of his face, the feeling of comfort and safety he brings me causes a lump to form in my throat.

"I didn't forget anything about my best girl." He throws his arm around my shoulder and pulls me close.

Burying my nose in his hard chest, I breathe him in. His woodsy scent mixes with his laundry detergent and it settles me in a way I didn't know I needed.

Leon's stare burns into my back as I snuggle with his brother and I force myself to pull away so he doesn't feel like the third wheel.

"Dunn," the server calls, and Leon rushes ahead to grab our order while Luca leads me to a booth at the back of the coffee shop.

As we walk past each table, I become more and more aware of the attention on the twins. I know their reps, they've had their football god status since before I moved to Rosewood and met them in high school, but I had forgotten just how hero-worshiped they were, and this right now is off the charts.

Girls openly stare, their eyes shamelessly dropping down the guys' bodies as they mentally strip them naked. Guys jealousy shines through their expressions, especially those who are here with their girlfriends who are now paying them zero attention. Then there are the girls whose attention is firmly on me. I can almost read their thoughts—hell, I heard enough of them back in high school.

What do they see in her?
She's not even that pretty.
They're too good for her.

The only difference here from high school is that no one knows I'm just trailer park trash seeing as I moved from the hellhole that is Harrow Creek before meeting the boys.

Tipping my chin up, I straighten my spine and plaster on as much confidence as I can find.

They can all think what they like about me, they can come up with whatever bitchy comments they want. It's no skin off my back.

"Good to see you've lost your appeal," I mutter, dropping into the bench opposite both of them and wrapping my hands around my warm mug when Leon passes it over.

"We walk around practically unnoticed," Luca deadpans.

"You thought high school was bad," Leon mutters, he was always the one who hated the attention whereas Luca used it to his advantage to get whatever he wanted. "It was nothing."

"So I see. So, how's things? Catch me up on everything," I say, needing to dive into their celebrity status lifestyles rather than thinking about my train wreck of a life.

"Really?" Luca asks, raising a brow and causing my stomach to drop into my feet. "I think the bigger question is how come you're here and why we had no idea about it?"

Releasing my mug, I wrap my arms around myself and drop my eyes to the table.

"T-things just didn't work out at Columbia," I mutter, really not wanting to talk about it.

"The last time we talked, you said it was everything you expected it to be and more. What happened?"

Kane fucking Legend happened.

I shake that thought from my head like I do every time he pops up.

He's had his time ruining my life. It's over.

"I just..." I sigh. "I lost my way a bit, ended up dropping out and finally had to fess up and come clean to Mom."

Leon laughs sadly. "I bet that went down well."

The Dunn twins are well aware of what it's like to live with a pushy parent. One of the things that bonded the three of us over the years.

"Like a lead balloon. Even worse because I dropped out months before I finally showed my face."

"Why hide?" Leon's brows draw together as Luca stares at me with concern darkening his eyes.

"I had some health issues. It's nothing."

"Shit, are you okay?"

Fucking hell, Letty. Stop making this worse for yourself.

"Yeah, yeah. Everything is good. Honestly. I'm here and I'm ready to start over and make the best of it."

They both smile at me, and I reach for my coffee once more, bringing the mug to my lips and taking a sip.

"Enough about me, tell me all about the lives of two of the hottest Kings of Maddison."

"Okay... how'd you do that?" Ella whispers after both Luca and Leon walk me to my psych class after our coffee break.

"Do what?" I ask, following her into the room and finding ourselves seats about halfway back.

"It's your first day and the Dunn twins just walked you to class. You got a diamond-encrusted vag or something?"

I snort a laugh as a few others pause on their way to their seats at her words.

"Shush," I chastise.

"Girl, if it's true, you know all these guys need to know about it."

I pull out my books and a couple of pens as Professor Collins sets up at the front before turning to her.

"No, I don't have diamonds anywhere but my necklace. I've been friends with them for years."

"Girl, I knew there was a reason we should be friends." She winks at me. "I've been trying to get West and Brax to hook me up but they're useless."

"You want to be friends so I can set you up with one of the Dunns?"

"Or both." She shrugs, her face deadly serious before she leans in. "I've heard that they tag team sometimes. Can you imagine? Both of their undivided attention." She fans herself as she obviously pictures herself in the middle of a Dunn sandwich. "Oh and, I think you're pretty cool too."

"Of course you do." I laugh.

It's weird, I might have only met her very briefly this morning but that was enough.

"We're all going out for dinner tonight to welcome you to the dorm. The others are dying to meet you." She smiles at me, proving that there's no bitterness behind her words.

"I'm sorry for ignoring you all."

"Girl, don't sweat it. We got ya back, don't worry."

"Thank you," I mouth as the professor demands everyone's attention to begin the class.

The time flies as I scribble my notes down as fast as I can, my hand aching all over again and before I know it, he's finished explaining our first assignment and bringing his class to a close.

"Jesus, this semester is going to be hard," Ella muses as we both pack up.

"At least we've got each other."

"I like the way you think. You done for the day?"

"Yep, I'm gonna head to the store, grab some supplies then get started on this assignment, I think."

"I've got a couple of hours. You want company?"

After dumping our stuff in our rooms, Ella takes me to her favorite store, and I stock up on everything I'm going to need before we head back so she can go to class.

I make myself some lunch before being brave and setting up my laptop at the kitchen table to get started on my assignments. My time for hiding is over, it's time to get back to life and once again become a fully immersed college student.

"Holy shit, she is alive. I thought Zayn was lying about his beautiful older sister," a deep rumbling voice says, dragging me from my research a few hours later.

I spin and look at the two guys who have joined me.

"Zayn would never have called me beautiful," I say as a greeting.

"That's true. I think his actual words were: messy, pain in the ass, and my personal favorite, I'm glad I don't have to live with her again," he says, mimicking my brother's voice.

"Now that is more like it. Hey, I'm Letty. Sorry about—"

"You're all good. We're just glad you emerged. I'm West, this ugly motherfucker is Braxton—"

"Brax, please," he begs. "Only my mother calls me by my full name and you are way too hot to be her."

My cheeks heat as he runs his eyes over my curves.

"T-thanks, I think."

"Ignore him. He hasn't gotten laid for weeeeks."

"Okay, do we really need to go there right now?"

"Always, bro. Our girl here needs to know you get pissy when you don't get the pussy."

I laugh at their easy banter, closing down my laptop and resting forward on my elbows as they move toward the fridge.

"Ella says we're going out," Brax says, pulling out two bottles of water and throwing one to West.

"Apparently so."

"She'll be here in a bit. Violet and Micah too. They were all in the same class."

"So," West says, sliding into the chair next to me. "What do we need to know that your brother hasn't already told us about you?"

My heart races at all the things that not even my brother would share about my life before I drag my thoughts away from my past.

"Uhhh..."

"How about the Dunns love her," Ella announces as she appears in the doorway flanked by two others. Violet and Micah, I assume.

"Um... how didn't we know this?" Brax asks.

"Because you're not cool enough to spend any time with them, asshole," Violet barks, walking around Ella. "Ignore these assholes, they think they're something special because they're on the team but what they don't tell you is that they have no chance of making first string or talking to the likes of the Dunns."

"Vi, girl. That stings," West says, holding his hand over his heart.

"Yeah, get over it. Truth hurts." She smiles up at him as he pulls her into his chest and kisses the top of her head.

"Whatever, Titch."

"Right, well. Are we ready to go? I need tacos like... yesterday."

"Yes. Let's go."

"You've never had tacos like these, Letty. You are in for a world of pleasure," Brax says excitedly.

"More than she would be if she were in your bed, that's for sure," West deadpans.

"Lies and we all know it."

"Whatever." Violet pushes him toward the door.

"Hey, I'm Micah," the third guy says when I catch up to him.

"Hey, Letty."

"You need a sensible conversation, I'm your boy."

"Good to know."

Micah and I trail behind the others and with each step I take, my smile gets wider.

Things really are going to be okay.

DOWNLOAD NOW TO KEEP READING

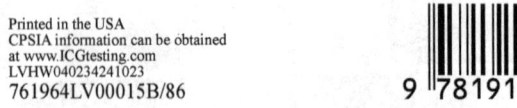

Printed in the USA
CPSIA information can be obtained
at www.ICGtesting.com
LVHW040234241023
761964LV00015B/86

9 781914 950858